INN

Against her father's wi... Jane Tudor obtained a p... a hostelry on the old ... Bridgend. But her new life, in contrast with her peaceful existence, proved a rude awakening, for the owner of the inn was Cap Coch, the notorious mass-murderer of the early nineteenth century. Within the space of six months her terrifying experiences had changed her from an ingenuous young girl into a mature woman whose bitter memories were assuaged only by the strength of a man's love.

This is a gripping novel based on fact, portraying vividly the life of the farming community of the Vale of Glamorgan during the Napoleonic era, overlaid with the violence, smuggling and murder that were commonplace at that time—in marked contrast with the sylvan settings of the Heritage Coast that we know today.

The author, Alun Morgan, has already had published three best selling books about Glamorgan. Of his first novel, *The Breakwater*, one critic wrote, "Exciting and gripping . . . I read it through in one sitting, a very surprising thing for me to do." *Inn of Fear* is a compelling thriller in the same mode.

Reproduced from Yates' map of Glamorgan, 1799 by kind permission of Glamorgan Archive Service.

INN OF FEAR

BY

ALUN MORGAN

COWBRIDGE

D. BROWN & SONS LIMITED

© Alun Morgan 1977

ISBN 0 905928 01 6

2nd impression August 1980

3rd impression March 1986

Printed in Wales by
D. Brown and Sons Limited
Cowbridge and Bridgend
Glamorgan

FOREWORD

According to historical evidence Cap Coch was a mass-murderer who paid for his crimes with a hangman's rope on Stalling Down, near Cowbridge; but legend has it that he lived to a great age, his crimes undetected until after his death.

It is against this conflicting background that the following story has been written, with a possible explanation for the anomaly. In the understandable absence of detailed information about the macabre events at the New Inn I have of necessity had to invent characters and situations, but I have tried to keep to the main, well-known facts, at least up to the arraignment at Cowbridge. After that conjecture has to take precedence, as it has in local lore, even to this day. Also, as with all historical novels that extend over a lengthy period, condensation of the time element was unavoidable to make the narrative readable. Other than that, like Cap Coch, I admit to nothing.

With the exception of Cap Coch and Sir John Nicholl all characters portrayed are the product of the author's imagination and have no relation to any person in real life.

By the same author

PORTHCAWL—ITS HISTORY AND DEVELOPMENT
LEGENDS OF PORTHCAWL AND THE GLAMORGAN COAST
THE BREAKWATER—A TALE OF OLD PORTHCAWL
ELIZABETH, FAIR MAID OF SKER
THE SHE GOBLIN

All published by D. Brown & Sons Ltd.

CHAPTER 1

MARY JANE TUDOR was beautiful from the day she was born, but in the process put paid to her mother, which augured ill for the future, so the old wives said. Edward, her father, after recovering from the grief caused by the loss of his wife, doted on the child, although he already had four daughters and two sons, all born in the space of six years.

The reason for Edward's devotion was apparent to everyone who came into contact with Mary Jane. From the beginning she was blessed with a happy disposition and a zest for life. She could never just walk, she had to skip, bounding from one task to another on the farm with an energy and gaiety that astonished her family. A laugh was never far away from her lips and she was kindness itself, attributes which ensured that her brothers and sisters never begrudged the special place she maintained in her father's heart. By the time she was sixteen she had golden hair down to her waist, eyes the colour of cornflowers, a dainty, up-tilted nose and small, white, regular teeth which she cleaned daily with pointed hazel sticks. It was not long before the fame of her beauty and nature spread among the hill farms of the Garw and Llynfi valleys, reaching even as far as the market town of Bridgend; and many were the hopefuls—farmers and tenants—who began climbing the steep slopes of Pwll y Cymmer, ostensibly to see Edward but in actual fact hoping to gain favour in the eyes of his daughter. Some of the landed gentry started sniffing about, too, making themselves known in their condescending way, a fact that worried Edward Tudor for he knew that dalliance was their aim, not marriage; but in that respect he had to be careful for he was a tenant himself, paying tithes to both landowner and church, with an annually granted permission to graze his sheep on the un-enclosed land to the north of the small-holding.

One thing troubled Edward more than any other. He loved Mary as much as any father could and never ceased to wonder that he had produced such a beautiful, happy and generous creature; but he was well aware of Mary's one weakness: she was inclined to be wilful, with a mind of her own. This was an admirable quality in many ways, for it meant that Mary was no fool and would not be led into bad ways by others, but it also meant that she would not always listen to advice and had a propensity for thinking that she was right and others wrong, a characteristic that eventually led her into great danger, an event that ultimately showed her the error of her ways.

For it was obvious from early on that Mary would not be content to remain long at Pwll y Cymmer. Set high on the slope of a hill, with distant views of the Bristol Channel, it was bearable in summer but savage and lonely in winter. The icy blasts from the mountain ridges whistled around the small croft, freezing the marrow of those who ventured out into it; and the never-ending tasks of gathering winter fuel and tending the animals meant a continuing life of unremitting toil. It was no place for a high-spirited girl and Edward Tudor knew it. One son had already left, taking the king's shilling, and two daughters had gone into service, one to Court Colman and one to Tythegston Manor. The remaining son, Jacob, showed no inclination to leave and the other two sisters, Sarah and Myfanwy, also seemed content with their lot and were, in any case, too plain to attract husbands. But Mary was a special case and so Edward steeled himself against the inevitable day when he would lose her.

The seeds of such an event were sown when Edward took Mary, then sixteen, for the first time to Bridgend. It was market day and Mary's blue eyes were constantly open in wonder at the sights and sounds of the busy little town. She gaped at the herds of cattle and marvelled at the size of the horses all, it seemed, much bigger and sleeker than poor old Illtud, their all-purpose cob, which had brought them down the valley in Edward's one and only cart. She was entranced by the stalls and street vendors, all displaying goods of a quantity and quality she had not thought possible. Edward bought her and her sisters a pair of woollen stockings each, direct from a mill on the river bank; and then, as a special treat, a length of blue ribbon for her hair. He watched happily as his daughter, with her usual impetuosity, wound the ribbon around her golden tresses; but it was a joy tinged with foreboding, for he saw also the admiring glances of the men. Young or old, there was hardly a male head that did not turn as they made their way through the crowds. Mary was aware of the admiration also, for she often blushed and her eyes shone. On the way home she was strangely silent and Edward knew that at last she had become aware of the power of her beauty. He prayed that it would bring her happiness and gave himself no more than two years in which to enjoy her company.

This was an accurate estimate for, after a few more visits to Bridgend with Mary and a particularly hard winter, when even the crystal-clear water of Afon Garw froze to its depths, his daughter began pleading to be allowed to follow her sisters into service. Edward, knowing that he was fighting a losing battle, resisted at first, pointing out that a good marriage to a local hill farmer was a better proposition. But with a flash of her eyes Mary dismissed the idea, saying that she wanted to see some of the world before settling down. She followed this up with an obvious argument: that with a son and two daughters her father was in no want for labour on the farm and that if she left there would be one less mouth to feed.

Accepting the inevitable Edward began inquiring around the countryside to find what work was available; but there was very little employment to be had, even the hiring fair at Aberkenfig producing nothing suitable for females. Then, one day, when he was quaffing a jug of ale in the tap room of the Wyndham Arms in Bridgend he heard that there was a vacancy for a general serving maid at the New Inn, a hostelry situated on the main coaching road a mile south of the town. He rode to the inn, pleaded his daughter's case with a Mistress Gronow, who appeared to be in charge of the establishment during the temporary absence of the landlord, and arranged for Mary to be given a three months' trial period, commencing the following week. He then rode home and broke the news to a delighted Mary.

Thus it was, on a day early in May, when the shadow of Napoleon was looming large on the continent, Mary Jane Tudor left the safety of her home and embarked on a life very different from that she had known. Fortunately for both her and her father neither had an inkling of what lay ahead.

CHAPTER 2

ON THE DAY that Edward was to take Mary to Bridgend he was, with the other inhabitants of the Garw Valley, placed on compulsory road maintenance and so was forced to entrust the task to Evan Philips, the pedlar, who volunteered to take girl and luggage in his gambo. Having sold most of his wares Evan piled some sacks in a corner of the little cart and, after a tearful farewell at the farm, Mary was made comfortable, her valise placed beside her, and transported to the Wyndham Arms, where arrangements had been made for her to meet an ostler from the New Inn.

As the little donkey clip-clopped its way between the green hedgerows Mary's sadness at the departure was replaced by a sense of excitement and adventure. She had no doubt that she could look after herself and had made a pretence of listening to her family's admonishments about entanglements with strange men, dismissing them mentally as unnecessary. In her valise she had a second dress, two petticoats, a white serving cap and a change of drawers; and in her purse a five-shilling piece, a parting gift from her father with strict instructions to use it only if she wanted to return home in a hurry. That, too, was unnecessary, she thought, for she was determined to make a success of her new career. Walking beside the donkey old Evan noticed her flushed, excited countenance but said nothing. He believed in minding his own business and allowing others to make their own mistakes, whatever the outcome.

As they breasted the common at Bryncethin and descended Litchard Hill, Bridgend came into view. Mary felt her heart throb with anticipation, a state of affairs that abated a little when they entered the town and found it strangely quiet. Gone were the cattle, the horses and the vendors; and then Mary realised: this was an ordinary Monday, not market day, and so all the bustling throngs were absent.

Old Evan appeared to read her thoughts.

"Very quiet this morning, Miss Mary."

"Very," said Mary. "I've only been here on market days."

"Ah! Then you'll notice a difference."

They entered the square in front of the Wyndham Arms.

"I've been told to look out for a tumbril," said Evan, looking around.

"A tumbril!" Mary's eyes opened wide. "Aren't those the carts they used in France to take all those poor people to the guillotine?"

Evan laughed.

"That's right, miss, but have no fear. There's no guillotine around Bridgend, at least not that I know of. Wait here and I'll go in and see who's to be found."

He disappeared around the back of the hostelry and a few minutes later Mary heard the sound of cart wheels on the cobbles. Into view came a two-wheeled contraption piled high with casks and sacks. Leading the two mules was a good-looking, dark-haired man of about twenty-five, of slightly more than medium height, with broad, powerful shoulders. He had brown, curly hair and his dark eyes stared unwaveringly at her.

"Here's your charge," said Evan, grabbing Mary's valise and hoisting it to the cobbles.

The man did not take his eyes off Mary, making her blush and feel uncomfortable. She had been stared at before but never with such intensity.

"Is *she* coming to the New Inn?" said the man with heavy emphasis on the word 'she'.

"None other," said Evan. "Mary Tudor from Pwll y Cymmer Farm."

"A farmer's daughter, eh!" The man smiled, but it was a crooked, insincere smile and Mary's dislike for him increased. "Welcome to the New Inn," he added. "I'm Daniel Mathias, ostler, cellar man and general factotum. At your service." He made a mock bow then reached out. "Allow me to help you down."

11

Mary would have avoided him if she could, but his strong, brown arms encircled her waist and heaved her down, as though she was a rag doll.

"Now where would you like to sit?" He indicated a small wooden seat at the front of the cart. "Here or on that sack of flour?"

Mary eyed the seat and decided against it. Sitting there she would be too close to the forward Mr. Mathias.

"On the sack," she said primly.

"Very well." Mathias helped her up and she perched herself on a large, bulging sack smelling heavily of hemp and grain. She clutched her bonnet with one hand and felt for the edge of the cart with the other to steady herself.

"You all right, Miss?" called out Evan.

"Quite all right," said Mary. "Kindly give my regards to my family when you see them."

"That I will," said Evan. "Then I'll be off." He jerked the donkey's head around and they disappeared up the street. Mary and Mathias were left staring at each other.

"Are you safe up there?" said Mathias, grinning.

"Yes, thank you."

"Then hold on."

But before Mary could brace herself a sudden movement of the mules sent her flying backwards, her dress over her face and her pantalooned legs high in the air.

Mathias stared at her legs then burst out laughing.

"I asked if you were safe."

Mary struggled upright, pulling down her skirt and righting her bonnet. She felt foolish and more angry than ever before in her life. She grasped the side of the tumbril with renewed determination.

"You didn't tell me we were moving off."

"I told you to hang on."

"I am now." Mary's knuckles grew white with the pressure of her fingers on the slat. She was determined not to give Mathias another free show of her charms. "Kindly proceed."

Mathias gave another short laugh then jumped on the small seat. He jerked the reins and they moved slowly out of the

12

square. Almost immediately they came to the narrow pack-horse bridge that spanned the river. The mules struggled to pull their heavy load up the steep slope and Mary noticed that the wheel hubs kept scraping against the parapet walls. Anything bigger than the tumbril would have failed to get across. Then they were in the green fields beyond and Mathias selected a path that followed the river bank. They went on for a good ten minutes or more then, under the spreading branches of a clump of trees, the ostler suddenly jerked the mules to a halt. He looked round at her, studying her, his eyes dark and inquisitive.

"Have you been away from home before?"

"No."

"Then your appointment at the New Inn is your first job?"

"Yes."

Mary began to feel angry again. She objected to being quizzed by a mere ostler.

"You're a good looking girl," said Mathias thoughtfully. "In fact, more than good looking. Are you sure you're doing the right thing leaving your farm? I thought you'd be better off marrying a farmer from round your parts."

Mary stared straight in front of her. Mathias was using the same argument as her father, but whereas her father had the right to say such things, Mathias was merely being impudent. She gave him a long, frigid stare.

"Kindly mind your own business."

"As you wish," said Mathias. "But I must tell you this: I doubt if the New Inn is the place for a girl like you. If you like, I'll take you back now. I'll tell Mistress Gronow you were taken ill or something."

Mary put on her best scathing expression.

"You'll do nothing of the kind! I have been appointed and nothing will prevent me taking it up!"

Mathias shook his head. He seemed about to say something more but changed his mind. He kicked the rump of the nearest mule and they moved off again. Mary stared at the back of his strong neck, fighting down an inclination to re-open the conversation. Something about Mathias' tone had intrigued her and

13

she wondered why he had warned her against the New Inn. Surely it could be no worse than any other hostelry, presenting no problems she could not handle with courage and common sense. Twice she opened her mouth to say something but twice pride prevented her. She did not wish to be beholden to a man like Mathias, and so they went on in silence, through lush, green fields and then over an expanse of boggy ground. Eventually they came to a heavily wooded part where the trees were so dense Mary could only hear the river, not see it. The over-hanging boughs once or twice nearly removed her bonnet and she had to hang on grimly as the cart lurched and swayed along the rough track.

Then they entered a clearing and for the first time Mary saw the New Inn. Behind a creaking sign heralding its name the hostelry seemed to lurk amongst the undergrowth, its walls clad with lichen. It was not large but appeared to have depth, for behind and to the right were stables and outbuildings, set in what looked like an orchard. Although it was May, smoke was spiralling from two of the chimneys. From the front door a path led across a forecourt to what appeared to be a main road and a squat, hump-backed bridge, under which the River Ogmore flashed and gurgled. Surrounding everything were tall trees, their topmost branches speckled with rooks' nests. It was a sylvan setting and Mary's heart felt gladdened. There could be no prettier spot for an inn and Mathias must have had some ulterior motive in not wanting her to come there. She decided she would have to keep an eye on him.

"Better go round the back," said the object of her thoughts. "The front door is for guests only."

He urged the mules through a gateway and they entered a grassy yard in which several chickens were pecking for worms. The tumbril came to halt outside an open door, through which Mary could see a large table and a tall Welsh dresser. She jumped down quickly before Mathias could help her, for she had decided the less favours she received from him the better. She could not reach her valise, however, and Mathias took it down for her. He was not grinning now and his face was impassive as he led the way into the building. Mary found herself in a large kitchen, in which was an enormous hearth festooned with cauldron chains and turning spits. In the hearth a log fire was smouldering. The place was strangely silent and Mary glanced enquiringly at her companion. He seemed to divine her thoughts.

"It's quiet here during the day. Wait till the evening, though. You'll have your work cut out then. I suppose I'd better take you to your room."

Carrying the valise he made for an inner door but, before he could lift the latch, it opened and a woman entered the room. Dressed entirely in black she was tall and commanding, with jet-black hair pulled so severely into a top-knot that her sallow skin seemed stretched to breaking point over her high cheek bones. Immediately Mary noticed two other peculiar characteristics about her: her hands were long and scrawny, almost like talons, and one of her eyes was a different size from the other, caused in part by a heavy, drooping lid. The woman lifted her head and stared at Mary with her good eye, which was as black as coal.

"I expected someone plain. Your father is not a handsome man."

Mary tried to think of something to say, but felt lost for words. The woman went on in a low, almost masculine voice:

"There will be no fripperies in this place. You are here to work. I take it you can work—or has your father deluded me on that score as well?"

Mary's spirits, high a moment or two ago, fell. She disliked this tall, severe woman who was casting aspersions on the integrity of her father. That made two people she disliked already and for a moment she wished she were back home. But she kept her voice steady as she replied.

"My father has not deluded you, ma'am. I have been brought up on a farm and I know how to work. I cannot help it if I am not as plain as you wish, but I assure you I will do my best in any task you entrust to me."

The woman's drooping eye-lid flickered. "We shall see. You are on a three months' trial period, but that can be waived if you do not give satisfaction. Take her bag to the attic, Mathias."

15

"Yes, Mistress Gronow," said Mathias, and disappeared through the doorway. Mary heard his boots clumping on a staircase and steeled herself again to meet the intimidating gaze of her new mistress.

CHAPTER 3

"YOU WILL RISE at dawn," said Mistress Gronow, "and help Davies in the kitchen. At present she is in Merthyr Mawr seeing to the supply of vegetables. Then you will clean the bedrooms and put the beds in order. After that you will wash down the passages and staircase and see to the downstairs rooms. In the afternoon you will gather eggs from the orchard and help Davies prepare the food. In the evenings you will serve drink and meals and attend to the wants of those who might be staying here. Do you know how to decant wines?"

"No, ma'am, said Mary.

"No matter, Mathias will show you. Most of our trade is in ale and porter, so you will not often be called upon to do that. When Mr. Robert is here you will serve him before any other. Is that understood?"

"Yes, ma'am. Who is Mr. Robert?"

Gronow's eyelid quivered with surprise.

"Mr. Robert is the owner of this inn. He has a house in Bridgend but mostly resides here when he's in the country."

"I'm told it becomes busy in the evening," said Mary, trying to sound bright and eager for work.

For reply Gronow reached down to her side and brought into view a bunch of large keys attached to her waist by a leather thong.

"I will show you the rooms. Follow me."

She left the kitchen and led the way to a dark hall which would have been spacious but for the intrusion of a staircase and a large grandfather clock. Under the stairs was a low door which Gronow unlocked. Mary followed her down a short flight of uneven stone steps and, although she could see little in the darkness, she knew from the vinegary smell that she was in the cellar. As her eyes

16

became accustomed to the gloom, relieved only by a diffused light emanating from an aperture set high up in one of the walls, she could see rows of barrels and smaller casks. In the centre of the flag-stoned floor was a rickety table piled high with glasses and pewter mugs, and a heavy, oak refectory chair. On a shelf in the corner was a brass candlestick, thick with grease.

"Mathias looks after the cellar," said Gronow. "He will pass what is required to you through that hatch." She indicated the aperture. "Then you will serve the guests. There—" the thin hands moved round in the direction of a cluster of smaller casks, "is Mr. Robert's personal cognac which he imports direct from France. It is for his consumption only. On no account are you to give it to anyone else. Do you understand?"

"Yes, Mistress Gronow."

"Neither will you mention that we have it to anyone who is here. Cognac is not easy to obtain these days with this war going on."

She swept back up the steps and when Mary caught up with her she carefully re-locked the cellar door. Leading off from the hall were three other doors, one of them, because of its size and massive iron hinges, obviously the main entrance. Gronow went to one of the other doors and flung it open, revealing a long, narrow room furnished with tall settles, stools and heavy wooden tables. The floor was six inches deep in soiled straw and smelled abominably of stale ale.

Gronow's aquiline nose wrinkled.

"This is the packmen's room. They have the money but will not pay for comfort so we do not provide it. You will change the straw once a week."

She turned to the other door, which was already open, and Mary found herself in another room, square in shape and much better furnished, with chairs and tables of solid, well-polished oak. A stone fireplace filled one wall, and a pleasant latticed window looked out upon the forecourt and trees.

"This is where the better class of traveller dines," explained Gronow. "You will keep it clean at all times. When Mathias supplies you with whatever is required he will pass it through the hatch, as I told you."

17

She pointed and Mary saw that the cellar aperture was now almost at floor level and was fitted with a sliding door.

"And here," said Gronow, walking through a short, narrow passage, "is where we put those who require privacy."

The third room, although small, was delightful in appearance, with a bow window fitted with damask curtains and a window seat on which were cushions of the same material. A small highly polished Jacobean table with matching chairs took up the centre space and Gronow was obviously pleased to show it off, for a look of pride came into her face.

"Sometimes we have important people dining here. Lords and ladies, even, travelling to London and waiting for connections with the stage coaches at Ewenny. When we have them you must be on your best behaviour. I shall be observing you closely during your probation period."

She cast a final approving glance around the room then returned to the hall. Mary heard her feet on the stairs and had to run to catch up with her. At the top of the staircase Gronow paused, slightly out of breath.

"You will sweep this landing every day and polish it once a week. You will also polish that chest. It is one of Mr. Robert's most prized possessions, having been made by a carpenter whose life he saved. If you do not do that he will be annoyed."

Mary paused to look at the six foot long chest, but barely had time to admire its solid construction and large lock before she heard Gronow's voice in one of the bedrooms.

"This is where the packmen sleep."

Mary entered a musty room, stale-smelling and depressing, with only a small window. On the bare floor boards were four low, roughly-made wooden beds, each covered by stained, unevenly-filled canvas palliasses.

"These mattresses are chaff-filled," said Gronow. "Shake them out every morning through the window, but not in the room. And don't stand too close to them because sometimes they become verminous."

She ushered Mary out and closed the door quickly as though to prevent contamination following them, and led the way to the next room which, repeating the pattern of downstairs, was better furnished, complete with basin and tall water jug. Two box beds were in this room and Gronow pointed at them.

"These mattresses are horse-hair filled. They present no trouble but examine them every morning. They must be repaired the moment you see the slightest tear otherwise the hairs come out. And now I will show you where people of quality sleep."

With pride once more in her eyes Gronow took Mary to the last room. This was tastefully furnished and contained a four-poster bed. It was the first time Mary had seen one at close quarters and she stared at it with awe. Noticing this Gronow's severe expression softened momentarily.

"I see you are impressed. This is my favourite room in the house."

Mary ran her fingers over the intricate carving of one of the posts and felt the brocaded coverlet with the soft feather mattress underneath. She glanced out through the window at the tree-lined river.

"It's beautiful, Mistress Gronow. It will be a pleasure to wait on the people who stay in this room."

Gronow regarded her silently for a moment, then the severity returned.

"See that you do. Now then, there are several things I must tell you. The most important is that you are to mind your own business. In this inn you may hear conversations not intended for your ears. On no account are you to repeat things, or indulge in gossip of any kind. Is that understood?"

"Yes, ma'am."

"You may hear things from many sources—from the guests, from Mr. Robert, from myself, from anybody. Whatever you hear you must keep to yourself, and if anyone tries to prise information from you, you must let me know immediately. There are busy-bodies about today who would do mischief if they could. You must be on your guard at all times."

"Yes, ma'am."

"And no doubt you will hear Mr. Robert referred to by another

19

name—Cap Coch, for example. Do you know what that means in English?"

"Yes, Red Cap."

"Correct. It is a name you will ignore if you hear it. Mr. Robert's normal headgear is a tricorn, although he does wear a red cap occasionally when he travels to the continent. The name is a calumny invented by his enemies. On no account will you refer to him by that name and neither are you to admit that you know of its existence. Is that perfectly clear?"

"Yes, ma'am."

"Very well. You are allowed into every room in the house except one. That is Mr. Robert's room. I shall show you where it is so that there can be no mistake. Follow me."

She brushed past Mary and returned to the landing. There she pointed to a door nearly as massive as the inn's main door.

"That is Mr. Robert's room. I repeat—on no account are you to enter it."

Mary eyed the heavy iron stays securely screwed into the woodwork. The door looked strong enough to withstand the impact of a cannon ball.

"You may see it open or ajar," went on Gronow. "You will still not go near it. Only I am allowed in to do the cleaning. Now you may go to your room. Unpack your things and be in the kitchen in half an hour, properly attired. Davies will have returned by then."

She nodded at the dark panelling of the wall and Mary's heart sank. Facing her was a narrow and very steep flight of stairs.

"Up there," said Gronow. "Your bedroom is the one on the right."

Mary went up the claustrophobic stairs, wondering what she would do in case of fire. To make things worse every step creaked and groaned under her weight, but when she reached her room she had a pleasant surprise. Although small, measuring barely eight feet by ten, it was comfortably furnished, with a pleasant little bed against one wall and a diminutive wardrobe against the other. She rushed to the small latticed window and was delighted to find that she could look out across the trees to green fields

20

beyond. Below was the gravelled forecourt at the end of which was the dark-green, slowly-moving river. It was, as she had first thought, a perfect setting for a country inn.

She pushed the window wide open and stared at the river. Unsettling though her reception had been at the hands of Mathias and Gronow, and with the further threat of a peculiar master who disliked being called Cap Coch, she felt happy and liberated; and if the going became tough she had the river as a friend. Called the Ogmore, one of its tributaries was the Afon Garw which passed the foot of Pwll y Cymmer, and so some of its water had come past her own home. In a way, therefore, it was a link with the life she had left, an assurance that her family was not far away in case of need.

Then she remembered that she had only half an hour to get ready. She sluiced her face in the wash bowl and threw her valise on the bed. Selecting her serving frock and apron she placed the rest in the wardrobe and dressed quickly. With a small hand-mirror she examined her hair and, emulating Gronow, pulled it tight into a bun, anchoring it securely with pins and a ribbon, then covered as much as possible with her lace cap.

She was ready, without frippery, to start work at the New Inn.

CHAPTER 4

IT DID NOT take Mary long to get into the routine of the inn. Davies, the cook, lived out in a cottage at Merthyr Mawr, arriving at dawn to begin her day's work. She brought with her William, an imbecile son who, although he could do little else, was adept at cleaning the kitchen utensils and drawing water from the well, thus relieving Mary of two considerable chores. Mary went out of her way to befriend the poor creature who, with his gaping mouth and vacant eyes, was at first timorous, then took to her with the trusting affection of his unfortunate kind, of whom there were many in the Vale, caused by in-breeding. This in turn endeared Mary to Davies, a buxom, kindly widow of sixty, and it was not long before the three of them were cavorting about the

21

kitchen, singing at their tasks, as though they had been friends all their lives. Mary also enjoyed cleaning the rooms and the furniture which she did with such zest that one day she earned the grudging approval of Mistress Gronow. She took most delight with the better rooms but turned her hand also to the packmen's abodes and, with much elbow grease and regular scrubbing, brought about an improvement there also, so much so that one pedlar complained that he had to think twice before spitting. Fortunately for Mary residential trade was slack during her first week at the inn. Travellers called for a drink or a meal but rarely stayed, a state of affairs she gathered from Davies not unusual in fine weather, when the itinerant traders preferred sleeping under a hedge to the luxury of a bed that cost twopence. Neither did the better class of traveller come to stay, except for a farmer from Maesteg who left after the first night; and so Mary had time to do her cleaning work thoroughly, much to her satisfaction and sense of achievement.

Very soon she noticed that Mistress Gronow was in the habit of retiring to her room for a nap every afternoon, and this gave her brief respites to look around and acquaint herself with her surroundings. The little bridge, she discovered, was very old and rarely free of traffic. Always there were pedlars, packmen or clothiers moving across, destined for Cowbridge or Swansea, their wares slung in sacks or panniers across their shoulders. She was surprised to find that many of them had Scottish or Cornish accents and spoke of travelling distances beyond her imagination. On the whole they seemed a happy, sociable lot, always ready to talk or pass the time of day. Farm carts were a regular sight also, their drivers constantly grumbling about the tolls, the state of the crops or the intransigence of their masters, who paid them only twelve shillings a week, with a little more at harvest time. Occasionally larger carriages passed, to and from Ewenny which, with the New Inn, lay on the principal coaching road that ran from east to west. Sometimes the passengers alighted to partake of refreshments and then the inn was in sudden turmoil to satisfy their needs, after which they would depart as suddenly as they had come.

Most of all Mary loved the times when animals used the bridge. Herds of cattle frequently passed, some of them quite large, and a few of the drovers appeared to be important and influential people, if their conversations over a jug of ale were to be believed. Then there were the sheep. Two days after she arrived Mary was awakened by what seemed to be a thousand bleats, accompanied by the barking of many dogs, and when she rushed to the window she saw that the bridge was packed tight with the woolly animals. Being a farmer's daughter she could not resist dressing quickly and running down to witness the spectacle and was amazed to see the bridge barred at one end and that the sheep were tumbling head first into the river. Then she saw they were being forced out through apertures in the stonework of the bridge and that a shepherd on the far bank was fishing out the weaker swimmers with his crook. On the bridge itself the pressure of the struggling mass, aided by dogs running up and down the parapet, was popping the sheep out two or three at a time, to hit the water with resounding smacks. Then, aided by a gentle current, they swam to the far bank, where they gathered in a frightened and complaining flock. Seeing Mary's intent expression a weather-beaten, besmocked old shepherd smiled at her.

"What's the matter, miss. Ain't you seen sheep-dipping before?"

"Never like this."

"Happens every year," said the shepherd. "We'll be doing the shearing in a day or two. Then we'll round up the Southerndown lot."

Mary watched for a few more minutes, fascinated, then tore herself away. There were tasks to be done and she did not want to offend Mistress Gronow.

One of the jobs Mary liked more than any other was to collect eggs from the orchard. She quickly came to know the individual hens and their favourite laying places, and enjoyed once more the feel of the warm, brown eggs as she slipped them into her basket. She enjoyed, too, the walk around the orchard, for the apple trees were in full bloom, conveying the promise of a bumper crop to follow. She was delighted also to find beehives at the far end of the orchard and prayed that the bees would do their work well, for she loved honey and knew that the wax would be a great aid in her polishing.

Then, towards the end of the first week, an event occurred that was to bring the slack period at the inn to an end. She had decided to visit Mathias at the stable for, being of a generous disposition, she had an uneasy feeling that she had been a little hard on him the first day, and wished to make amends. She had seen little of him since their first encounter, glimpsing him only occasionally through the cellar hatch as he handed out jugs of ale or porter, but always he had been polite and well-mannered. In addition there were one or two questions she wanted to ask him so, one day, after raiding the hens' nests to her satisfaction, she approached the stable, placed her egg basket on a mounting block at the entrance, pushed open the split-level door and called out.

There was no answer so she went a little way in and waited for her eyes to become used to the darkness. The familiar smell of hay and straw assailed her nostrils and she heard the unmistakable sound of horses moving in their stalls, but of Mathias there was no sign. She looked up at the loft but that was empty as well.

She was about to turn and go out when she felt something in the vicinity of her neck. She swung round just in time to feel her ribbon being pulled and the next moment her hair had cascaded down to her shoulders. Leaning on a stall, grinning hugely, the ribbon in his hand, was Mathias.

"This was loose," he said profferring her the ribbon. "It was hanging down below your cap."

Mary snatched at the ribbon, fury mounting within her, her previous good intentions abandoned.

"Why did you do that? You frightened me."

"I'm sorry. I didn't mean to." But he was still grinning.

"Oh you—" Mary was temporarily lost for words. "Why didn't you answer? I called out to you."

"I stood up when I heard you. Didn't you see me?"

"How could I see you in the dark? I can hardly see you now."

"Sorry." At last Mathias sounded genuinely contrite. "I'd forgotten about coming in out of the sun. I meant no harm.

24

Anyway, you look nicer like that. I like you with your hair down."

Mollified slightly by his tone Mary nevertheless moved towards the door. She still did not trust Mathias at close quarters, but now was as good a chance as any to put her questions.

"Mathias," she began.

"Daniel," he interjected. "Call me Daniel. It sounds more friendly."

"Very well—Daniel. Tell me, why did you try to prevent me coming here?"

"Did I? I don't remember."

"Oh, yes, you do. You even offered to take me back to Bridgend."

"Well, perhaps I thought you were a bit young and inexperienced."

"I'm eighteen and I've had plenty of experience of housework, and I wish you to understand that I like it here. I enjoy my work and am quite happy. I'm glad I didn't listen to you."

"Pleased to hear it. How're you getting on with Mistress Gronow?"

"Very well."

"Good for you."

Mary smiled. She did not wish to make an enemy of Mathias and quarrelling was against her nature. Then she caught sight of a pony's head above a stall and, forgetting her caution, walked towards it. She stroked the animal's head.

"Isn't he lovely. What's his name?"

"It's not a he, it's a she. Poppy."

"Is she ours?"

"Yes. We use her in the trap."

Mary resumed her stroking. Over her shoulder she said:

"Tell me, Daniel, what sort of person is Mr. Robert?"

"What sort of person? Why d'you want to know?"

"Well, he's my master and I haven't met him yet."

Mathias plucked a straw from a bale and stuck it in his mouth.

"He's on the big side—a powerful man. Ruddy complexion, fairish hair going grey. About fifty. Looks a bit like a farmer—"

"I mean, what sort of a person is he to work for?"

25

"Oh! You won't have any trouble on that score. Do your work well and he'll treat you right. He's very generous to those that please him—especially women."

"Why do some people call him Cap Coch?"

Daniel removed the straw.

"Who told you that?"

"Mistress Gronow."

"Did she also tell you that he doesn't like to be called that?"

"Yes."

"Oh, well, if she's told you that there's no harm in letting you know a bit more. Anyway, it's common knowledge around here. Robert goes a lot to France. He shares a schooner with some men down at Ogmore. They bring back brandy and other things. It's smuggling but so far he's got away with it. But that's not the point. Going to France these days is a tricky business. One day we're at war with them, the next day at peace; and to make sure of his skin Robert wears a red cap—you know, like the French Revolutionaries wear. That way he makes them think he's sympathetic towards them, so he gets his brandy."

"Isn't he running a risk?"

"He's running a risk of being thought a revolutionary. That's why he objects to being called Cap Coch. Smuggling's one thing, revolution's another. If the authorities thought he was an agitator he'd be behind bars."

"Is he a revolutionary?"

"If he is he's too clever to admit it. All I know is you won't catch him wearing his red cap around here. A tricorn he wears."

"That's what Mistress Gronow said."

"Did she also tell you not to talk about it?"

"Yes."

"Then why are you talking to me?"

"Just curious, that's all. If it's generally known I see no harm in asking."

"No harm but be careful who you talk to. Curiosity killed the cat."

Mary studied Mathias's good-looking face to see if he was mocking her again, but he appeared to be serious.

26

"I'm not all that curious," she said. "But if I am to please my master it's as well to know certain things."

"Quite right. Anything else you want to know now that you're here?"

Mary resumed her stroking of Poppy.

"No thank you. Oh, I do like Poppy. I think she likes me, too."

"Then I think I deserve a reward for answering all those questions. How about a kiss?"

In a flash Mary was out through the door. Mathias tried to grab her but she eluded him. Laughing she slammed the door in his face and retrieved her basket. She ran towards the inn but before she could get there she was confronted by a frowning Gronow.

"What are you doing here, girl?" Gronow's suspicious eyes fastened on Mary's dishevelled hair and dress, on which a few hen's feathers were still adhering.

"Nothing, ma'am. Just collecting eggs."

Gronow drew herself up to her full height.

"Then take them to the kitchen and go and make yourself presentable. Mr. Robert has returned and wishes to see you. If you keep him waiting he will be angry and you'd better make a good impression, believe me."

CHAPTER 5

Mary stared at herself in the mirror. She had washed quickly and brushed the chicken feathers out of her dress but her hair still hung down about her shoulders. All the week she had kept it tight in its prim and proper bun, as a serving maid should, but Mathias had said he liked her hair loose. The question was, would Gronow approve and what of the as yet unseen Mr. Robert? She glanced again at the mirror and made up her mind. She pulled the comb several times through the springy, almost unruly tresses and put her cap at a more jaunty angle at the back of her head. If anyone objected she could easily change it back again. Quickly she went down to the dining room.

In the hall Mistress Gronow was waiting for her. The one good eye swept Mary up and down, taking in her hair and dress with one glance.

"Your hair," snapped Gronow. "What have you done with it?"

"I've let it down," said Mary, suddenly flustered by Gronow's tone. "I didn't have time to do it properly."

Gronow seized her shoulder and propelled her towards the dining room door.

"There's no time now. Mr. Robert can't be kept waiting. I'll speak to you later."

She pushed Mary through the doorway into the dining room which was heavy with tobacco smoke. As her eyes focused through the blue haze she became aware of a heavily-built man standing in front of the fireplace. From Mathias's description she recognised him immediately as Mr. Robert. He was not tall but gave the impression of bulk and strength. Clad in a dark-blue, high-collared coat with long tails, cut away in front to show a yellow, embroidered waistcoat, his legs encased in yellowing buckskin trousers thrust into tall riding boots, he looked more like a prosperous country gentleman than an innkeeper, an impression heightened by a ruddy complexion, clear blue eyes and hair pulled forward over the forehead in the new French fashion. When he spoke his voice was deep and had an accent Mary could not place, more like the West Country pedlars she had met.

"And so this is Mary Tudor. Has she given you satisfaction, Mistress Gronow?"

"She does her work well," said Gronow grudgingly. "I told her to be ready for you but she's not fully presentable at the moment, in spite of my warning."

"Oh!" Robert's expression remained the same but his eyes danced with amusement. "In what way, Mistress Gronow? I see nothing amiss."

"Her hair," snapped Gronow. "She had it up tight as she should. Now she's let it down. She had no permission from me."

"Let her hair be," said Robert, taking a sip from a brandy glass he was holding. "She's presentable enough. Better looking

28

than the last one we had. You're too hard on your girls, Rachel. You'll lose this one, too, if you're not careful. If she does her work well, let her be."

Mary could almost feel Gronow writhing beside her. Then Robert addressed himself directly to her.

"So you're a farmer's daughter, I hear."

"Yes, sir."

"Good. I'm from farming stock myself. Would still be but the inn keeps me busy—and pays better than the land. Have you got used to everything around here now?"

"Yes, sir."

"It's not so bad, is it? We're in the country. Plenty of fields and farms round about. You'll see lots of animals and farm carts. It should stop you feeling home-sick. You're not home-sick, are you, m'dear?"

"No, sir. I like it here."

"Good. Then you'll stay, I'm sure. Serve me civilly and do your work for Mistress Gronow and all will be well. Now then, let me introduce you to someone you'll see a lot of from now on —whilst I'm here, that is. Ebenezer, Benjamin! Pay your respects to Mary Tudor, our new girl."

Mary looked in the direction of Robert's gesticulating arm and immediately felt a thrill of apprehension. Seated at a table near the fire were two of the most villainous-looking men she had ever seen. One, a thin individual in a greasy top-coat, knee-breeches and dirty white stockings, had long, lank, black hair, as greasy as his coat, an aquiline nose, cold, staring eyes and thin, cruel lips. The other, dressed equally shabbily, was fat but had the same cruel face, made worse in his case by a hare-lip. To Mary's horror she saw that the latter had an iron hook in place of a hand and that one leg of his breeches was tied loosely around a wooden peg. Both men were still wearing their hats—hard, felt tricorns— and they stared appraisingly at her, grinning slyly. Stiflling her revulsion Mary tried to smile back.

"They're not much to look at, I grant you," said Robert jovially, "but they're good friends of mine so treat them well. Take your hats off you ignorant bloody pair."

The thin one immediately removed his headgear, but the other was too slow for Robert, who reached across and knocked the tricorn to the floor, taking with it a dirty and moth-eaten wig, revealing a pate as bald and shiny as a freshly scrubbed piglet.

"The bald one's Benjamin," explained Robert. "No hand, no leg and no hair. No bloody tongue either, and deaf with it." He raised his voice. "Show Mary where your tongue was, Ben."

Benjamin obediently opened his mouth and, to help with the view, pulled down his lower lip with his hook. Mary closed her eyes in horror.

"Not the best looking pair, you must admit," said Robert, "but they've stood by me through thick and thin many a year now, and I'll stand by them or my name's not Robert."

Benjamin retrieved his wig from the floor, dusted it down and replaced it on his head, together with his hat. Both men glanced knowingly at each other then resumed their lascivious grinning. Mary tore her eyes away from the hideous pair and looked again at Robert, expecting to be dismissed. Instead he drew up a chair and handed her his empty glass.

"Fetch me a brandy, there's a good girl, and when you come back I want you to remain. You may as well know something of what goes on around here."

"Is that wise?" Gronow's voice cut across the room like a knife.

"Why not?" Robert's tone was mild. "There's nothing special about today's business, is there? Who's waiting to see me?"

"Nathaniel Evans, Martin Llewelyn and Gwladys Davies."

"All with the usual, I suppose."

"Evans and Llewelyn have been dispossessed and Gwladys Davies wants to borrow money to buy a coffin for her husband."

"A coffin, eh! So old Davies snuffed it while I was away, did he?"

"Three days ago. She's been here every day to see you."

"Well then, there's nothing special about all that. The sooner Mary realises that her master is kindly disposed the better."

There was a sudden and muffled sniggering from the two reprobates at the table, stifled immediately by a glare from Robert. He turned to Mary.

30

"Go now, m'dear, and fetch the brandy. When you come back you'll realise what a safe place you've come to, where much good is done. Then, when you next see your father you can tell him that he need have no fears about his daughter's welfare."

Mary hurried from the room and, when she returned with a full glass of brandy, found that the table had been drawn up in front of Robert. On it was a large ledger and a writing set made out of ivory, complete with three quill pens. Robert took the brandy and motioned her to sit at a nearby settle in the ingle-nook. Gronow then entered the room with a gnarled, bent old woman and led her to the table.

"Well, Gwladys, said Robert. "Right sorry I am to hear of the death of your husband. How did it happen?"

"He was gored by Squire Edward's bull on the way to Cow-bridge market. I told him not to go that day, but he would and Squire won't give no compensation—not a penny. Two weeks it took him to die. I can't afford a proper coffin and church won't bury him without one. A pauper's burial he'll have otherwise." She wiped her eyes with the end of a ragged shawl.

"Where will you go now?" asked Robert gently.

"I can live with my son. I'm not worried about the future. It's the coffin I'm worried about. Daniel was regular at church-going —went all his life. Now they won't bury him without a proper coffin."

"Oh, yes, they will. I'll see to that, Gwladys. I'll have a word with Parson Newman. How much does a good oak coffin cost these days?"

"Tom Howells of Ewenny can do one for five shillings."

"Then you shall have five shillings. Give her five shillings, Ebenezer."

Ebenezer fumbled in a leather purse then handed the money to Gwladys, who broke into a flood of tears of gratitude. Robert took up a quill, dipped it carefully in the ink and made an entry in the ledger.

"Go now, Gwladys, and do what is necessary. If I have time I'll come to the funeral."

Still weeping the old woman was led from the room by

Gronow. A moment later she reappeared with an equally old man dressed in a shepherd's smock.

"Ah! Nathaniel Evans," said Robert. "What ails you?"

"It's Squire Edwards," said Evans. "He won't let me graze on Southerndown Common, and me looking after his sheep all these years."

"Edwards again! What's going on on the other side of the river? Why has he stopped you grazing?"

"He says I'm too old for work. That may be, but Squire said I could keep a few sheep when I'd finished, but now he's gone back on his word. He's got a new shepherd and won't let me keep the half dozen he promised me. There's even talk he wants me out of my hut—"

"How many sheep did he say you could keep?"

"Six, and two pigs. They're all on the old side—ones I'd saved from the cliffs the last year or two. Squire says I'm not to mark them, but if I don't they'll get mixed up with his."

"How much money have you got saved up?"

"Money? Nothing, Master Robert. Not a shilling to my name."

"Give him two, Ebenezer. That'll be enough to keep him until I see Edwards. Don't worry, Nathaniel, you'll keep your sheep and hut. The Squire won't throw you out after I've spoken to him."

The old man's lips trembled as he stumbled out his thanks. Robert waved him away and made another entry in the ledger.

"Fetch Martin Llewelyn. I want to see him particular."

Gronow glided out and returned with a tall, gangling man who kept writhing his cloth hat between his hands.

"Well, Martin," said Robert. "What have you been up to whilst I've been away?"

"It's not what I've been up to, Master Robert. It's Sir Roger who's been up to things—and that John Nicholl."

"Why? What've they been doing?"

"They've enclosed some of the land to the north of Candleston and thrown me out."

"Did you have notification of the enclosure?"

Llewelyn shuffled his feet.

"I didn't, though I've been told it was pinned to church door these last six months, but I didn't see it."

"Nor any of your friends?"

"No master. Few of us can read down there."

Robert's eyes narrowed and for several moments he did not speak. Then: "Are you sure it's Sir Roger de Cantelupes and John Nicholl we're talking about?"

"I am sure."

"Got to be careful here. Their land meets down at the coast so I've got to know my facts to go about things the right way."

"It is them all right. There's no doubt about it."

"You know Sir Roger's been having trouble with the sand, don't you?"

"That I do, but that's no excuse for getting me off. I can do more with it than he can."

"Has he offered you an alternative?"

"Only down by the dunes, but that's no good. It's sand there, too. Even the trees are dying of the bloody stuff."

"Well, Martin, I'll try and help. I can do something with Sir Roger but I ain't sure of Nicholl. He's not been here long enough for us to get properly acquainted. Anyway you've left it late."

"I know, but if anybody can do anything it's you. Sir Roger only wants my bit because there's soil there. He's had his eye on it for some time."

"How far has the sand encroached on that place of his?"

"It's right up to the walls. Another gale and he'll have to dig himself out."

"Is that so?" Robert drummed on the table with his fingers and for the first time Mary noticed how large and powerful his hands were. As though talking to himself he went on: "So Candleston Castle has come to the end of the road, along with its master. I've always said they'd go together. Very interesting. Very interesting indeed." In a louder voice he added: "I'm glad you've come to me, Martin. You've told me something I wanted to know. I'll help you, but don't forget Nicholl's a lawyer. I doubt if I'll get past him. But I'll see what can be done. Go now and I'll get in touch with you later."

33

Llewelyn bowed and shuffled from the room. Robert pushed his chair back and stood in front of the hearth, stretching to his full height. He smiled down at Mary, an expression of triumph and satisfaction on his bland face.

"There you are, m'dear. Now you can see you've come to a good place. Your master has some influence around these parts."

Mary smiled back. That a show of power and authority had been put on for her benefit was obvious, although why for her in particular was mystifying. But whatever the reason she warmed towards Robert, for a man who used his position to aid his more unfortunate countrymen was to be admired. He was an obvious champion of the oppressed; and if he had revelled in an ostentatious display of influence then that could be forgiven. She remembered the look of gratitude on the faces of the supplicants and so there was genuine admiration in her answering smile.

Then she caught sight of Benjamin and Ebenezer. They were grinning again at her. Why on earth, she wondered, did such a kindly man as Mr. Robert have two such dreadful men as companions?

CHAPTER 6

MARY WROTE to her father telling him how happy she was in her post and describing Mr. Robert's kindness to the people who had asked his help. But soon after there occurred an event that was to plant a seed of doubt in her mind, although she did not realise its true significance until later.

It came about with the onset of a rainy spell when the pedlars, as Mary had been forewarned, preferred the comfort of a bed to the damp embrace of a hedgerow. By now Mary was used to the routine of the inn and the sudden influx of visitors left her unruffled. She had also become well-known to the local farming community and, as at Pwll y Cymmer, many were the hopefuls who began to call to solicit her favours. Some of the better-class yeomen tended to be over-familiar with her, asking for assignations or trying to pinch her bottom, all of which Mary took in good spirit, retaliating only when the overtures became too personal. Then she was not averse to slapping a face or using her tongue, for which she discovered a new-found sharpness; but by and large most of the ripostes were given and received with great good humour and the New Inn gained a popular and appealing attraction. With the more persistent farmers Mary found the ploy of threatening to tell their wives or sweethearts effective and so no real or undesirable molestation occurred; and she was particularly gentle with the more backward labourers who called merely to gawp at her over a jug of ill-afforded ale. One lad in particular who was so obviously in love with her that he was always continuously tongue-tied in her presence, was rewarded with an occasional extra measure, surreptitiously slipped to him when Mistress Gronow was not looking.

The packmen were usually too tired or too engrossed in their business to mount sustained offensives against her virginity, although some tried. Mary got on well with most of them and found their stories of far-away places fascinating. By and large they responded to her kindnesses, for most were far from home and had patient wives and families dependent on their hard-earned money. They were not ungenerous but careful, although one or two, after finding that Mary had run a warming pan over their mattresses, slipped her a penny before leaving. They, too, passed on word that a good-looking and kindly serving girl was at the New Inn, and so trade gradually increased, a fact that did not go unnoticed by either Gronow or Robert.

One particular evening, when the summer rain was falling with a persistency that dampened everything, making the trees drip and the inn smell of mildew, several packmen called within a short time of each other. Oozing water and soaked to the skin they congregated in the room put aside for them, where they drank ale and supped on bread and cheese. Because of their condition their usually lively spirits and animated exchange of gossip were absent, and after a while one of their number, an old, white-haired man, picked up his pannier bags and removed himself to the dining room, where he was confronted by a startled and surprised Mary.

"I'm sorry," said Mary. "You're not allowed in here."

"Och, awa' wi' ye, lassie," said the packman. "Din ye ken I'm soaked? I want the warmth of a fire."

Mary glanced at the door, afraid that Gronow might appear.

"I think you'd better go back to the other room. If Mistress Gronow sees you—"

The door opened and Gronow came in. She took one scathing look at the packman then glowered at Mary.

"Why has this man been allowed in here?"

Flustered as always by Gronow's intimidating presence Mary blurted out:

"I did tell him, Mistress Gronow, but he won't go."

Gronow came up to the fire and turned the full power of her gaze on the old man, who returned it without flinching.

"The girl has told you," said Gronow. "Packmen are not allowed in here. Go to the room assigned for you."

The pedlar dropped his bags in front of the fire.

"To hell wi' ye, woman. I'm no' shifting from here."

"Go this moment or I shall call the master."

"Call who you like. Ye dinna expect men tae sit like wet scarecrows in a room wi' no fire."

Gronow drew herself up to her full height, looking like a menacing, black wand.

"Very well. Just wait and see what happens to you."

"Wait! How much does it cost for a man tae sit in front of a fire in this hell-hole of a country?"

"In this room you must pay the price of a bed—a good one."

"Are ye referring tae the flea-ridden thing I slept in last time? I wouldna put a dog tae sleep there?"

"No. The bed that goes with this room costs threepence."

"Threepence, eh! Daylight robbery." The packman reached into a voluminous waistcoat pocket and produced a leather purse. "Well, ye shall have it and good riddance tae ye. I'm off hame the morrow. Back to Bonnie Scotland and stay there for ever, thanks be tae God."

He held out the silver coin but before Gronow could take it he snapped his fingers tight.

"How many beds in the room, woman?"

"Two."

"Then I'll tak the both. I want peace and quiet the nicht. I deserve it after what I've been through. And I want a dram or two of whuskey. I tak it ye've got whuskey, woman."

"Welsh whiskey."

The packman rolled his eyes in despair.

"Welsh whuskey! An abomination in the sight of the Lord. But I'll tak it. Here's a shilling, woman. Let the girl get me a dram or two and reserve that room for me. Ye'll never see me again, which will please Angus McGregor as much as it pleases ye."

Gronow took the shilling and nodded to Mary, who hurried over to the hatch to order the whiskey from Mathias. When she returned Gronow had gone and McGregor had moved his chair nearer the hearth where the heat made the steam rise from his clothes in clouds. He winked at Mary.

"Ye've a right bitch there, lassie. I'm sorry for ye."

"Oh, she's not too bad," said Mary loyally. "She's only doing her duty."

"Duty! The only duty that woman understands is money." He drained the glass at one go, grimacing as the fiery liquid hit his stomach. "Och! This Welsh stuff is teerible, but it warms ye. Get me another one."

He handed Mary the empty glass, and produced another shilling from his purse.

"Keep me supplied, lassie, and when that runs out ask for more. Keep old Angus going and there'll be a penny or two in it for ye. I'm no' going tae stint the nicht."

Mary was quickly back with the replenished vessel. McGregor eyed her admiringly.

"Are ye the lass I've been hearing about? Mary—is that ye'r name?"

Mary nodded.

"Ye certainly are bonny," said McGregor. "Nearly as guid-looking as the highland lassies I ken. Weel, Mary, keep the whuskey flowing and I'll no forget ye before I go. I promise ye that."

37

Mary did as she was told and was pleased to do so. She liked the old Scotsman with his twinkling eyes and bluff manner and admired the way he had dealt with Gronow. The room gradually filled, mostly with farming folk, and she was kept busy serving them and answering calls from the packmen's room; but she kept an eye on McGregor's glass, refilling it as necessary. After an hour or two he was obviously under the influence of the drink and became an object of ribaldry on the part of some of the men. They cajoled him to sing, which McGregor did, although no one could understand the words. He ended up doing a sort of high-land reel on the hearth then collapsed back on his chair, exhausted and out of breath.

"Well done, Angus," shouted someone. "We'll be sorry to see you go. When d'you leave us ?"

"Crack o' dawn," said Angus, downing his ninth whiskey. "An' I'll tell ye this. Right sorry I am in some ways. Ye've been good to me round here—at least most of you have. I've done well out of ye. But now I'm off tae bonny Scotland—for ever."

"How long have you been in Wales, Angus ?"

"Eight year. I've no' been hame in all tha' time."

"Your wife won't know you when you get there."

"She'll know me all reet. Back to the croft it is for Angus, an' no stirring after that."

"What'll you live on ?"

MacGregor stared at the questioner and so did Mary, who was carrying a tray of drinks at that moment. It was Ebenezer, who was standing by the hatch holding a tankard of porter.

McGregor's eyes, trying hard to focus through the smoke, became sly and cautious.

"I'll manage. I've enough put by."

"What'll you do with your goods ?" persisted Ebenezer. "Or have you sold all your stock ?"

"No, I've no' sold everything. I've kept enough to see me through the journey hame. Leather sells well wherever ye are."

"Then I wish you good luck." Ebenezer raised his tankard in salutation and all the other men did likewise. McGregor responded with his glass, obviously pleased with his popularity, but after downing one more whiskey he hoisted himself to his feet and announced his retirement to bed.

"Where's the lassie?" he shouted. "Where's Mary? She promised tae tuck me up for the nicht."

There was much bantering at that, which McGregor received with a wide grin.

"Och, away wi' ye, ye dirty-minded bastards. I'm too old for that sort of thing."

"Never too old, Angus."

One of the men fetched Mary, who blushed at the loud laughter that greeted her. McGregor slung his panniers across his shoulder, nearly falling in the fire with the effort. Mary supported the swaying figure and, amid many calls of good wishes, escorted the old Scotsman from the room. On the stairs McGregor and his bags took up the entire space so she had to walk behind him, fearful that he might fall backwards on the candle. Once in his room McGregor made straight for one of the beds and collapsed upon it.

"Och, lassie, I canna drink much these days. Not used to it, d'ye ken. I've saved my pennies for eight years and noo I've almost lost the taste. Still, a good nicht an' I enjoyed it. An' I'm warm, lassie, warm as toasted cheese. Have ye warmed this bed?"

"I slipped up just now," said Mary, unlacing his boots. "You were so wet I was afraid you'd catch cold."

"Bless ye, child." McGregor produced his purse and fumbled inside it. "Here, tak this for helping me." He thrust a threepenny piece into her hand.

Mary took the coin and made to lift McGregor's legs on to the bed but he resisted her.

"'Tis not enough. I want you to have this as well."

He reached down beside the bed and, after two clumsy attempts, succeeded in undoing a strap on one of the panniers. Inside was a jumbled collection of boots, slippers and gaiters, all made of clean-smelling new leather. McGregor felt about inside then cursed and undid the other pannier.

"I want ye to have a book mark. A special one. There's a guid one here somewhere."

He fumbled about so long among a multitude of belts, sheaths and aprons that Mary began to feel anxious, a vision of an angry Gronow in her mind. She allowed McGregor to search a little longer then blurted out:

"Mr. McGregor, I must go. I have lots of work to do."

Reluctantly McGregor straightened up.

"I understand, lassie. I know what a bitch ye've got lordin' over ye. Ye shall have it in the morning. It's special for ye, for the kindness ye've shown. A real lowland calf leather book mark embossed wi' shamrock. Cost all of a shilling an' ye'll treasure it all ye'r life."

"Thank you, Mr. McGregor," said Mary, drawing the blanket over the now recumbent figure.

"Ye must have it to remember me by," said McGregor sleepily. "Ye shall have it in the morning." His head went back on the pillow and three seconds later he was snoring. Mary took the candle and tip-toed from the room.

Downstairs another two hours of work awaited her, which she did with her customary efficiency, and at midnight succeeded in getting to bed herself. Like McGregor she was asleep almost as soon as her head touched the pillow.

Then, some time in the early morning a sound awoke her. She glanced towards the window and saw that it was still dark. She listened and heard the noise again. It was a scratching sound which appeared to emanate from the passage at the bottom of the stairs. Puzzled, she tried to make out what had caused it, for she knew there were no rats in the house and few mice. Again there was a scratching so she pushed the blanket aside and went to the door, opening it an inch or so to peer into the darkness below. This time she heard another sound, like heavy breathing. Then silence, a heavy, leaden silence which only places in the country experience.

A surge of curiosity prompted Mary to go down and investigate, but she stifled it immediately. She had been warned to mind her own business; and anyway the safety of the establishment was not her concern. Then she heard the unmistakable sound of the front door bolts being quietly drawn and a waft of fresh air struck her face, to cease again almost immediately. Whoever it was in the passage had gone downstairs and left the building. She closed the door and went over to the window.

A quarter moon cast a dim, pallid light over the landscape. The trees, dark in shadow, had ceased their dripping and were waving gently in a slight breeze. Mary stared at them and at the forecourt. There was nothing unusual to be seen but she remained by the window for several minutes, wondering. Suddenly she caught sight of a movement in the bushes at the base of the trees and pushed her nose against the whorled pane to see better. A figure was darting between the shrubs, suspiciously, obviously trying to keep out of sight. For a fleeting moment the clouds cleared the moon and at that moment a man emerged from the shadows and ran out of view behind the pine-end of the inn. It had only been a brief glimpse but there was no mistaking who it was. It was Mathias, the ostler.

Mary continued to stare but there was no further movement. The time, she imagined, was about three o'clock. What Mathias was doing out there instead of being in his bed in the stable was something to ponder at. Probably he had been visiting some girl in Merthyr Mawr village; she would not put that past him, knowing what sort of man he was. But equally he could have been connected with the noise she had heard in the inn. Whatever the reason, she decided, it was obvious that from now on she would have to treat Mathias with even more circumspection than she had in the past. Still thinking about the event, but heavy with fatigue, she went to bed and resumed her sleep, which remained fitful and broken until she rose again at dawn.

After dressing quickly she hurried downstairs to help Davies with the preparation of the breakfasts. The other three pedlars who had lodged in the cheap room appeared, sleepy-eyed and coughing and spluttering as was their wont; but of McGregor there was no sign. After serving the three Mary hurried up to his room, convinced that he had overslept, but his bed was empty. It was ruffled and untidy, as she expected, but the Scotsman and his panniers had gone. Mary felt a sense of disappointment, for she had looked forward to seeing the packman off and receiving his present. She could only surmise that, in his eagerness to return to Scotland he had set off early and forgotten all about her. She shrugged and made to go downstairs again.

Then she caught sight of two scuff marks on the floor. They were long and irregular, as though two gigantic snails had glided across to the door. Annoyance rose within her, for only the day previous she had bees-waxed the floorboards and now she would have to go over them again. She followed the marks to the door, intending to see if the passage had been marked as well. At the door she bumped into Mistress Gronow.

"What are you doing here, girl?" Gronow's voice was sharp, stabbing into her like a knife. "You should be downstairs serving the breakfasts."

"It's Mr. McGregor, ma'am," said Mary. "I came to wake him up but he's not here."

"I know. He left before day-break."

"Before day-break! But he—"

"He what?"

Mary's intuition came quickly to her aid. She decided to say nothing about McGregor's promise of a book-mark.

"Nothing ma'am. But something's marked the floor. I don't know what's done it but it was perfect yesterday."

Gronow glanced down at the floorboards.

"He probably dragged his bags along it. Typical of a packman. You can wax it again later. Go back to the kitchen and help Davies."

Gronow swung round and disappeared from view. Mary took one look around the room, still feeling puzzled and slightly hurt. Then she caught sight of something lying on the floor by the bed where McGregor had slept. She went towards it and picked it up.

It was a leather book-mark, beautifully made in rich, smooth leather, embossed at the bottom with a red and green shamrock.

CHAPTER 7

MARY KEPT THE book-mark without compunction, knowing that it was McGregor's parting gift, although why he had left in such a hurry was a mystery to her. Perhaps in his eagerness to leave for home, aided by a befuddled mind caused by over-indulgence in whiskey, he had forgotten all about her. Perhaps, too, he had put it ready to give her and then mislaid it in the dark and that was why she had found it on the floor. Whatever the reason she was certain that the book-mark was now hers by right, although she decided to say nothing about it, even to Davies; and as far as the strange noises she had heard and the mysterious cavortings of Mathias, the sooner she forgot about them the better. She had been told to mind her own business and that was what she proposed to do. The book-mark was a gift she would treasure and, although she had never possessed a real book of her own, she resolved to purchase one as soon as possible at Bridgend market, probably a small bible. She ran to her room, placed the book-mark under her pillow, then returned to the kitchen to re-commence her tasks.

The thought of possessing a bible suddenly made her realise that she had been so engrossed in her work at the inn she had completely neglected her religious up-bringing. There had been no church near Pwll y Cymmer so Edward, her father, had turned to Methodism, his children doing likewise. Many itinerant preachers had come up the valley, holding open-air meetings, and Mary remembered the emotion-charged services with awe and pleasure. Accordingly she resolved that, at the very first opportunity, she would make amends for her grievous omission and attend service in the near-by Merthyr Mawr church. There could be no transgression in that for the Methodist preachers had urged their listeners to go to Anglican services, and in the absence of a Wesleyan minister that was the best thing to do. As soon as she had the chance, therefore, Mary asked and received from Mistress Gronow a grudging permission to attend service on the first Sunday that trade at the inn was slack.

The opportunity to do so came sooner than expected, for July started with cloudless skies and warm sunshine. Mary prepared for the occasion by ironing her best dress and purchasing a new bonnet inexpensively from a travelling haberdasher. She enquired as to the distance to the church and was told that half an hour's brisk walking would get her there but, not wishing to arrive hot and bedraggled, she gave herself an hour and, final approval having been granted, started off on as fine a summer evening as she could have wished for.

First she ascended the steep little hill that led from the inn to the cross roads which local people said was the haunt of Mallt y Nos and the spirit hounds,* then entered the narrow, leafy lane that led to Merthyr Mawr. Its surface had been badly furrowed by cart wheels and so she had to watch her step; but the birds were singing and the sun cast slivers of light through the hedge-rows. On either side were the meadows and rich fields of the Nicholl estate which, she had been told, was the richest in the district; and so her country-bred spirit felt lighter and gayer than at any time since leaving home, a mood enhanced by the knowledge that she was about to make up for her recent lack of religious endeavour. Because of this she enjoyed every inch of the walk, not hurrying but pausing now and again to examine the hedgerow flowers and savour their scent. Before she realised it she came upon the thatched cottages of the village and there she paused, suddenly surprised at the quietness of the place. She had expected to see people hurrying to church but there was no one about. All the cottages had a quiet shut-up look, as though it was a normal working day and everyone was out in the fields.

Still puzzled she went on through the village, which consisted of only a few dwellings; then, rounding a bend, came upon the church. It lay back from the road and it, too, had a deserted appearance. Mary paused by the lych-gate then walked up the path to the porch. She swung back the heavy entrance door and entered the church. A damp, musty smell greeted her and she saw

* *See page* 205.

immediately that all the pews were vacant. There was no one there, not even a verger and Mary felt a pang of disappointment. She must have been misinformed about the time of the service.

She dropped a penny in the collecting box, went up the aisle and knelt before the altar. She prayed for her father, sisters and brothers, especially for Jack serving in the army, and then thanked God for her good fortune in finding a happy and reward-ing position at the New Inn. This brought on a further bout of conscience for she had received several tips recently and had put only a penny in the box. She decided to put in another one on her way out.

Then, just as her prayer was ending, she had a sensation that she was being watched. She rose, turned and saw standing only a yard or two away a stout, jovial-looking man of about fifty dressed in clerical garb. How he had come up the aisle so noise-lessly she did not know; but the slight shock she experienced at seeing him was dissipated immediately by his friendly, welcoming smile, although most of his teeth were rotting and black.

"Good evening, my child," said the cleric. "Forgive me if I've interrupted your devotions."

Mary straightened her bonnet and smoothed down her dress.

"Oh, no, father. You've not interrupted me. I was just leaving."

"Not before you tell me your name and where you live."

"Mary Jane Tudor, sir. I live at the New Inn. I'm the serving maid there."

"Ah!" The parson's eyes lit up. "Then I believe I've heard of you. They said a good-looking girl was serving there. And you are good-looking, my child. Very, indeed."

Used to compliments Mary nevertheless blushed.

"Thank you, sir."

"Allow me to introduce myself. I am Parson Newman. And no doubt you've heard of me. Most people in the parish have."

Mary nodded. Parson Newman's name had been mentioned several times by the regulars at the inn. It was well-known that he preferred hunting to sermons and something stronger than communion wine, but he was well-liked for he was good to the poor and had a jovial, earthy disposition. Some of the farmers had

45

criticised him for laziness and pluralism but he was adjudged no worse and no better than many of the churchmen of the time.

"And where did you come from originally, Mary?" asked Newman.

"From Pwll y Cymmer in the Garw Valley, sir."

"Not far away, then. Are you a regular church-goer?"

"I'm afraid not. I'm Methodist really."

"A Methodist, eh! Well, I can't say I entirely approve of that. If some Methodist preachers had their way there would be no more churches, would there?" He chuckled.

"Oh, I don't believe that. Most of the preachers I heard encouraged us to go to church."

"Ah, yes! when they're not around. I have little brief for all this open-air preaching. Currying favour with the masses I call it. Why, some of them are even hinting that there will be no need for priests soon—that people can obtain forgiveness direct from God. Can you see that being any good to the majority of the ignorant and inarticulate farm workers we have around here?"

Mary did not entirely agree but thought it unwise and presumptuous to say so. She merely shook her head.

"They've robbed us of many good people," went on Newman. "Our congregations are dwindling all the time. That is why the church is in a parlous state; and I even hear rumours that some of them would like to break away altogether and ordain their own ministers. Can you imagine that! Ordination outside the body of the church! Impossible. The government would never allow it."

Mary smiled sweetly but pulled her gloves further up her arms, hoping that the parson would take it as a sign that she wanted to go for, as there was no service, she had set her heart on walking as far as the coast. Newman took the hint.

"But I am keeping you. You must forgive me. I care for the church, you see."

He fell into step beside her as they went down the aisle. When they reached the door he asked:

"What made you come here this evening?"

"I thought there was a service on. That's what I was told."

"Then you were informed wrongly. I have other churches to look after, you see, which means there is a service here only once every three weeks or so. The army of the church is not always as thick on the ground as one would wish, and I have to do the duty of several priests."

Mary said nothing. She had heard that Newman saw to it that no other priest came to the parish to share in the stipends. She merely made a sympathetic murmuring sound.

"It's a lot of work," the cleric went on. "There are some nights I don't get to bed until midnight. I'm here now only to collect some sermons I had forgotten. I should really be elsewhere but this damp weather we've been having has given me a heavy cold."

He took out a large handkerchief and blew his nose as though to emphasise the point.

"Well, now, I'm sorry you've had a journey for nothing. Come next Sunday—there will be a service here then. Perhaps I can expect you then?"

"I certainly will come if I can get time off."

"Then I shall speak to Mr. Robert about it. We must wean you away from Methodism. Perhaps a few more men would attend if they saw you in the congregation." He laughed jocularly, his ample stomach shaking his cassock.

Mary smiled again. In spite of all that she had heard she liked Newman. He was not like some other clerics she had met who were cold and distant with their parishioners. She had no doubt that, if she ever felt in need of religious comfort, it would be to Newman she would turn.

"Thank you again, sir," she said, curtsying.

Newman put a podgy hand on the latch but seemed reluctant to open the door.

"And what will you do now? Having walked all this way for nothing where will you go?"

"Oh, I would very much like to go as far as the beach and possibly see Candleston Castle on the way."

"A good idea, but don't be too disappointed. It's a manor house really, not a castle, and what's left of it is nearly falling down. Sir Roger de Cantelupes, who owns it, lacks sufficient capital to put it in proper order. Only last week a shepherd broke his leg when part of the wall fell on him, so take care. And take care, too, if you walk much further. The dunes are treacherous and there are quagmires near the river. Keep to the path."

"Thank you for warning me, sir. I shall take care."

Newman lifted the latch and at last allowed her out into the sunshine. On the path she turned and waved and he waved back. Then she hurried to the lych gate, eager now to start her walk. Although there had always been a distant view of the sea from Pwll y Cymmer she had never actually stood on a beach and seen and heard the waves. Now, with time to spare, she had the opportunity of achieving a life-long ambition and she hoped that she would have the beach to herself so that she could savour its delights to the full and, greatly daring, perhaps take off her shoes and stockings and paddle in the water. Determined to make the most of her brief period of freedom she started off down the twisting lane.

This time she walked quickly although still giving herself time to savour the sights and smells of the hedgerows. The dandelions, she noticed, were in profusion, an indication, it was said, of a wet summer to come. The blackberry bushes, too, had a multitude of blossom and Mary made a mental note that she would return there in the autumn to collect the berries. Mistress Gronow would surely allow that, especially if tarts and pies could be made for the inmates of the New Inn. She noticed, too, as she walked, that other bushes appeared similar in appearance to the blackberries but much lower to the ground. She knelt at one to inspect it more closely, marvelling at its multiplicity of blossom and lack of thorns. She surmised that these were dewberries but was not sure, so she broke off a twig intending to take it home and show to Davies.

Then the lane straightened and ran in front of her without a bend for several hundred yards. Here the hedges were much thinner, with only a few large trees interspersed along their length, an indication, Mary concluded, that she was approaching the sea. She thought she could glimpse sand hills in the distance and the air seemed to have a tangy flavour, so she hurried her footsteps intending to traverse the straight part quickly so that she could see what was round the next corner.

Suddenly there was a clap of noise like a cannonade and Mary came to a startled halt. Quickly she glanced around, for the noise had come from behind. Horrified, she saw that the sky to the north was a black mass of threatening cloud; and even as she looked a jagged fork of lightning descended, followed a moment later by a peal of thunder that seemed to make the ground shake. Despairingly she looked to the south, the direction in which she had been walking. There the sky was as blue as before. So engrossed had she been that she had failed to notice the quick materialisation of the summer storm and now she was stranded an hour's walk from the inn, in her best dress and a new bonnet. Menacingly the first raindrops began to fall, large but mercifully warm. With a cry of anguish she took off the bonnet and looked around for shelter. The only likely place was a large elm a hundred yards distant. She ran to it and tried to work out the best course of action. Above all she wanted to save her bonnet.

Another fork of lightning reiterated what she already knew: that the storm lay between her and the New Inn; so it was pointless to try to return there. A more likely solution was to run down the lane to Candleston Castle, which could not be too far distant, possibly just around the corner, and shelter in a doorway, if such a course were possible. But the blackness was now racing towards her and heavy drips were already coming through the branches. Then she realised with a start that she was doing what a country woman would never do: stand under a large tree in a thunderstorm. Quickly she moved to a smaller hawthorn, with branches so low that her hair became entangled in a needle-sharp thorn. Suddenly it became so dark that she could hardly see the opposite hedge.

Then the rain began to come down heavily and it was obvious that even a run to the castle was out of the question. At first the thick foliage of the hawthorn afforded good shelter and Mary prayed that the storm would be over before the rain percolated through the branches; so, optimistically, she held the bonnet close to her breast, trying to shelter it with her arms. But a

49

sudden, terrifying shaft of lightning, followed almost immediately by a roll of thunder and an intensification of the rain told her that she was in for it. To make matters worse the thorn-infested branch tore down her hair and scratched her forehead. Gradually the droplets began to descend on her, slowly at first, then with increasing rapidity. Within five minutes she was wet through and the bonnet a bedraggled mass in her hands.

How long she stood there she did not know. Lightning and thunder were now of such force that she adjudged the heart of the storm to be immediately overhead. The rain had lost its early warmth and was now cold; and, most uncomfortable of all, she began to feel her feet squelching in her thin, summer shoes. She was now so wet she contemplated the idea of walking home, for even in the open she could not be in a worse plight. She took a tentative step towards the roadway but one of her shoes became stuck in the mud and she had to stoop to replace it. A particularly loud clap of thunder drove her back again.

Then, above the sound of the rain lashing on the surface of the lane she heard the noise of horses' hooves and the rumble of carriage wheels. She flung strands of her bedraggled hair away from her eyes and stared down the lane in the direction of the sound. Gradually, as her eyes became accustomed to the gloom, she could make out two horses pulling an ancient four-wheeled carriage, its driver sitting high, hunched against the rain. The horses were at the canter and bore down on her quickly. As they drew near she threw caution to the winds and frantically waved her bonnet.

At first it looked as though the driver had not seen her, or if he had thought it best to ignore her, for the carriage rumbled past sending up sheets of spray. But fifty yards down the lane it came to a halt, the door half opened and a head and shoulders appeared. An arm waved and a stentorian voice shouted:

"Come here, you."

Mary gathered up her dress and ran down the lane after the carriage. The driver stared down at her from his tall perch as she approached, his face distrustful and suspicious. The door opened fully and from within came an expletive.

"Hell! I thought it was a woman. What the devil are you doing out on a night like this?"

"I was walking, sir," said Mary. "I got caught in the storm."

"Get in girl. You look like a drowned rat."

Thankfully Mary climbed into the carriage and collapsed on a seat opposite the only occupant, a handsome man of about forty wearing a beaver tricorn and a heavy, triple-cloaked great-coat. Thick brown hair, penetrating dark eyes and a cleft chin conveyed an immediate impression of strength of character, as did the voice which was deep and commanding. In the man's hand was a double-barrelled pistol.

"It's lucky for you I saw you. Jenkins wouldn't have stopped. Don't you know it's dangerous to leap out at carriages around here? You could have had a ball between the eyes."

"I'm sorry, sir," said Mary. "I didn't know quite what to do. I'm wet through."

"I can see that. Are you hurt? There's blood on your head."

"Is there?" Mary felt her forehead. "Oh, it's nothing. Just a scratch."

The man pocketed the pistol, reached for a riding crop and banged on the roof of the carriage.

"You'd best come home with me. We'll decide what to do with you when we get there. Allow me to introduce myself. I'm Sir Roger de Cantelupes."

CHAPTER 8

WITH A FEW more questions Sir Roger elicited from Mary her name and occupation, information received with little emotion from the dark, inscrutable eyes, although they seemed to soften a little when Mary added that she had been walking in search of the sea. But there was no time for further conversation for within what seemed only a few minutes the carriage wheels grated on a stony surface and they came to a swaying halt outside an archway framing a double-fronted door. Mary's companion leaned forward and bawled through the window.

"Leave the horses, Jenkins. Get the door open and light the lamps. Stir that blasted fire, too."

Jenkins's sodden figure lurched through the rain and Mary heard him wrestling with a massive iron lock. The doors creaked open and eventually some lights appeared from within. A quavering voice came faintly to them.

"Ready now, Sir Roger."

"Come." Sir Roger helped Mary down and as he took her arm she had the sensation that she was dreaming. Riding in an aristocrat's coach was unbelievable, but that she was actually about to enter his home was something that did not bear contemplation. A flash of lightning, silhouetting the massive grey pile above her, added to her feeling of unreality.

The doors thudded to behind her and she found herself in a damp-smelling hall. She followed her benefactor to a large, high-ceilinged room. There three lamps were already lit and Jenkins was bending under the lintel of a tall stone fireplace, prodding the embers of a half-dead log fire.

"It'll soon come, Sir Roger," he said in his plaintive, high-pitched voice. "Give it another minute or two."

Sir Roger threw off his heavy coat and Mary stared at him with interest, for she had never been at close quarters to a nobleman before; and Sir Roger de Cantelupes, although dressed in an unfashionably short jacket, with his dark hair tied at the rear in a small pig-tail, was every inch her idea of what such a person should look like. He went to a tall sideboard and Mary heard the chink of glasses.

"Here, drink this."

Mary took the proferred drink which she recognised from the smell as brandy. She took a cautious sip and immediately felt the fiery liquid begin to warm her. Another sip and a glow of well-being stole over her body. She felt less cold although she was still conscious of her bedraggled appearance, especially the way her wet dress clung to her, revealing all her contours and making her feel almost naked.

Sir Roger seemed to sense her thoughts. He hurried over to the fire and took the poker from Jenkins.

"Get a warming pan and air some of Lady Diane's dresses. Underwear, too, if you can find any. Leave the fire to me."

He stirred at the embers then threw on some fresh logs. Soon a few flames began to rise.

"Come stand by the fire."

Mary did as she was told and was thankful to find that the stonework of the hearth exuded warmth. Between the brandy within and the warmth without it would not be long before she was dry again.

"I am indebted to you, sir," she said. "There is really no need for you to prepare other clothing for me. I shall soon feel better and ready to return home."

"You may be ready," said Sir Roger gruffly, "but the storm won't. Summer storms hang around for a long while. Anyway, I won't allow you to go without Jenkins and he's wet through himself. You may stay an hour or two." He threw on more logs. "And now I shall leave you for a short while. I have something important to attend to. Jenkins will see to you."

He disappeared into the darkness of a low alcove, leaving Mary to sip her brandy and turn herself like a roasting spit, first drying one part of her and then another. As she turned she glanced around the room and was surprised to note how sparsely it was furnished. Except for two large, leather armchairs by the hearth, the sideboard, a tall Welsh dresser and a long oak dining table surrounded by heavy chairs, there was little else. The quality of the furniture was of the best but the carpet was old and shabby and the whole gave the appearance of having seen better days. A large, oil-painted portrait of a beautiful, fair-haired woman in hunting dress stared down at her from the opposite wall.

Suddenly a door opened and Jenkins appeared, armed with a copper warming pan. He shuffled across the room and, for the first time, Mary noticed how old and decrepit he was. Nigh on seventy, with scant grey hair, stoop shoulders and bandy legs, he was in keeping with the furniture. He stooped by the fire, knees cracking, and began filling the bowl with embers, carefully selecting the hottest bits. Occasionally he glanced up at her.

"How's Mistress Gronow getting on at that place o' yourn?"

"Very well, thank you," said Mary cautiously.

"Does she treat you right?"

"Oh, yes."

"Bit of a dragon though, ain't she?"

"Now and again, perhaps."

"Oh well, I suppose she's got to be in that place. That hat of yours looks a bit gone to me."

Mary glanced down at the bonnet she was still carrying.

"It was a new one. I wore it for the first time today."

"Put it on the chair. I'll see what I can do with it later."

Mary laid the bonnet on an arm of one of the chairs and went on sipping her brandy, which was now making her feel light-headed.

"I'm sorry to cause you so much trouble," she said. "Really I must go soon. Mistress Gronow will be wondering where I am."

"Let her. Master wants me to take you home, so you'll have to wait for me. He don't want you getting knocked on the head."

"Is there any danger of that?"

"At night there is. You don't know the rascals we get round these parts. Anyway the master likes the look of you, otherwise he wouldn't want you to stay."

"Likes the look of me?"

Jenkins cracked himself upright and carefully placed the heavy lid on the pan. He grinned.

"You're the first woman to enter them doors for nigh on three years, so regard yourself as privileged."

"I am. I mean I do feel privileged. But why should he ask me, a—a—"

"A serving girl? May be so, but a good-looking one. Have no fear. You'll come to no harm. Sir Roger's a gentleman. It's just that he's lonely. I know him and he's been a bit short of female company recently. He'll just have a chat with you and a bite to eat then he'll let you go."

"Is that a portrait of his wife?"

"That's her. Beautiful, warn't she? Died four years ago last month."

54

"Has Sir Roger never married again?"

Jenkins shook his head.

"He fell to pieces when she died. She was good as well as beautiful, see. Sir Roger's never been the same since, but now, at last, I think he's getting over it. Pity there weren't any children to comfort him, but that's how it is. The Lord is good to some but not to others."

"But he's still young, isn't he? There's still time to marry again, surely."

"And who'll have him? None of the nobility, I can tell you. He's as poor as a churchmouse. I'm the only servant he's got—and I do for footman, groom, valet, cook, laundryman and all the rest. Sometimes he ain't even got enough money to pay me."

"How can that be with all the land he owns?"

"Land! Have you seen it? A foot deep in sand most of it. No one can stop the damned stuff. Not a day goes by without some part of it going under. It's right up to the house walls in parts—and he hasn't got money for repairs. No rents, see. No one can work on the land so he don't get no rents. That's why he'll never get another wife—at least not from the nobility. One or two ladies've been interested in him but once they found—or at least their fathers did—that Sir Roger's skint—" He drew a finger across his throat.

"I'm sorry," said Mary.

Jenkins felt the under part of the warming pan.

"Anyway, this is ready, so that's enough of talk. I'll tell you this though: if Sir Roger don't get a wife soon he's finished. No heirs, see. He's the last of the line. But I don't hold out much hopes. What between the sand and everything else—and what he'll do when I'm gone I don't know."

He shook his head again and made a clucking noise; then, holding the warming pan in front of him like a spear, he walked unsteadily across the room.

"Follow me. There's some of Lady Diane's dresses left. You can have the choice of what's there. Bring that lamp with you but be careful—it leaks."

Mary hurriedly finished the last of the brandy and went after

55

him, gingerly holding the foul-smelling lamp. They ascended a dark flight of stairs, lined on either side with portraits, and entered a large bedroom, empty save for a few chairs and a four-poster bed at the foot of which was a long oak linen chest. Jenkins placed the warming pan on the bed, which was complete with coverings and pillows, then took the lamp from Mary and balanced it on the shelf of a cold-looking marble fireplace. He lifted the lid of the chest and took out a pile of clothing.

"I've tried to look after these but the moths've had most. There'll be something you can wear though. Lady Diane was about your size. How about this?"

He selected a fine blue silk gown and Mary gasped.

"I can't wear that!"

"Why not, unless you're fussy about wearing a dead woman's clothes. You ain't got much choice though, have you? Try it on, but air it first." He folded the dress neatly and placed it on top of the warming pan, tucking it in at the sides. "Give it a few minutes otherwise you'll end up with the rheumatics like me. There's some underclothing at the bottom, but choose them yourself. I'm not much shakes with ladies' things. Don't forget to air them as well though. Come down when you're ready."

As soon as he had gone Mary darted towards the chest and examined its contents. There were three or four other dresses inside but none as beautiful as the blue gown. Carefully she extracted a small pile of undergarments and found them to consist of petticoats and pantaloons. She seized a pair of pantaloons, held them against her body and looked around for a mirror. Fortunately there was one, a tall, dressing mirror set into the wall by the bed. She was relieved to note that the garment would just about fit, so she did the same thing with the petticoat and the blue dress then, satisfied, she placed all three on the warming pan. Quickly she took off her own clothing and rubbed herself all over with the towel Jenkins had left behind. Finally, completely dry and glowing with exertion, she clambered into Lady Diane's garments, now comfortingly warm, and surveyed herself in the mirror. Except for being an inch or two on the short side the gown fitted perfectly, but when she looked at her hair she let out a gasp of dismay. Still wet and shapeless it hung down like rats' tails.

Frantically she retrieved the towel and began rubbing away at her hair. After a few minutes it began to crackle and glow so she took a comb from her purse and brought the tresses down in long, flowing sweeps to her shoulders. She was pleased to note that, although still slightly damp, it had waves in just the right places and reflected the dim light of the lamp. She gave it a final pat, adjusted her dress slightly, and stood back to admire her handiwork.

The sight that met her eyes pleased even Mary's fastidious nature. She could not have looked better even if she had spent hours on her preparation, and suddenly a sense of excitement and adventure mounted within her. Here she was, a poor farmer's daughter, dressed in a gown the texture of which made her feel a lady of quality, of a shade that exactly matched the colour of her eyes, with hair and complexion enough to turn any man's head, about to descend and sup with a nobleman in his own manor. And if, as Jenkins had said, Sir Roger had liked her a little when wet and bedraggled, what would he think when he saw her now? She held in her stomach for a moment to suppress a nervous tremor, then gave the dress a final smooth down, picked up the lamp and made her way downstairs.

Sir Roger was sitting in one of the armchairs when she arrived in the great room, his legs in the hearth and a long clay pipe in his mouth. He did not see her at first, but when she neared him he looked up. Immediately his eyes narrowed. He removed the pipe from his lips, stood up, looked her up and down, then tugged at a bell pull near the fireplace. His expression left Mary in no doubt that she had impressed him and she thought for a moment that he would remark on her appearance, but in this she was disappointed. In a dry voice he merely said:

"Are you completely dry now?"

"Yes, thank you."

"Please sit down. Jenkins will be here in a moment with something to eat."

Mary sat and arranged her dress more comfortably. Sir Roger watched her every action then permitted himself a smile.

"Are you comfortable? I mean, does the dress fit?"

"Very well, sir. It's almost as though it was made for me."

"My wife was about your size."

"It is indeed most kind of you."

Sir Roger resumed his smoking and they sat in silence for a few minutes, so it was with relief that Mary heard Jenkins enter the room. He was bearing a silver tray on which was a large bowl and a plateful of bread.

"It's not much," said Sir Roger. "It's only some cawl. Jenkins hasn't had time to prepare anything decent. Have it by the fire. It will be cold at the table."

Jenkins stooped and placed the tray on Mary's lap.

"It's good and hot. Do you good. Eat it all up and then you won't catch cold after your soaking. Anything else, sir?"

Sir Roger waved him away. Mary felt for her spoon and glanced hesitantly at her host.

"Aren't you having anything, sir?"

"Not hungry. You carry on. Would you like some wine with it?"

"No, thank you."

"Then do as Jenkins says. Eat it all up."

Mary dipped her spoon into the leek-infested broth and nervously raised it to her mouth. Sir Roger seemed to be studying the fire so she gulped down the hot liquid and found it delicious. She wondered for a moment if she should try and make polite conversation but decided against it. Speaking to nobility was an art she had not yet mastered so she concentrated instead on eating daintily. After several long puffs at his pipe, evidently much enjoyed, Sir Roger knocked out the dottle.

"So you were looking for the sea."

"Yes, sir."

"Dangerous down by the coast. Take care if you ever go there, especially by the river mouth."

"So I have been told."

"Who told you?"

58

"Parson Newman. I had intended going to service in Merthyr Mawr church."

"Oh, so you've met him have you? What did you think of him?"

"He was very pleasant—very kind to me."

"He would be. He likes a pretty face."

Mary concentrated on the cawl.

"And what about Robert, your master? How do you get on with him?"

"He's very kind to me, too."

"Good. Glad to hear it. Do those thugs of his leave you alone?"

"Thugs?" For a moment Mary was puzzled, then she remembered Robert's unprepossessing helpmates. "Oh, you mean Benjamin and Ebenezer. Yes, they leave me alone."

Sir Roger stared at her silently, the dark eyes boring into her. Then, abruptly, he turned his head again and resumed his contemplation of the fire. It seemed to Mary that he had completely forgotten her existence, so she concentrated on her meal. Sir Roger did not look at her again until he heard the spoon being placed in an empty bowl. Then his glance was sideways.

"I see you've finished. You haven't eaten much bread."

"The cawl was quite sufficient. I thoroughly enjoyed it."

"Good. Would you like some more brandy before you go?"

"Oh, no thank you, sir. I've had quite sufficient."

"Then Jenkins shall take you back." He rose and pulled the cord and remained standing with his back to the fire until the servant appeared.

"Are the horses still harnessed, Jenkins?"

"Yes, sir," said Jenkins, taking the tray off Mary's lap.

"Then you may return the young lady to the New Inn."

"Her clothes are dry," said Jenkins. If she comes with me to the kitchen—"

"No need for that. She can keep the dress."

Mary's eyes widened in astonishment. She doubted whether she had heard correctly.

"Oh, no, sir. If you wish I shall wear it until I get home and return it tomorrow."

59

"Keep it, I say. I have no further use for it."

"Quite right, sir," said Jenkins quickly. "It's only food for moths here. Come along. Follow me." He caught hold of Mary's elbow and tried to lead her away, but Mary stuck her ground. She opened her mouth to say something more but Sir Roger turned his head. The pressure of Jenkins' hand increased and she felt herself being propelled towards the door.

"Thank you, sir," was all she managed to say before Jenkins got her as far as the door. She had a fleeting glimpse of Sir Roger refilling his pipe and then she found herself in the kitchen.

Jenkins made a scolding, cackling sound.

"When you get given something, miss, take it. Don't ask questions."

"But how can I? It's his wife's."

"She's got no further use for it, has she? He wouldn't have given it to you if he hadn't wanted to. Anyway, it's one thing less for me to look after. Here's your own things."

On a wooden clothes-horse before a decrepit range was her dress and underclothing. Jenkins neatly folded each article and gave them to her. Finally he produced her bonnet from inside an oven.

"I did my best but it's not much shape."

Mary studied her hat which was dry but shapeless.

"Oh, well, I didn't pay much for it. But what's a bonnet compared with the dress Sir Roger's given me?"

Jenkins nodded approvingly.

"A fair exchange. I told you he liked you, didn't I? Come now, I have things to do when I get back."

He led her out to a courtyard, where the patient horses were standing. It was almost dark but the storm had receded and it had stopped raining. Before getting into the carriage Mary glanced around her. On three sides of the courtyard the walls were crumbling. Above her a beam holding part of the roof was naked and exposed. A pile of slates stood near a buttress. Near the pillared gateway three gaunt trees struggled for existence in an expanse of sand.

Candleston Castle was indeed falling about the ears of its owner.

CHAPTER 9

MUCH TO Mary's relief the coach arrived unseen at the New Inn and she was able to slip without hindrance to her room. She had no wish to divulge her adventure or the acquisition of the dress to anyone, least of all to Mistress Gronow. But after changing and secreting the precious article behind an apron in the wardrobe she ran into that redoubtable matriarch on the stairs, and was immediately assailed with questions as to where she had been. She explained about the storm but refrained from mentioning Candleston Castle and was saved from further interrogation by the crowded state of the inn, which had filled up because of the storm. She plunged into her normal task of serving everybody and, after four hours of continuous work, managed to get to bed at midnight.

She lay for a long time in the dark thinking about the day's experience. She had, she thought, acquitted herself fairly well on the whole. Serving girl she might be but she had been brought up properly and knew how to behave, and she wondered if Sir Roger had really liked her, as Jenkins had said. From that her mind lapsed into fantasy, in which she had a vision of herself walking along Merthyr Mawr lane and finding Sir Roger thrown from a horse. She had tended his wounds and then, at the castle, nursed him back to health; whereupon he had taken her in his arms and declared his undying love for her. On that happy note she fell asleep and in the morning woke refreshed.

The moment of wakening brought Mary no premonition of what lay in store. Her first reaction was to examine the gown, which appeared just as beautiful in daylight as in the flickering lamp-light of Candleston Castle. Then she prepared for the day's toil, her mind occupied composing a letter home describing her adventures and imagining what her sisters would say when they knew. She went down to the kitchen, threw some wood on the fire and began scouring the pots prior to Davies's arrival.

Suddenly the door opened and Robert appeared. Mary was surprised for she had not expected anyone to appear at that time of the morning and in any case the innkeeper rarely entered the kitchen. His face was serious.

"I'm sorry, m'dear, if I frightened you, but you'd best come with me. There's someone here to see you."

Something about Robert's tone made Mary uneasy and, to make things worse, he walked towards her and put a thick arm around her shoulders. In future years she was to remember the pressure of that arm for it was the precursor of events that were to change her, in the space of four months, from a happy, ingenuous girl into a mature woman of bitter memories.

"You're not to worry, m'dear," said Robert in an unusually hesitant voice. "It's only a bit of—er—news from your family. They've been took ill, it seems, or so I'm told, and I think it's best for you to return home for a while."

The walk to the dining room took only a few seconds but it seemed an age to Mary. When she got there she saw old Evan Philips, the pedlar, standing in the middle of the room, twisting his woollen cap in his hands. He forced a smile, but Mary knew from his expression that something serious had happened.

"What is it, Evan?" she asked fearfully.

Evan went on twisting his cap, his mouth open but no words coming out.

"Tell her, Evan," said Robert. "It's best not to dilly-dally."

"It's your father, miss," blurted out Evan. "He's very ill and so are your sisters."

Mary felt for a chair and sat down.

"How serious is it?"

"Not good. It's the choking sickness."

"Do you mean diphtheria?"

"Yes, miss. At least that's what the folks up there think it is."

Stark fear gripped Mary. No one ever recovered from diphtheria, especially adults. She had seen too many families decimated to know that.

"Oh, God! Can nothing be done?"

"Everything possible is being done. They've been made comfortable."

"And my brother? You haven't mentioned my brother. Is he ill, too?"

Evan glanced at Robert who, after a moment's hesitation, nodded.

"I'm afraid he's dead, miss. Some say he brought the sickness to the house."

Mary felt life drain from her body. Again she felt Robert's heavy arm about her shoulder and, as though from a great distance, she heard his voice.

"I'll send her straight away, Evan—with Mathias in the trap. She'll be there before you will."

She sat there silently. No tears came for the shock had been too great for that. Already the loss of Jacob made her feel as though half her body had been torn away and there was worse to come, she felt sure. The icy coldness within her permeated her whole body, making her shiver. Then she felt her cloak being placed around her.

"Come now," said Robert. "The trap's ready. You must stay home until everything's been put to rights."

Mary remembered little of the journey. She was vaguely aware that, in contrast with her black despair, the morning was a fine one, with a strong, clear sun that betokened great heat to come. She was conscious, too, that Mathias drove skilfully, urging Poppy on whenever possible but holding her back when the water-filled ruts threatened the flimsy wheels. She took some small comfort from his silent strength.

They made Bridgend in good time but the long haul up to the Garw Valley seemed endless. There the track was often inches deep in mud formed by the rain of the previous evening, and on several occasions Mathias had to dismount and lead the horse. Wisely he said not a word throughout the drive, but when eventually they came to the bottom of Pwll y Cymmer he reined in the horse. He applied the handbrake and turned to her.

"Mary, you and I have had our arguments, but I want you to know that I'll help you as much as possible."

63

"Thank you." Mary stared at the farm track in front of her, her only wish being to continue as quickly as possible. But Mathias made no move and so she glanced impatiently at him.

"Is anything the matter ? Why don't we go on ?"

Mathias drew in a deep breath.

"I must prepare you for the worst. Neither Mr. Robert nor Evan had the heart to tell you before so they asked me to do it. As we're nearly there you must know now. Both your sisters have passed away, too."

Mary swayed and would have fallen had not Mathias's strong arm encircled her.

"I'm sorry," he muttered. "I left it until the last minute, but I had to tell you now. You must be brave. It's not good at the farm, I'm told."

Mary bent forward in her seat, the agony now too great to bear. Mathias kept his arm around her and with the other disengaged the brake. The willing Poppy pulled them up the steep slope and soon they came to the gate. Two old women were standing there, be-shawled and weeping. Mary recognised them as the wives of tenants from further up the valley. At the house was a knot of men, some of them dressed in black. They bared their heads as the trap came to a halt. One of them, Rhys ap Williams, helped Mary down from the cart.

"Glad you've come, Mary. I'm afraid it's bad, real bad."

"How's my father ?" cried Mary.

Rhys, who in the absence of a doctor in the valley acted as apothecary and general medicine man, shook his head.

"Failing, miss."

Mary would have rushed to the door but Rhys snatched at her.

"Don't go in, miss. Leastwise not yet. Old Rhiannon's in there now fuming the place out. The Commissioner do say it ain't safe for a day or two, but Rhiannon thinks—"

Mary tore herself away from him and began grappling with the heavy door latch. Rhys looked helplessly at Mathias.

"I'll go in with her," said Mathias. "She can't go in alone."

He helped Mary with the door and they both entered together.

The first room, the kitchen, was full of acrid fumes. Old Rhiannon, who had laid out the dead for so long that she was considered immune to any illness, was methodically dripping water on a herb and fern fire to make more smoke. She glanced up at the newcomers and placed the bottle on the mantel shelf.

"Can't come in here!" she quavered. "Can't come in here!" Then she recognised Mary. "Oh, Duw, it's not you, is it? Stay outside, girl—for a while at least."

"Where's my father?" Mary stumbled forward in the darkness then came to a sudden halt. Dimly she could make out three bundles lying on the flags. She went towards one but was seized by Mathias.

"Don't touch them. You mustn't touch."

"Quite right," scolded Rhiannon. "Listen to what he says. Them's your sisters and brother. They've gone, so it's no use touching them."

Overwhelmed at last, the flood of tears came. Mathias held her tight for, in spite of the warnings, Mary would have flung herself at the inert forms. Over his shoulder he said:

"Where's the father?"

"In there." Rhiannon pointed towards a door and, using his full strength in order to be gentle, Mathias led Mary towards it. He kicked the door open with a foot and they entered the main bedroom. Lying on the deep box bed was Edward Tudor, his mouth wide open. Even in the poor light the red, mucous-infested cavity looked hideous, as did the protruding grey membrane that was choking his life away. Mary collapsed in Mathias's arms. He allowed her to sink to the floor but still held her, preventing contact with the skin-covered skeleton that was only a minute or two away from death.

Mary did nothing but sob for a while, then she cried out:

"Why wasn't I told? I would have come sooner."

"He didn't want to worry you," cackled Rhiannon, who was standing by the door. "Anyway, they all thought it was the influenza at first and then it was too late."

Suddenly the stentorian wheezing faltered and Edward turned his head. The dazed, suffering-filled eyes searched the darkness and found Mary's face. The old man smiled and slowly his hand travelled across the blanket towards her. Mathias's grip on her arms tightened and, although Mary fought, he succeeded in restraining her. Edward struggled to draw breath but instead there was an unnerving sound as the air rattled into his throat. That went on for a minute or more then his eyelids drooped and he fell back lifeless. Beneath his hands Mathias felt Mary's body stiffen. He allowed her to remain there for a little while longer then gently drew her to her feet.

"He saw you before he went," he whispered. "We were just in time. You made him happy. But you mustn't stay here—your father would not have wished it. Come. He wants you to live."

Mary was now past resistance. Still weeping she allowed Mathias to half lead, half carry her from the room. She paused again by the corpses in the kitchen and once more Mathias had to pressurise her into walking. They emerged into the bright sunlight and there she fainted. Without hesitation Mathias gathered her into his arms. The men kept their distance for, although compassion still showed in their faces, they were afraid to risk contamination.

"How's Edward?" called out Rhys.

"Gone," said Mathias, walking towards the trap with his burden. "He went whilst we were there."

"What'll you do with the girl?" asked Rhys, following him. "She can't stay here now."

"I'll take her back with me. She must stay at the inn until something can be done. I'll contact her sisters later."

"Best thing, too. Sooner you get her away from here the better, 'machgen 'i."

"What about the farm? What'll happen to that?"

"Iestyn Griffiths is taking over the lease. He's already seen the landowner."

Mathias smiled grimly. Normally slow in their actions country folk lost no time when it came to taking possession, contamination or not. Gently he lifted Mary to the seat and climbed in beside her.

"And the chattels. What about them?"

"Commissioner do come in the morning," said Rhys, "to decide what's best to do. More than like he'll have the beds burned."

"Then I'll return tomorrow and see him. Arrange the burials at the same time, I expect."

"Don't let Mary come. 'Tain't safe."

"I won't. Don't worry, I'll look after her."

"You're a good boyo. We do think highly of Mary around here."

Mathias flicked the rein and Poppy began her sure-footed progress down the hillside. At the gate the two old women were still there, still weeping. Mathias nodded briefly to them and then they were on the roadway. As the wheels lurched upon the firmer ground Mary stirred and then began to struggle.

"Please! Don't take me back. I must stay here."

"You can't. There's nowhere to stay, and anyway it's dangerous."

"But I can't leave them. I can't leave my family."

"You must. Neither your father nor sisters would wish you to return there. Not yet anyway."

Mathias increased his grip on her slim form and slowly she began to yield to the pressure. Poppy broke into a canter and they moved off down the road with the sun beating down hard on their heads. After half a mile it was obvious that she had given in completely to her fate for she buried her face deep in the lapels of Mathias's jacket and wept without ceasing. He stared down at her. In spite of the blotches caused by crying she still looked beautiful, but what surprised him most of all was her hair. Whereas previously it had been springy and full of life, now it was lank and lustreless. It was as though, suddenly, the happy, ebullient spirit that was its source of vitality had been driven out; and Mathias wondered how long it would be before it returned.

"I'll help you," he said quietly. "I'll help you all I can. If you let me, that is."

But Mary did not hear him. Wildly her mind was trying to work out what she had done to bring such savage retribution on her family.

CHAPTER 10

THE ENORMITY AND suddenness of the tragedy made Mary ill and, for three days after the funeral, she lay in bed in a state of shock. Davies, the cook, brought dainty morsels from the kitchen to tempt her appetite but she ate little. Gradually the initial sensation of numbness wore off only to be replaced by searing memories of the times her father had been kind to her, and of her own occasional wilful disobedience. Now it was too late to make amends and she knew that she would reproach herself for the rest of her life. But she also remembered that her father had loved her and that she had not been entirely bad, and so the healing process of time slowly began.

She was visited once by Robert, who filled the tiny room with his bulk and bland assurances that she must now regard the New Inn as her home; and also by Gronow who, unbending momentarily, told her that she must recover her strength before commencing work. But her greatest pillar of strength at this time was Mathias, who called to see her daily, helping her write letters to the surviving relatives and bringing news of Pwll y Cymmer. True to his word he had returned there the following day and arranged for burial at Bryncethin and then seen to the sale of the chattels. This brought in very little for the only expensive items, the feather beds, had been burned and the few goods worthy of disposal had been the chairs and a dresser. This brought in a sum of just over four pounds, which Mary kept intending to share it later between her brother and two surviving sisters. Mathias also brought the family bible, for which she was grateful. Then, on the fourth day, of her own volition, Mary forced herself to start work. Although still unwell she acknowledged that she had to go on living and so she compelled herself to do the familiar tasks with all the energy she could muster; but it was obvious to everyone that she was a changed person. Gone was the light, skipping step and the ready laugh; now she was wan and listless, with lack-lustre eyes and hair that still hung down in lifeless tails. To Mathias, who observed her more closely than anyone, it would be a long time before she became well again.

But the death of her loved ones was only the first of a series of calamities that were about to befall her, and the second came very quickly upon its heel. It occurred one evening only a week later, when a group of young noblemen descended upon the inn. They had been en route for London, but the main coach at Ewenny had broken a wheel and so they had returned to the New Inn to await its repair. Already inebriated when they arrived they vociferously demanded a meal in the parlour and then, in the tradition of their kind, set about making nuisances of themselves.

At first they were quiet enough, for Davies's roast lamb and mint sauce demanded full justice, but gradually the wine took effect and they became boisterous and over-loud. This was no surprise to Mary, who had to wait on them, for experience had taught her that some of the well-to-do were often more boorish in their behaviour than plain country-folk, who were supposed to be their inferiors; and so she prepared herself for a certain amount of horse-play. But what transpired went beyond the realms of decency and, in her weakened state, retarded her attempts at returning to normal.

Gronow had already warned her to be on her best behaviour, for two of the noblemen were influential local landowners: Lord Carne, who had come into his estate only two years previously at the age of twenty, and was often seen careering about the lanes in a carriage and pair; and Sir Philip Kenfig, a tall, effeminate youth, who owned tracts of land to the west of the county, reputed to be the leader of an aristocratic gang of ne'er-do-wells. Their two companions were from London and all four spoke with what Mary thought were affected English accents.

The first incident occurred at the end of the meal. Carne had called for port and Mary was leaning across the table to clear the dishes, when she felt a hand travelling up the rear of her legs underneath her skirt This had happened on previous occasions and she had always countered it with a sharp slap of a face but now her hands were full of dishes and before she could do anything about it the hand plunged between her legs and touched her private parts through her thin, cotton drawers. She screamed and wrenched herself sideways, only to fall into the lap of one of the Londoners who immediately pulled down her bodice, disengaging one of her breasts. In a trice Mary was on her feet and across the room.

"How dare you! You're worse than any farm worker."

A gale of laughter accompanied her from the room. She ran to the kitchen and stood there, trembling.

"What's the matter, merch fach?" asked Davies, noticing her white face.

"Those men! They molested me."

"They would. It's that Sir Philip and his lot. You want to watch them. No woman is safe when they're around."

Mary sank into a chair.

"I'm not going back there. I don't feel well."

"You don't look it. Sit there and have some tea. It'll make you feel better."

But at that moment Gronow entered the room, bearing the dishes that Mary had failed to clear.

"Why did you leave these behind?"

"They messed about with her," said Davies loyally. "She's not fit to serve tonight."

"She'll have to," snapped Gronow. "You're making a mountain out of a mole hill. You must expect that sort of thing in an inn, particularly from the aristocracy. You should know that by now."

"She's not fit," repeated Davies stolidly. "Remember what she's just been through."

"Fit or not she'll have to serve. They want port. Go and get it immediately."

Gronow whisked from the room leaving Mary and Davies staring at each other. Slowly Mary got to her feet.

"I'll have to do it. I must keep my place here."

Davies nodded sympathetically.

"I know. But don't let them muck about any more with you.

Come and tell me if they do. I'll go and see Mr. Robert and tell him you haven't recovered yet. He'll understand."

Still trembling Mary went to the cellar. Mathias was nowhere to be seen but he had left an uncorked bottle in anticipation on the table. Through the aperture she could hear the voices of her tormentors raised in ribald conversation. She took a deep breath, put the bottle and four clean glasses on a tray and made her way back to the parlour.

The conversation ceased immediately she entered. Four pairs of eyes stared at her from grinning faces. Warily Mary advanced to the table, keeping as far as possible from the nearest man, and deposited the tray on its shiny surface. She was about to turn when Lord Carne spoke.

"One minute, my surly miss. Why did you take exception to my friend fondling you?"

Mary shot him as scathing a glance as she could.

"Don't you like to be fondled?" went on Carne. "If not you're in the wrong job. Don't tell me you haven't had a hand up your skirt before."

Mary did not deign to answer. She swung round and made for the door, only to find it barred by one of the Londoners. Desperately she glanced around the room, but there was no escape.

"Come here," said Carne. "Let's have a look at you. A tavern maid who doesn't like to be touched is a rarity."

"She dem well nearly broke my arm just now," said Kenfig. "She twisted like a ferret. Nearly snapped it off at the wrist."

"Better your wrist than anything else," said one of them and they all burst out laughing.

"Imagine what Kenfig would have to say to his wife," added the one at the door, "if he'd gone home and told her he'd broken his arm in a girl's fanny."

That set them roaring.

"It's all right for you," said Kenfig wryly, "but I tell you she's dem strong."

"All the more reason for making her apologise," laughed Carne, pouring himself a glass of port. "Come on! Let's see you make her apologise, Kenfig."

"That I will," said Kenfig. "Here, you, apologise for what you did."

"No!" Mary tried to reach the door but was stopped by its burly guardian. "Let me pass, please. I have work to do."

"D'you know," said the fellow laconically, "I don't think she will apologise. I'll wager you a guinea she don't."

"Oh, yes she will," said Kenfig. "I'll dem well make her."

Seeing his expression Mary backed against the wall. Kenfig got unsteadily to his feet and stood in front of her.

"Now then, my girl, say you're sorry or we'll see the colour of your drawers."

In desperation Mary tried to push past the door sentry but he held her fast.

"Here she is, Kenfig. What'll you do with her?"

"Put her on the table," said Kenfig. "'Pon my soul a good look at her fanny will do us all good."

"Excellent idea," said Mary's captor. "Come on, give us a hand."

The other Londoner rushed forward and between them the two dragged Mary to the table. She was lifted up bodily and then pinned to its hard surface by their combined weight. Kenfig advanced towards her and raised her frock but she kicked him in the stomach and sent him sprawling across the room. He was soon back, his face vicious and determined.

"Oh! so you'd kick me, would you? Right, my little dragon! Hold her fast and see if she likes this."

Keeping safely to the side of the table this time he drew up her frock until it was nearly over her face and then tore the petticoat almost up to her middle. With rough bony hands he searched around her waist and untied the strings of her drawers. Then he partially drew them down.

"Lift her up, I say. I can't get them off."

How the violation of her person would have ended Mary could only conjecture in later years. Suddenly there was a crack like a pistol-shot and the door flew open. Robert stood there, staring around the room with bloodshot eyes. Then, with a bellow like a bull, he hurled himself forward and seized Kenfig by the shoulders. With a quick heave of his powerful arms he

72

flung the nobleman across the room with such force that he struck the wall and sank to the floor. A short, vicious punch staggered one of the Londoners and the other was floored with a wide sweeping blow to the chin. In a trice all three were on the floor and only Carne was left, still sitting at the table. Coolly he raised his glass and swallowed some port. Unhurriedly he reached into his pocket and produced a pistol.

"Come no nearer, Robert, or I'll put a ball in you."

Ignoring him Robert helped Mary off the table. She pulled down her dress and leaned against him feeling sick. Robert jerked a thumb over his shoulder.

"Try anything with that, Carne, and so much the worse for you." Standing by the door was Ebenezer, holding a brace of pistols, and Benjamin, armed with a blunderbuss, his hook precariously encircling the trigger.

Carne carefully replaced the pistol in his pocket.

"Out-gunned as usual, I see, Sioni. No matter. I never was one for violence."

"I want you out," snarled Robert. "Out! All of you. Now!"

"Oh, come!" Carne readjusted the lace in his sleeve. "You're taking it too much to heart. We meant no harm. Just a little sport with the girl."

"No one sports with her!"

"Why not?" Carne spread his arms wide. "She's no relation of yours, is she? What's a tavern girl for but to provide a little fun now and again?"

"Pay your bill and get out," roared Robert.

"'Pon my soul," said Kenfig, staggering to his feet at last. "What villains of innkeepers you have in your part of the county, Carne. If he was in mine I'd have him in irons."

Robert took one of Ebenezer's pistols and pointed it at him.

"Well, you're bloody well in my part of the county now. If I catch you here again I'll put you in the river."

The two Londoners produced handkerchiefs. One dabbed at his mouth, in which a tooth had been loosened, and the other tried to stem a flow of blood from his nose. Robert moved towards the door, gently shepherding Mary.

"Ebenezer! Benjamin! Give them two minutes. If they're not out by then relieve them of their wallets, take what's due, and see them to the door."

Benjamin rattled his hook enjoyably against the trigger. Mary was nearly through the door when she heard Carne's voice, cool and modulated as usual.

"You've gone too far this time, Sioni. I'll get you one day, see if I don't."

Robert swung round, a hideous leer on his face.

"Try it on, Carne. I'll cross swords with you any time."

Then he led Mary to the kitchen where a concerned Davies fussed over her and made her drink a cup of tea. But as she held the cup in shaking hands Mary had a sudden fear of the future. In aiding her Robert had made powerful enemies, and the menace in Lord Carne's voice had been unmistakable. Also, it was the first time she had heard the innkeeper referred to by the contemptuous name of Sioni. Powerful and influential though Robert was he could not affront nobility without some form of retaliation.

How long, she wondered, would the New Inn provide a safe refuge for her now that her own home had gone?

CHAPTER 11

MARY WAS GRATEFUL to the innkeeper for his timely intervention but any notion that he was a true benefactor was dispelled shortly afterwards when an incident occurred that heightened her feeling of insecurity and gave her further alarm about her position. That the inn's normal routine was about to be disrupted had already been made apparent by the arrival in the kitchen of a flushed Gronow, her usual icy demeanour showing traces of agitation. With a voice tinged with excitement she announced:

"Mr. Robert's brother is arriving today. His ship has anchored off Newton. At high tide he will arrive at the river mouth in the long boat and Mr. Robert will meet him there. I want everything ready—good meals and the best wine. He has had nothing but ship's biscuits for the last year."

"Is he coming to press men?" asked Davies sourly, who had not forgiven Gronow for forcing Mary back to the dining room. "The last time he was here half a dozen men disappeared from Ewenny."

"Of course not," snapped Gronow. "He would never do a thing like that—not in Mr. Robert's area, anyway."

She glided out before Davies could say anything more, but when the door closed the cook pulled a face.

"Uffern! That woman's a bloody fool. She fancies her chances with Mr. Robert's brother, did you know that? The last time he was here she acted like a sixteen year old. He don't want her though, the scrawny cow. And you can forget that bit about the wine. Rum is all he drinks—by the barrelful. You'd better go and check we've got plenty."

Obediently Mary set off for the cellar, where Mathias was engaged in driving a tap into a firkin. He looked up when she entered and studied her. He had heard about the encounter with the noblemen but had already made up his mind to say nothing to save her from embarrassment. He put on a light-hearted demeanour.

"Don't tell me! You've come to see if there's plenty of rum in the cellar."

"How did you know?"

Mathias pointed at the firkin.

"What d'you think that is? The last time Robert's brother was here he got through one of those the first day. Good thing he's only staying for two, otherwise I'd have to go to Bridgend for more."

"Does he get very drunk? I mean, does the rum—?"

"Oh, no," said Mathias quickly, divining Mary's thoughts. "He doesn't get nasty. He just gets comatose."

"Comatose? What's that?"

"Half asleep—not with us. Too drunk to move."

Mary smiled. Now that Mathias had proved himself a true friend she had lost her previous suspicion of him; and she had been amazed to discover how well-read he was. One day, she resolved, she would speak to him about it for he had the makings

75

of being something better than an ostler and part-time cellar-man. All he needed was a push in the right direction.

"Then I hope he'll be comatose very quickly," she said.

"Mind you," said Mathias ruminatively. "I can't say I blame him. If I were cooped up on a man-o-war off the French coast for years on end I'd drink a firkin or two myself. Anyway, that's what he'll do. You won't see much of him. They'll both spend their time upstairs in Robert's room and Gronow will wait on them. You're not allowed in there, by the way. You know that, don't you?"

"Yes. The holy of holies. I wonder why."

"Ah!" Mathias gave the tap a final blow. "I wonder why, too. Not many people have been in there. There! All set for Nelson's favourite bo'sun."

"Is he really?"

"Is he what?"

"Nelson's favourite bo'sun."

Mathias exploded in a laugh.

"Oh, Mary! You mustn't believe everything people tell you. He certainly is a bo'sun on one of Nelson's ships but I doubt if the good admiral's ever heard of him. Probably never seen him."

Mary blushed, knowing that she had been foolish, but the sight of Mathias's kindly expression told her that he was not mocking her, so she laughed, the first time since the calamity at Pwll y Cymmer.

"Quite right! It was silly of me to think that. I'll go and help Davies in the kitchen."

"Don't miss Robert when he leaves," Mathias called after her "He's a sight for sore eyes when he meets his brother. He'll be in his Sunday best. Watch out for him."

"I'll do that."

She did not have long to wait. By mid-morning the innkeeper appeared downstairs, bellowing like a bull for Ebenezer.

"Where's that bloody lay-about? I'll flay him alive if he don't come this instant."

Davies and Mary ran to the kitchen door to see their master set off. He was indeed in his Sunday best, with dark green velveteen jacket, amply cut with large pockets, puce-coloured silk breeches, white stockings and black, buckled shoes. The only incongruous item was his normal day-to-day tricorn, which contrasted strangely with the finery of the rest of his apparel, and Mary could only surmise that he was so attached to it that he could not resist wearing it even on this gala occasion. He was about to bellow again when Ebenezer appeared.

"Damn your bloody eyes," said Robert. "Where the hell have you been?"

"Plenty of time, master," said Ebenezer. "It ain't high tide for an hour yet,"

"At the rate you row we'll not even make the weir. Get the boat ready, you verminous bloody toad."

"Aye, aye, sir," said Ebenezer, saluting, making it obvious that a nautical aura was already developing at the inn. Mary and Davies went to the front door to witness the embarkation.

First Ebenezer got into the small rowing boat, which was always moored near the bank, and began dusting down one of the seats with a filthy red and white spotted handkerchief. Then Robert clambered aboard, making the tiny craft rock dangerously. Ebenezer pushed off with an oar and the incongruous pair glided along on the dark green turgid water dangerously close to the shallows. A few more expletives from Robert and Ebenezer corrected course. Soon they were out of sight.

"You'll hear them when they get back," said Davies. "If I know Mr. Robert he's got a bottle in each of them pockets of his."

And so it turned out. An hour later, even above the roaring of the kitchen fire, Mary heard voices raised in song. Again she ran to the front door and saw the rowing boat coming around a bend in the river. Robert and his brother were sitting together in the stern, their arms around each other's shoulders, singing uproariously. As Davies had prognosticated they had a bottle each and it was immediately obvious that the first, boisterous stages of drunkenness had already been reached. Ebenezer rowed steadily on and brought the boat safely to its mooring. He held the prow as the two brothers lurched ashore. Robert's brother was in the full uniform of a naval bo'sun and Mary noticed that he was just as big and powerful as the innkeeper. He had the same heavy jowls and beetling eyebrows, but his hair was black and pulled tight into a pomaded pigtail. They clambered up the bank, placed their arms again about each other and staggered into the inn.

"That's the last you'll see of them for a bit," said Davies, who had joined Mary at the door to witness the arrival.

But in that she was wrong. The great heat which had started when Mary was at Pwll y Cymmer had been maintained, even intensified, as one sun-drenched day followed another. The inn, in spite of being sheltered by tall trees, became stuffy and airless; and so it was no surprise to Mary when the two brothers, after being served with dinner by Gronow in Robert's room, re-appeared downstairs and went to the rear of the inn where there were roughly hewn rustic seats and tables underneath the apple trees. There they went on talking and drinking for a while until their voices died away and snores indicated that rum, a heavy meal and the heat had combined with inevitable effect. Even from the inn the nasal cacophany could be heard, drowning the hum of the myriad of insects that frequented the river banks.

Feeling lethargic herself Mary was glad that no one was staying permanently at the inn. After washing the utensils she found that she had time on her hands. She thought for a moment of going to bed but that would be a waste of a fine summer's day; so instead she decided to go and sit by the bridge. She had come to like it there for the view was beautiful in all directions and there was always something to see: a drover band, a shepherd with his sheep, horsemen and sometimes carriages. And as Mary seated herself on the parapet the thought of carriages reminded her of Sir Roger de Cantelupes, the first time since the tragedy. Would he ever pass by, she wondered, and if so would he notice her? Probably not, for the gift of a frock and shelter from a storm did not mean that he wanted to resume her acquaintance. It was presumptuous of her to think so. But it would be nice to see him just once more and, if he remembered her, she would be very pleased. With these idle thoughts Mary settled herself more comfortably on her stony seat and gave herself over to the warmth of the afternoon.

Presently she heard the sound of animals coming down the hill from the direction of Laleston. There were many of them and at first she surmised that they must be sheep, but as they rounded the bend she saw that they were pigs, at least thirty of them. Pushing and grunting they wandered from one grassy verge to the other, a motley band of big ones and little ones. Behind them, brandishing a stick, was an old man whose face was familiar. A moment's reflection told her that he was the shepherd who had been one of the supplicants at Robert's 'court', and she even remembered his name: Nathaniel Evans, who had been worried about the loss of his hut and his sheep. Why, she wondered, was he now struggling with such recalcitrant animals as pigs? She drew up her legs to let the herd pass but with much shouting and thrashing with his stick Nathaniel drove them into a hedged enclosure just short of the bridge. He took off his bedraggled felt hat, mopped his brow with a sleeve of his smock and peered at Mary. Slowly recognition dawned on the gnarled sun-burnt face.

"Why, you're the gel from the inn. Mary, ain't it?"

"That's right," said Mary. "And you're Nathaniel Evans."

Nathaniel smiled broadly, pleased that she had remembered his name.

"Da iawn, merch fach. It's a good memory you have. But do me a favour, will you? Get me a jug of cwrw da right away. I'm parched and I can't leave these animals."

"Certainly." Mary clambered down from her perch. "You shall have one immediately." She ran to the inn and poured out the biggest jug she could find. When she handed it to Nathaniel he did not stop drinking until the vessel was nearly empty. He sighed, wiped his lips and handed her a coin.

"Diawch! Only Iesu Grist himself knew how thirsty I was. Diolch yn fawr."

"How are you, Nathaniel?" asked Mary, seating herself again on the parapet.

"Weddol. And you? But you don't look too good to me. Not as well as when I saw you last. Have you been ill?"

"I'm afraid so." Mary told him about the loss of her family

79

and the old shepherd listened with obvious concern. When she had finished he said:

"Terrible for you, merch fach. Time alone will heal your wounds but you must look after yourself. Eat good food and don't work too hard—leastwise not until you're better. Mr. Robert is a kindly man. He'll look after you. How is he, by the way?"

"Very happy at present. His brother is here—his ship is berthed off Newton."

"Ah! High jinks it is then with them two. I've never seen men knock back the liquor so quick."

"So I've noticed. But are you all right, Nathaniel? I mean, when you were here last you were in danger of losing your home and some sheep."

"Dammo, yes. Thanks to Mr. Robert I kept everything. No more nonsense after he spoke to squire. He's a great man, Mary, a great man. He looks after us poor, you know."

"I'm so glad. But I thought you had retired from work—giving up being a shepherd to stay at home."

"So I have, but the odd job brings in a penny or two. Right now I'm taking these pigs from Sker Farm to Cowbridge."

"Then you've still a long way to go. Can I get you another ale?"

"Uffern, no! I must be on my way or I won't get home till nightfall." He drained his jug and handed it back. He seized his stick then paused, his expression thoughtful. "By the way, would you like a little pig for a pet?"

"A pig? For a pet?"

"Yes. Black Evan's daughter's pig he was. It's lame, see, the scryncyn of the litter. Do you know what a scryncyn is?"

Mary nodded. A scryncyn was a runt, the last of the litter, the one who got trampled upon by the rest of the family.

"Wait," said Nathaniel. "I'll show it to you." He went to the rear of the herd, stooped and picked up a tiny piglet. He cradled it in his arm and, to Mary's surprise, it neither squealed nor wriggled. "See, it's like a baby."

"It's very young," said Mary dubiously. "And very pretty. But what could I do with it?"

80

"It'll follow you around," said Nathaniel. "Watch." He took a length of hemp from his pocket and tied one end around the pig's neck. He walked in a circle and, after an initial resistance, it followed him docilely, although it limped badly with a rear leg.

"Poor little thing," said Mary. "If it was a pet why are you taking it away from its owner?"

"Black Evans is getting rid of his entire stock and he won't even let his daughter keep it. He's short of money, see—in debt up to his ears. I've carried it most of the way—I don't want to do the same as far as Cowbridge. You'd be doing me a favour to take it off my hands."

"But won't it be missed when you get there? I mean—"

"I'll say a fox got it. A scryncyn don't fetch much. Mind you, one day it'll have to go for bacon, but until then you can let it wander round the orchard. It'll look after itself and as I say it'll be a pet. Something of your own to take your mind off things. Pigs is intelligent animals—it'll give you something to make you laugh."

Mary stared again at the poor little creature. Back on the farm she had always realised how attractive small animals were, even pigs, but this one was particularly appealing. Perhaps Nathaniel was right: to have a pet even for a short while would take her mind off things. But would she be allowed to keep it?

"I wonder, Nathaniel," she said. "Do you think Mr. Robert would approve? I mean—"

"Tell him I gave it to you and then everything will be put to rights. If he's not keen I'll be round again in a week and I can have it back then if you don't want it."

"All right. I'll take it. Let me see if it will follow me."

Mary jumped down from the wall and took the rope. She walked up and down a few times and the pig followed her uncomplainingly. Delighted, Mary relieved Evan of the jug.

"See you in a week's time, then. I'm sure I will be allowed to keep it until then at least."

They waved goodbye to each other and Nathaniel started the herd moving. Mary watched for a moment as the animals crowded into the narrow confines of the bridge, then started off for the inn, the piglet limping behind her without even a glance at its disappearing brethren.

"Come on, piggie," said Mary. "We must see about you right away."

She placed the jug on the window ledge and walked around to the rear of the building, intending to ask permission immediately to keep her acquisition. She was pleased to note that Robert and his brother were now awake, although silent, obviously resting before further labour with the bottle. Robert saw her first and stared wide-eyed at her as she walked across the grass towards him.

"Please, Mr. Robert," said Mary, "could I keep this little pig ? It's been given me for a pet. It's lame and I—"

"Where did you get it ?"

Robert's voice was so gruff that Mary stared at him with surprise. His face began to take on a menacing expression.

"From Nathaniel Evans," she stumbled out. "He gave it to me and said I could keep it. It belonged to the daughter of Sker Farm—"

She got no further than that. Robert leaped to his feet.

"Get the bloody thing off these premises. Get it off now, do you hear ? Take it back to where it came from. Now!"

Suddenly frightened, Mary picked up the piglet. That Robert would have refused permission to keep the animal was something she had been prepared for, but not this vicious show of temper, especially from a man who only the previous week had leaped to her defence. So taken aback was she with the change of demeanour that she felt ill. But Robert had not finished with her.

"Get it out of here," he roared. "Take the bloody thing back, and don't you dare bring anything else here again, do you hear ? Nothing! If you do I'll have you out of the house in seconds and back to where you came from."

Mary shrank back from him. Robert was so gone with temper she was afraid he might strike her. She ran back towards the bridge, the pig in her arms. There was no sign of Nathaniel so she had to go up the hill, eventually catching up with him and the herd a quarter of a mile along the Ewenny road. Panting, she held out the animal, then burst into tears.

"Mr. Robert won't let me keep it. He was very angry."

"Angry?" Nathaniel's face puckered in astonishment, then slowly a look of understanding came into it. "I should have guessed. Did you tell him I gave it to you?"

"Yes. But it made no difference."

Nathaniel took the pig.

"I'm sorry, merch fach. Dry your eyes. It's sorry I am that I've been the cause of trouble for you. I should have known better."

Still weeping Mary returned to the inn and went straight to her room. She flung herself down on the bed and gave herself over completely to misery. At no time in her life had she felt so frightened and lonely.

CHAPTER 12

"YOU'RE WANTED in Mr. Robert's room."

The words, laced with venom, made Mary drop the rushes she had been gathering from the kitchen floor. She straightened up and met the dark, intimidating gaze of Gronow.

"Now!" said Gronow. "He wants to see you now."

Flustered as always by Gronow's presence and doubly alarmed by the vindictive tone of her voice, Mary felt what little courage she still possessed evaporate like spindrift. Barely twenty four hours had passed since the innkeeper had ranted at her and now he wanted to see her in his room, a place previously forbidden to her. She blurted out:

"But I thought I wasn't allowed in there."

"Well, you are now. Don't ask me why. Go immediately."

Mary wiped her hands in her apron and ran out of the kitchen. Whatever the reason Robert wanted to see her the fact that she had to go to his room had obviously been an affront to Gronow, one she would not easily forgive. One dark cloud after another seemed to be gathering on the horizon. Any more and she would think of handing in her notice—that is if she was not dismissed immediately. Where she would go she did not know, but anything would be better than the life that seemed to be materialising. She mounted the stairs with trembling legs and knocked timidly on the heavy, iron-studded door—too timidly, for there was no reply. She knocked again and an unmistakable voice roared a command to enter.

She pushed open the door and was immediately surprised to see how small the room was. It was smaller than the parlour and cluttered with furniture, well-made and expensive. A narrow box bed took up one wall, a Queen Anne table and chairs filled the centre and a deep, heavy chest, similar to but smaller than the one on the landing, prevented easy access to the window. But what the room lacked in size it made up for in opulence, in addition to the furniture. On every conceivable resting place there was silverware and exquisitely-cut glassware, more than she had ever seen before; and under her feet she felt the fine texture of a Turkish carpet. It was a comfortable den such as some rich and tasteless nobleman might have furnished in his palace, replete with choice treasures and trappings. Recovering from her surprise she heard Robert addressing her.

"Ah, Mary! Right glad I am you've come. I want to apologise to you, m'dear, for being so angry with you yesterday. It was wrong of me and I can only say that I had—er—drunk a little too much rum. You can blame my brother for that. He always makes me do things I'm ashamed of. He'll bear me out."

Mary glanced at the brother who was regarding her with an expression that seemed to be both amused and appraising.

"That's right," he said. "Don't pay any attention to him when he's with me. He don't ordinarily touch rum, see, and when he do he forgets himself. He didn't mean no harm."

"A true word," said Robert magnanimously, "and to show you how sorry I am, Mary, I'm going to give you an extra sixpence a week. Will that do to make amends?"

"Yes," said Mary and, not knowing quite what else to say, added: "That's very good of you, sir."

Robert seemed relieved at her quick acceptance.

"There you are, brawd. I told you she was the forgiving sort, didn't I? And pretty, too, ain't she?"

"Very," said the brother.

"It's like this, Mary," said Robert in an ingratiating voice. "You did wrong to bring me that pig, see. Some people might get the wrong idea—think I'd asked you to get it for me. Steal it, like, and you know what the law does to people who steal something valued at more than five shillings, don't you?"

"But it wasn't stolen," cried Mary. "It was given to me by—"

"Never mind who gave it to you. You know I'm well liked round here, don't you, m'dear? But there are people who would do me an injury. Now if someone said I'd stolen that pig, or got you to steal it for me, where do you think we'd end up—you and me?"

"In prison, sir."

"Not in prison, Mary. On the gallows more like, up at Groes Gibbet. Leastways I would. You wouldn't like to see your master strung up now, would you?"

"Oh, no! Of course not. You've been very good to me."

"Well, then, that's the reason I was angry. You didn't give me no warning see, and that's why I flew off the handle. Now do you understand?"

"Yes, sir."

"And you won't do it again?"

"No, sir. I've learned my lesson."

"Good girl. I can't tell you how much I like you, Mary, and how sorry I am over your great loss. Now you like it here, don't you?"

"Yes, I do."

"Well, then, you must stay here. I've already told you to regard the place as your home, now that you've got none to go to. But you must understand my position, Mary. Nothing must happen that would give my enemies a chance to—er—place a finger on me, so to speak. Look around this room and tell me what you see."

Mary glanced again at the myriad of valuable objects.

"Great wealth, sir."

"Not as great as some, m'dear, but great enough, all obtained by honest toil. Now do you understand why some might be envious of me?"

"Yes, sir."

"Well, then, you can see why I was angry. As long as it don't happen again you and me'll get on famously. Now, Mary, go down to the cellar and get a bottle of brandy and then every-thing'll be fine between us. We'll have no more misunderstand-ings. I've had enough rum to last me a lifetime and I want a change of liquor."

Mary nodded and ran from the room. Tears were in her eyes but now they were tears of relief. Mr. Robert had been kind to her, almost like a father, and her position at the inn was secure after all. She could understand the previous day's outburst now and saw the sense of her master's words, although why he had enemies she failed to understand. He helped everybody and was highly thought of; but, of course, he did possess great wealth, as his room had shown, and some people were always jealous of possessions and position. She would make sure that she, at least, would never be the cause of a calamity befalling him. She reached the cellar, wiped her eyes, and found a bottle of brandy already de-corked by the ever-thoughtful Mathias.

Back in Robert's room the brothers had left their chairs and were poring over a chart unrolled on the table, its ends weighted down with books. Mary had no great knowledge of geography but she recognised it as one of the English Channel. She hovered around for a moment, not knowing where to place the bottle and wondering whether she should have brought fresh glasses. She was saved from such a decision by Robert's great hand reaching out and seizing it. He took a prodigious swallow, belched and placed the bottle on the table beside the chart. Engrossed, he and his brother went on studying the map, oblivious of her presence. Not knowing quite what to do she remained standing, the tray still in her hand.

Then she caught sight of the chest by the window. Its lid was open and, out of curiosity, she moved a step or two nearer it, expecting to see further wealth enclosed in its confines. But what she did see made her gasp in surprise, for the chest was a miniature armoury. Set in the lid, carefully attached by straps about their scabbards, were three swords, two cutlasses and a rapier. On the wood of the furthermost side was a brace of ornate pistols, complete with pouches and cleaning rods, and two smaller hand guns. Along the two inner walls was a motley collection of knives and daggers, straight and curved. But what took her eye most was a partition in the centre of the chest on which was a dark blue cloak, carefully folded, and a red stockinette cap such as French revolutionaries wore. Hastily Mary averted her eyes and returned to the table, fearful that she had seen something not intended for her eyes.

After a few more moments studying the chart Robert straightened up and reached again for the bottle. Another copious swig and he caught sight of Mary and the open chest. His eyes narrowed and he looked from her to the chest and back again. Then he grinned.

"Mary, guess what this brother of mine's been up to. Last night he split his hammock. He can't sleep in an ordinary bed, see, so he takes it with him wherever he goes. God knows what he'll do when he marries. No woman'll have him on them terms. Anyway, last night he forgot to take his bloody boots off and put his foot through the canvas. Will you repair it for him?"

"Certainly," said Mary.

"It's in the corner. Canvas ain't the easiest thing to sew but you've got some stout needles, I'm sure. Do the best you can, will you, m'dear?"

Mary smiled.

"Of course, I'll see to it immediately."

"You're a good girl. And now I've got some special news for you so listen carefully. In a few days I shall be going away for a while for I've some business in France to attend to. While I'm gone I want you to clean this silver—all of it. Gronow will give you the key of the room and if she objects tell her I've given you permission. You've proved a reliable girl and I know I can trust you. Will you do that for me?"

Before Mary could reply Robert's brother spluttered out a cloud of rum.

87

"Be careful, now. Gronow won't like that. Take care what you're about."

"Shut your gob," said Robert cheerfully. "I always know what I'm about."

"So far you have, but don't get too cocky. Many a good man's been brought low by the spite of a woman."

"Pay no attention to him," said Robert to Mary. "He ain't a womaniser as you can see. But remember what I say. If Gronow tries to stop you tell her I want you to clean the silver particular. If that don't stop her nonsense I'll have things to say when I get back. And now, m'dear, I've kept the best bit of news till last. There's a certain gentleman around these parts very taken with you, very taken indeed. You know who I'm referring to, of course."

Mary shook her head, not taking in his words immediately, and Robert's grin widened.

"You ought to. He tells me he's promised to show you the sea, and when he do he wants you to wear that dress he gave you."

Mary felt the blood rush to her face.

"Ah!" said Robert. "I thought that'd make you sit up. Sir Roger'll be here at two o'clock sharp to call for you, and I want you to go with him. You've had a rough time recently, what with one thing and another, so a trip to the sea'll do you good. Just make sure you're ready in time."

"But the dress," gasped Mary. "The dress. It's an evening gown. It won't do—"

"If he wants you to wear it, m'dear, see that you wear it. I ain't a prophet but to my way of thinking he's taken a fancy to you."

"But—"

"No 'buts'. Do as I say. Go with him."

To prevent further conversation Robert went to the corner of the room and unhooked a roll of canvas from a nail. He bundled it up and thrust it into her hands.

"Repair this first. You'll have plenty of time to get ready by this afternoon." He leaned forward, engulfed her with an arm and lowered his voice. "Play your cards right, m'dear, and you might do yourself a power of good. Sir Roger ain't the best catch in Glamorgan but by Saint Christopher you could do a lot worse."

He squeezed her hard then propelled her towards the door. As he closed it behind her he winked.

"Remember what I say. Play your cards right. There's many a girl who's bettered herself with her looks and you've got plenty of them. And don't forget—I've put in a good word for you, and you know that counts round here."

He winked again and shut the door.

CHAPTER 13

MARY REPAIRED THE hammock and returned it to Robert's room only to find that both brothers had dozed off in their chairs, empty bottles beside them. She tip-toed in, deposited the hammock on the floor and returned to the kitchen to have an early meal, only to find that she could eat little for her mind was on Sir Roger's impending visit. Why, she wondered, was he really coming? Was he merely being kind or did he have serious intentions towards her? Surely that was out of the question because of the disparity in their stations; but she could still visualise Robert mouthing the words: "Play your cards right, m'dear, and you might do yourself a power of good."

She said nothing to Davies about her assignation, although she felt guilty about the deception, and was relieved that Gronow was nowhere to be seen: coming on top of being allowed in Robert's sanctuary the attentions of a nobleman would undoubtedly not be well received in that direction. As soon as she was able she slipped to her room to prepare for the coming encounter.

First she washed and put on her newest and cleanest underwear, then she tried on the gown, pinning it in one or two places until it fitted to her satisfaction. Half an hour's deft needlework completed the operation and made sure that it would retain its shape, although she knew she would have to unpick the cotton before getting out of it again. She looked at her hair in the mirror and realised with dismay that it was still lifeless and what was more she now had no decent bonnet to cover it, for her best still showed the effect of its soaking. She compromised by sweeping her hair upwards and pinning it at the top in a mode she had seen fashionable ladies wear. It seemed to suit the gown and so she felt better. Finally she threw her cloak over her shoulders and sat on the edge of the bed until she thought it was about two o'clock then, trembling slightly, she made her way downstairs.

The inn was unusually quiet and she wondered whether it was better to go outside and wait, for she still dreaded meeting Gronow. But it was still warm and close and she was afraid the heat would make her perspire, so she hovered by the dining room window, keeping an anxious eye on the forecourt. Mercifully, after only a few minutes, she heard wheels on its rough surface and Sir Roger's coach came into view. She saw Jenkins dismount and approach the front door and, fearing a loud knocking, she ran to meet him. The old servant eyed her up and down.

"My! I would hardly have recognised you. You look a real lady."

Taking it as a compliment Mary's morale received an instant boost.

"Thank you. It's very nice of you to say so."

"Come. Sir Roger's waiting."

Stumbling a little as usual he led the way to the carriage and opened the door for her. Sir Roger was sitting in the far corner dressed, as far as she could make out, in the same suit as when she had last seen him. He doffed his hat.

"Welcome, Mary. Has your master told you I wish to take you to the seaside?"

"Yes, sir."

"Then make yourself comfortable and so I shall." He patted the seat beside him. The coach smelled slightly of mildew but it was comfortable, with seats of the best leather. Sir Roger banged on the roof with a silver-topped cane and they moved off. "We shall go as far as Ogmore. It's as pleasant a run as any. I have a hamper of food and we can sup on the beach. You'd like that, wouldn't you, not having seen the coast before?"

"Oh, yes," breathed Mary, the same sensation of unreality enveloping her as it had at Candleston.

"Good." Sir Roger sat back in his seat and turned his head to the window. As the green hedgerows flashed past on either side Mary surreptitiously studied his profile. It was as strong and commanding as she remembered, the cleft chin now even more prominent in the bright daylight. She thought how much had happened since she had last seen him and wished that she was happier within herself so that she could enjoy her new adventure to the full; but she kept thinking of her family and wondering if Sir Roger had heard of her loss. He answered that by turning to her, when the coach reached Ewenny, and saying:

"I'm sorry to hear of the death of your father and several members of your family. Please accept my sincerest sympathy."

Mary smiled her thanks.

"Most unfortunate," said Sir Roger. "Diphtheria is a terrible disease but usually it strikes children. It must have been a particularly malignant form to have had such an effect, but it does happen. There have been several cases recently of adults having been stricken. It must have been a terrible ordeal for you. I take it you will remain at the inn for some little time now."

"I have nowhere else to go. My father's farm has been given to a new tenant."

Sir Roger studied her for a few moments before replying.

"Most sad. I thought that might happen when I heard the news. That is why I decided to invite you today. I thought it might do you good. Are you glad you came?"

"Yes, sir. It will do me good, as you say."

"Good. Excellent. I hope you don't mind my saying so, at a time when your mind is clouded with unhappiness, but you look very beautiful in that dress. Thank you for wearing it."

"Thank you for giving it to me. It is my most treasured possession."

Again his gaze hovered on her, but the carriage began bumping and they were both thrown about.

91

"This is a rough part," explained Sir Roger. "The road becomes smoother a little further on."

In this he was correct, for after a few more minutes of lurching and swaying the carriage picked up speed and they went bowling along a straight and level section of the road. To her left Mary could see tree-clad hills and on the other side there were occasional glimpses of two slow-moving rivers. Beyond the rivers were sand-dunes, immense waves of them extending as far as the eye could see. Seeing Mary's interest Sir Roger smiled.

"See those damned things? Dunes. That's what's choking the life out of Candleston. I wish I could do something about it—but I can't, unless God sees fit to change the direction of the prevailing wind."

Mary murmured something she hoped sounded like an expression of sympathy. He went on:

"One of the river's the Ewenny. It meets the Ogmore lower down. That's where we shall picnic. It's a pleasant spot and you shall see as much of the sea as you wish. There! Do you see those ruins? That's Ogmore Castle. Norman. Don't go near it. It's the haunt of some very undesirable ruffians. I'll have to get them cleared out one day."

They passed the castle and suddenly the sea came into view. It shone and glittered in the distance like Robert's silverware. Mary leaned forward to get a better look.

"You're on the wrong side," said Sir Roger. "You should be sitting where I am and then you'd see more of the scenery. Come, move nearer me and then you'll see more."

Mary obediently slid along the seat until she was very close to Sir Roger, who pressed himself into the upholstery to give her a better view. The carriage slowed down slightly as they came to a gradient, and a panoramic view began to unfold. To the west stretched a magnificent beach, completely empty and deserted, and beyond it even more dunes. Now Mary could see the full expanse of St. Georges Channel. Sir Roger pointed through the open window.

"If you look carefully you'll see a ship. It's the man-o'-war Robert's brother serves on. Can you see it?"

Mary craned her head forward. There was a haze over the sea and she could only make out a black speck.

"It's a long way away."

"About four miles. It's anchored off Newton. That's the only safe berth around here. If only this damned river was navigable we could have a port here, but as it is it's hopeless—only small craft can use it. Can you see the other side of the Channel?"

Mary screwed up her eyes.

"I think I can see something."

"It's difficult today. On some days the visibility is so good you can see the coasts of Devon and Cornwall. You can even pick out the fields and houses, but today it's misty. Still, that's a sign of continuing good weather. There! Can you see the Tuskars?"

Mary leaned forward even more and to support her Sir Roger placed an arm around her shoulders.

"The Tuskars are the most dangerous rocks around here. Many a good ship's been broken up there. It's the burial ground of hundreds of vessels—so many no one can tell the exact number."

"It doesn't look dangerous," murmured Mary. "It all seems very calm and peaceful."

"Ah! Today's a summer day. Wait until you see it in the winter when there's a storm raging."

He took his arm away, reluctantly Mary thought, and she sat back again in the seat. It was as well that she did for suddenly the carriage came to a sudden, lurching halt. The sound of many voices came through the window and she saw that they had stopped opposite what appeared to be an inn. It was a solitary structure, built on the slope leading down to the river. Sir Roger leaned out.

"What's the matter, Jenkins? Get on, man."

There seemed to be great activity going on around the inn. Its yard was packed with men and horses and there was a continuous line of people extending down to the river, where several small boats were moored. Everyone seemed to be carrying something, either a box or a bale.

"Some trading goes on here," said Sir Roger. "Possibly a little smuggling, too. It doesn't do to dwell here too long."

At that moment two men detached themselves from a group in the yard and came towards the carriage; and Mary recognised them immediately as Benjamin and Ebenezer. What the two ruffians were doing so far from the New Inn she did not know, unless they were involved in some form of trading, probably illegitimate. They came up to the carriage window and peered in. Grinning, with knowing and impish expressions, they doffed their tricorns.

"Good afternoon, Sir Roger," said Ebenezer, his sly eyes darting continually from one to the other. "It's a nice day. I see you have a companion with you."

Sir Roger ignored him. He reached for his stick and banged on the roof. The carriage remained motionless.

"How are you, Mary?" Ebenezer's small eyes seemed to be dancing with mirth. "Well, I trust."

"Get on, Jenkins," roared Sir Roger.

For several moments nothing happened. Mary could see that Sir Roger was becoming angry, making her afraid to say anything. Then, with a lurch, the carriage moved off. The still-grinning faces of the two reprobates were lost to view. Swaying dangerously they left the road, circumnavigated a large cart piled high with sacks and boxes, and re-gained the road. Slowly the horses picked up speed. Sir Roger said nothing, but his out-thrust chin told Mary that he was still annoyed at the encounter. She said nothing and continued to stare at the view.

In a short time the gradient steepened and the horses began to labour. Gradually more and more of the sea came into view until Mary could make out the full outline of the western coast. Beneath them the river moved sluggishly in its estuary, but where it met the waves there seemed to be great turbulence. Suddenly they swung off the roadway and went careering down a track, brakes hissing noisily. They came to a halt and Sir Roger got out.

"Here's your beach. I think you'll like it here."

He helped Mary down and she saw that they had stopped on a

flat, grassy bank on the edge of the sand. Small waves tumbled gently on the shingle and her nostrils were filled with the smell of salt. She took a deep breath.

"It's beautiful here. Thank you for bringing me to such a lovely place."

Visibly pleased at her remark, his good humour now fully restored, Sir Roger smiled.

"We'll take a walk. Get the food ready by the time we come back, Jenkins. In one hour or thereabouts."

He took Mary's arm and helped her down the embankment to the beach. It was the first time her feet had touched sand and she felt strangely exhilarated by its feel through her thin shoes. Slowly they made their way down to the water's edge. There she glanced down at the shingle.

"Look at those shells! And those pebbles! They're all different colours."

"Collect a few. Take them back with you and they'll remind you of today."

"Oh, may I ? They're not somebody's property ?"

"Not that I know of, except possibly the king's, and I doubt if he'll object."

They both laughed and Mary set to with her task. She picked up a red-hued pebble but a few paces further on saw a better example and dropped the first.

"Oh dear! I don't know which to have first. They're all so beautiful."

"Let's walk a little further," suggested Sir Roger. "Then you can make up your mind which you want. You can always pick them up on the way back."

They kept to the area where the hard sand met the soft, moving inland only where rocks impeded their progress. Every now and again Mary stooped to pick up a treasure she could not resist, and Sir Roger dawdled good-naturedly along with her. Her joy, when she found a particularly pleasing example, seemed to communicate itself to him, and Mary knew that he had pleasure in merely watching her. Mr. Robert would have said that she was playing her cards right, but she knew that her enjoyment was genuine, with no ulterior motive other than being grateful to the man who had given her such pleasure. She was enjoying herself so much that she forgot about the time and was startled when Sir Roger took her arm and stopped her walking.

"I think we've gone far enough now. We'd better turn back."

Surprised, Mary saw that they had come up against a headland and that no further progress was possible on the beach. Above her towered an enormous cliff. She looked over her shoulder and saw their footprints extending along the sand as far as she could see, interspersed with little round holes where Sir Roger had placed his stick. Of the carriage and the original beach there was no sign. She gasped.

"I didn't realise we'd come so far."

"Are you hungry?"

"I am now. I wasn't earlier on but I think the salt air has given me an appetite."

"Come then. We shall see what Jenkins has in store for us."

He placed a hand under her arm but soon afterwards withdrew it as though he was afraid of appearing too forward. Mary mentally gave him full marks for that: he was, as Robert had said, a gentleman. Together they retraced their footsteps, with Mary still finding something of interest every few yards. At last they came within sight of the carriage and Mary saw that Jenkins had set up a table below it on the beach, replete with tablecloth, crockery and a bottle of wine.

But what took their eye was not the table or Jenkins setting out the food, but a little knot of men bending over something further up the beach.

"What are they up to?" said Sir Roger, half to himself. Out loud he called out: "Who are those men, Jenkins?"

Jenkins straightened up and shook his head. It was obvious that he had been too busy with his chores to notice the group.

"Come," said Sir Roger to Mary. "They've found something of interest or they wouldn't be there. Let's go and see what it is."

They walked towards the men, who straightened up as they approached. They were a dirty, tattered lot, obviously beggars or beachcombers. At their feet, half buried in the sand, was something that looked like a large, torn bale.

"What have you there?" asked Sir Roger.

One of them touched his forelock.

"Don't rightly know, sir. We've just found it."

He stooped and scraped away some of the sand and an object came into view that looked ominously like a human arm. He scraped again and revealed a bloated torso, then worked his way up until he came to a sand-encrusted face, old and gnarled, with a halo of white, matted hair. On the forehead was a huge gash which had once bled profusely, for the congealed blood was still caked over one cheek. Suddenly Mary gave a cry and started back.

"What's the matter?" exclaimed Sir Roger. "Do you know who it is?"

Mary stared at the face a moment longer then turned away, unable to look any more, for there was no doubt about it now. The face was McGregor's, the packman who had given her the book mark.

CHAPTER 14

WHEN MARY LOOKED again she was horrified to see McGregor's mouth drool open and emit a sound. At first it was just a croak then it increased in strength and crescendo until it was a ear-piercing, frightening shriek. She turned and ran, but the sand slowed her down, giving her the sensation that her limbs were incapable of movement. Suddenly she fell headlong into a soft patch and writhed and twisted in an attempt to get up, but some weight seemed to prevent her. Then she woke to find herself in her own bed, twisting and turning, her heart racing fit to burst and her body bathed in perspiration. The bedclothes were a tangled mass, mute testimony to the nightmare that had wracked her. With trembling hands she reached for the tinder box, scratched alight the rag and lit the candle.

That it was nearly dawn she knew for the first faint shafts of sunlight were appearing over the trees, but she was glad of the flickering comfort of the candle. Gradually, as she became calmer, the memory of the discovery on the beach returned. Sir Roger had brought her back to the inn and explained her distress to the innkeeper and Gronow, neither of whom seemed to comprehend why the death of an itinerant should have had such an effect on her; but at Sir Roger's insistence, and with Davies's help, she was given a dose of laudanum and put to bed. She must have slept the greater part of the night and the scream she had heard was part of the nightmare, a figment of her imagination; but how often now, she wondered, would she see the poor, battered face of old McGregor, who had been so kind and generous to her?

That he had been murdered there was no doubt. Sir Roger had thought so, too, pointing out that if the packman had accidentally hit his head and then fallen in the river, all blood would have been washed away. But the blood around the wound had congealed so thickly that neither river nor seawater had had any effect on it, and in any case the gash was so deep there could be only one sensible conclusion: and so the frightening possibility arose that he had been killed at the inn. With a spasm of fear Mary recalled the strange noises the night McGregor had disappeared: the scratching and the heavy breathing; and then there was the mystery of Mathias's nocturnal wanderings and Gronow's glib explanation of the scuff marks on the floor. Gronow was capable of anything, she was certain of that, but what of Mathias? Surely the ostler, who was now her friend, could not be a murderer. Such a thought was impossible; but whoever had done it she prayed that he would be punished, for God would surely not allow an innocent old man to be slain without retribution. Sir Roger was going to report the matter to the authorities so there would be an enquiry; and if dreadful deeds were being perpetrated the sooner the better.

Gradually the light strengthened and Mary knew that she had to get up. She dowsed the candle, dressed and went downstairs to the kitchen. Lethargically she carried out her tasks until Davies arrived who, after fussing over her for a few minutes, informed her that they must hurry to prepare breakfast because Robert and his brother were leaving that morning, the one to travel to France, the other to rejoin his ship. About an hour later the two men appeared in the dining room, wan and listless after their two days' debauchery; but what surprised Mary was Robert's garb. No longer was he wearing his country gentleman's outfit: now he was attired in the rough clothes of a sea-faring man, complete with woollen hooped jersey and white canvas trousers. Around his waist was a heavy belt from which hung the cutlass she had seen and the two ornate pistols. On his head was the red cap, the whole effect being that of a pirate rather than an innkeeper. Dully he asked how Mary was and tried to eat his breakfast, but neither man seemed to have a stomach for food, which was understandable; and when Mary cleared the plates they were still half full.

Mathias then arrived outside with the trap and loaded on it two leather portmanteaux and the hammock which, as far as Mary could see, was stuffed full of bottles. The brothers lugubriously mounted and Gronow arrived to see them off, smiling ingratiatingly. Obviously she had not yet given up hope of captivating the bo'sun; but in mid-smile she was pushed brusquely aside by Ebenezer and Benjamin who proceeded to park themselves on the running boards of the trap, grinning like monkeys. The heavily-laden vehicle set off with only a desultory wave from its occupants and Gronow returned dark-faced to the house and was not seen for the rest of the day.

Then, for six weeks, a period of comparative peace descended on the inn. Without Robert bellowing orders, his henchmen sniggering and joking, and a lack of custom caused by the continuing fine weather, the level of activity dropped considerably, a matter for which Mary was glad. She wanted time to think and assess her position. Already she was puzzled why the innkeeper had left knowing that an enquiry was pending, an enigma that deepened as the days went by without anything happening. No official called, not even an excise man or a soldier. It was as though the authorities were uninterested in the event, or had deliberately decided not to investigate, a state of affairs that angered her. McGregor might have been nothing more than a packman—a nonentity in the eyes of the law—but he was a human being; and it made her blood boil to think that no attempt was being made to find his assailant. There was little she could do about it but she made a mental note to voice her discontent when next she saw Sir Roger.

Already she was the object of a few snide remarks in the inn about her visit to the beach. The local farm workers, after pressing her for details about the gory find, occasionally ended with questions as to when she was going out again with Sir Roger, all of which made Mary even more annoyed, for it was obvious that the death of the old Scotsman meant less to the community than local gossip. She tried to find refuge in work, especially in the task of cleaning Robert's silver. Several times she obtained the key of the erst-while forbidden room from a glowering Gronow and escaped there as though to a sanctuary, diligently polishing every object until she could see the reflection of her face. The innkeeper's chest, she noticed, was locked and padlocked, and she wondered how much of his armoury he had taken away with him.

One other matter puzzled her as the days went by: she had heard nothing from Sir Roger. He neither called nor sent a message, which was strange, for he had warned her that she might be summoned by the coroner as a witness; and as the time passed without a word from him she became anxious, not so much because his interest in her might have waned but because there was no progress in the cause of justice. After a week had gone she decided that, whatever he thought of her, she would visit Candleston and find out why.

This time she set off along a more direct route, a footpath that followed the course of the river. It was a well-worn track but now that it was high summer the brambles and nettles had made great progress, so she had to guard against thorns and stings. Once or twice she thought she had lost her way, for the path twisted tortuously, but eventually she came out into a clearing and saw the walls of the castle. She had come upon it from the rear and was amazed to see the decayed state of the outer bastion, which had great, gaping holes where the stonework had fallen away. Sand had made inroads everywhere, covering the surrounding sward and the roots of the trees, which showed signs of strangulation. The whole area presented a gloomy picture and the building was ghostly and forbidding, even in bright daylight. It was obvious that unless restorative work was quickly put in hand the entire place would be a ruin. She knocked on the heavy double-fronted door but the sound echoed back emptily and there was no response. She went through the courtyard and knocked again on the kitchen door, but that, too, had no effect. Disappointed, she made her way back to the path, intending to return immediately to the inn. Then, after going less than a hundred yards, she saw Mathias sitting on a stile. He waited until she came up to him then lightly vaulted off on the other side.

"Hullo, Mary. Been for a walk?"

"Yes. I'm getting to know where all the paths lead to".

"Have you been as far as the castle?"

"Yes."

"Sir Roger's not there. He's gone away." Mathias's voice was laconic. He said the words as a statement of fact, not as though he was prying, but Mary felt slightly irritated. Everyone knew of her outing with Sir Roger.

"Has he?" was all she said.

"Have you had a good look at it? The castle, I mean."

"Yes." Mary advanced to the stile and was about to climb over but changed her mind. Friend that Mathias now was she did not want him to see that she was wearing a new pair of lace-edged pantaloons, specially put on for her visit to Candleston, so she remained facing him, the rough woodwork between them. Mathias studied her for a moment, then:

"Can I have a word with you, Mary?"

"Certainly, Daniel." Mary leaned on the fence, wondering what was coming. Mathias seemed apprehensive and having trouble framing his words. To help him she added: "Nothing serious, I hope."

"I don't think you'll like what I'm going to say."

"Oh! Why not?"

"It's about Sir Roger."

"What about him?"

"He's an imposter."

Mary's eyes opened wide.

"An imposter? What are you talking about?"

"Well, didn't it strike you as strange that he wasn't there after all that talk about an enquiry?"

"What about it? I expect he had to go away suddenly."

"Oh, Mary! Can't you see? He doesn't want an enquiry. He's been bluffing you."

"Why shouldn't he want an enquiry?"

"Because he's afraid of what the authorities will find out if they start delving too much."

"What will they find out?"

"For one thing that he's no right to the name. The Cantelupes died out years ago. He just appeared here a few years ago and laid claim to the title. Nobody bothers to dispute it because the only inheritance—if you can call it that—is that thing of a castle and some wind-swept land. Some say he's illegitimate— a bastard. Don't tell me you haven't heard that at the inn."

Mary swiped at a passing butterfly. She would not admit it to Mathias but since the trip to the beach she had heard snatches of talk about Sir Roger's mysterious background; but she had put it down to the usual country gossip.

"What if I have? Is it any concern of ours? I hardly think he could stay at Candleston without some right in law."

Mathias let out an exasperated snort.

"Well, there are other things he's afraid of as well."

"What other things?"

"Where he gets his money from, for a start. He's not too scrupulous about it."

But he hasn't got any. He's poor. Jenkins, his servant, told me—and other people."

"He's got a bit though and he doesn't get it from the land. You can take it from me, Mary, he'll never be able to provide for you."

"Provide for me! What are you talking about? Anybody'd think he was going to marry me."

"Then why is he so interested in you? He went to the beach with you, didn't he?"

Mary bridled then checked herself. It had suddenly occurred to her that Mathias might be jealous, in which case it was futile to become angry. A more gentle approach was required.

"Sir Roger's merely been kind to me," she said quietly. "He sheltered me one night during a storm and when he heard what had happened to my family he took me to the sea to do me good. He's never mentioned marriage nor is he ever likely to. You're as bad as all the others."

Mathias seemed relieved.

"I'm sorry. I didn't want you to get hurt, that's all."

"That's all right, Daniel. Thank you for thinking about my welfare. I assure you I shan't get hurt. And if Sir Roger is il-legitimate as you say then I am sorry for him."

"My apologies if I seem to be prying into your affairs, but I know how upset you've been over this business of McGregor. That's another thing I must talk to you about. If you're ever in trouble like that again you must go and see Mr. Nicholl, not Sir Roger."

"Mr. Nicholl who lives in that big new house? Why should I go to see him?"

"Because he's the most influential man around here—a member of parliament and the local magistrate. He'll help you."

"But he's in London most of the time, isn't he? Anyway, what's the point of going there? I can hardly walk up to him and complain that nothing's been done about Mr. McGregor, can I?"

"Not now perhaps, but if anything like that happens again you must go and tell him. He'll be in Merthyr Mawr for the rest of the summer."

"If anything like that happens again! Is there any danger of that?"

"I don't know. I hope not. But McGregor's body has disap-peared from the beach. Did you know that?"

103

Mary stared at him.

"No, I didn't know."

"It's true. So you see what that means. No body, no murder—and so now no enquiry."

"Is that why I've heard nothing?"

"Yes. That's why I'm telling you. If ever you're in difficulty go and see Nicholl. Don't be afraid—you can trust him. He's a lawyer."

"Thank you. I'll remember your advice."

Again Mathias's dark brown eyes appraised her.

"There is one final thing—a request."

Mary studied the good-looking, sun-burnt face, wondering what was coming next. Her mind was churning with doubts. The ostler, who had just warned her against Sir Roger, was also the man she had seen the night McGregor had disappeared. She was reminded of a dictum of her father's: it was difficult to know whom to trust these days. Cautiously she replied:

"What is it?"

"I'd like you to come to a noson lawen with me."

"A noson lawen?"

"Yes. In September. At Turberville's barn."

"But that's several weeks away."

"I know, but all the best girls are getting booked up; that's why I'm asking you now."

"And you consider me a best girl?"

"Yes."

Mary tried not to smile at the compliment. Although perplexed she knew she owed Mathias a favour for helping her at Pwll y Cymmer and it would have been unkind not to have accepted. Surely, she thought, there could be no harm in going to a public evening of song and dance with him. There would be too many people present for anything sinister or dangerous to happen. She nodded.

"Very well, Daniel. I'll go with you."

"Good." Daniel's face lit up with pleasure. "Thank you." He held out his arms. "Let me help you over and I'll walk back with you."

Mary climbed on the stile and he swung her down to the ground, amazing her again with his gentle strength. But just as they were setting off a robin alighted on the stile Mary had just vacated.

"Oh, dear!" said Mary. "A robin, now, in mid-summer."

"Not unusual. I saw one yesterday."

"It is unusual. They say it's a sign of bad luck."

"More like a hard winter to come I'd say."

Mary stared at the little bird, which eyed her cheekily back.

"I expect you're right."

"Anyway," he said, "don't worry about it. We've both seen it now so if there's any bad luck going we'll share it."

He laughed and they set off for the inn with Mary walking in front, conscious that every plucking blackberry branch was revealing the fact that she was wearing the new pantaloons she had not wanted Mathias to see.

CHAPTER 15

AIDED BY THE absence of the innkeeper and his vociferous cronies, a farming community working in the fields until night-fall and country air seasoned occasionally with salt when the westerlies blew, Mary slowly recovered her strength. Her light, skipping step still failed to materialise but her complexion improved and the first glimmerings of lustre reappeared in her hair. Her recuperation was also helped by a visit from her two surviving sisters, who arrived together one day at the inn. Mary gave them tea in the kitchen and, in spite of the sorrow that still engulfed them, they all felt strengthened by the family bond between them. She was delighted, too, by the unexpected appearance one day of Jack, her brother, on furlough from his regiment pending a posting to Ireland. Mary was secretly glad of that for, although the Irish were still recalcitrant and suspected of harbouring a French army, a period of service there seemed safer than being sent to Europe, where the intermittent, desultory war still dragged on. Coming on top of everything else, she knew, the death in battle of her brother would be the final calamity that would destroy her; so she thanked God silently and plied Jack with food and ale until the time came for him to leave for Bristol where he was to embark on a troopship.

Then, in mid-August, the innkeeper reappeared, noisily and spectacularly. Hearing the commotion Mary, Gronow and Davies rushed out to find the forecourt full of mules, each one heavily laden with pannier bags. In the middle of a throng of disreputable-looking men, still wearing his hooped jersey, canvas trousers and red cap, was Robert, half drunk and roaring at the top of his voice.

"Ebenezer, Benjamin, get three of them mules off-loaded. You others take the rest of the stuff to you know where. If there's as much as a parcel missing when I come down tonight I'll have your bloody gizzards for breakfast. Get it there by nightfall—or else."

His two henchmen hurried to do his bidding, although it was obvious that they were the worse for drink as well. The other men began leading away the rest of the mules and then Robert caught sight of the women.

"Avast there, you land-lubbers. How've you been since I've been away?"

They all smiled at him.

"Well, I see," he shouted. "And you, Mary. How are you? You're looking better. Good! Now get indoors and prepare a meal for us or we'll start eating these bloody animals."

Gronow led the way back in. They had to pick their way between piles of boxes and bales in the hall but no sooner had they reached the kitchen when they heard Robert bawling again.

"Come here, Gronow, you skinny bitch. I've got something for you—and bring Mary with you."

The two women went to the dining room to find Robert fumbling with a pannier.

"Damn these bloody straps. Here, Ebenezer, you did them up. Undo them, you shifty-eyed bastard."

Ebenezer, not very deft himself, succeeded in loosening the

106

buckles. Robert plunged his hands into one of the bags and drew out a small parchment-covered parcel.

"Here you are, Gronow. For you. We've had a good trip, see, so here's your reward. Open it, woman, and see if you like it."

Gronow parted the folds of the parchment and gasped. It was a necklace of pearls.

"Well!" roared Robert. "Say whether you like 'em or not. Put 'em on and let's have a look at you."

Gronow slipped the necklace around her neck. It went well with her sombre dress and black hair.

"They're beautiful," she breathed. "Truly beautiful. Thank you indeed."

Robert roared with delight.

"That gives me the right to knock you about for another year. Now, Mary, I have something for you too—something special."

He delved again into the bag. This time it was a larger parcel, wrapped in cloth. He thrust it into her hands.

"Got that in Dieppe. The best in France. Have a look at it."

Mary pulled aside the string and unwrapped the cloth. It was her turn to draw sudden breath. Slowly she unfolded a damask shawl, richly embroidered with a floral motif.

"For me ?"

"Who else ? Put it on."

Mary placed the shawl around her shoulders, at the same time fingering its superb quality.

"I—I don't know what to say. It's the most marvellous material I've ever seen. How can I thank you ?"

Robert winked.

"By wearing it when Sir Roger comes here. He'll be here presently to see you—before another ten minutes are up, I'd say, if what I heard is true."

His words had an immediate stupefying effect on her.

"Sir Roger! Coming here ? To see me ?"

"None other. I met him at Ewenny, coming off the London coach. He was mighty agitated about seeing you. Got something important to tell you, he said. He's just going down to Candleston to tidy up, then he'll be here."

Mary's hands shot up to her hair.

"Oh, dear! What does he want? I'm not ready—"

Robert slapped her on the back.

"You look fine. Just wear that shawl. He'll like you in that. Come on, you two. We've work to do."

Swaying slightly he left the room, followed by his two companions. Mary heard them clattering up the stairs with some boxes. She glanced quickly at Gronow, expecting to see a scowling countenance at the news of Sir Roger's visit, but Gronow was fondling her pearls with a look of euphoria on her face. Mary took advantage of the respite to go to her room.

Hardly had she had time to run a comb through her hair when she heard carriage wheels on the forecourt and Robert's stentorian voice.

"Mary! Come down. Your visitor's here."

Gathering her new possession closely about her shoulders she hurried downstairs. The innkeeper was in the hallway, rummaging about in a sack. He beckoned her.

"What've you been doing to Sir Roger? He's all excited and bothered.

"I—I've done nothing."

"Well, he ain't the cool, calm fellow he used to be." He winked. "If you ask me he's going to make you a proposal—right now! Think well about it and if he do don't turn him down. He's in the small room waiting for you."

He struck her on the bottom with such force that she was propelled half way to the dining room. Her mind in a whirl she hesitated by the parlour door, which was open. She could see Sir Roger with his back towards her, facing the window. Hearing her he turned and came towards her with arms outstretched.

"Mary! It's so good to see you again. How are you?"

Instinctively Mary placed her hands in his.

"Well, thank you, sir. I have improved in health since you saw me last."

"I can see that. You look positively radiant. Sit down, please. I have much to tell you."

Mary sat in a chair by the table. Sir Roger closed the door and drew up another chair beside her.

"How long is it since we were together that day at Ogmore? It must be six weeks. I'm sorry I could give you no word about leaving. It was too sudden and unexpected. I had no alternative but to rush off without seeing you."

"That's quite all right," Mary said, still flustered.

"But it's not all right! I left you in the middle of that affair of McGregor. I fully intended instigating an enquiry, as you know, but there was no time. Now I understand nothing's been done about it."

"I believe not. I called at the castle to see you but could get no answer."

"Dammit! I should have warned you. I'm sorry. They haven't found the culprit, I know. Some fellow told me at Ewenny. A great pity. And the body's disappeared, too, I understand."

"Yes."

"Probably it was taken out by the tide. It will never be found now. I'm doubly sorry, Mary, for you were fond of him, weren't you?"

"He was kind to me."

"I wish I could have done more, but there it is! However, I have something of greater import to tell you. I'm pleased to say my fortune has taken a turn for the better. I've just had a successful business trip to London. For once everything seemed to come right—unusual for me. If all goes well I shall have left my impecunious state behind for ever. You knew I was impecunious didn't you, Mary?"

"Well—"

"Of course you did. It was no secret. But now all that's changed. I shall never be really wealthy but I shall have an income large enough to do the things I've always wanted to do— renovate the castle for example."

"Oh! I'm so glad to hear that."

"There should be enough left over to employ labour and improve the land, so that will bring in extra income. My prospects are now good, Mary. I'll show the people around here a

109

thing or two! And that brings me to the main point—why I'm telling you this. I cannot complete my schemes without someone to help me—someone who will share the work that lies ahead." He paused. "Someone who will sustain and fortify me, be part of me. In short, Mary—a wife."

Mary held her breath. Although forewarned she had not expected Sir Roger to be so direct and animated. Suddenly, almost roughly, he seized her hands.

"Will you be my wife, Mary? I cannot promise you much at first for the task will not be easy. But the rewards will come. Candleston will be rejuvenated and you can be its lady. In time you will have servants of your own. I will do all in my power to make you happy. I will—"

"Sir Roger!" cried Mary. "Stop! Please stop! You don't know what you're saying. I can never be your wife. I am a serving girl working in an inn. If your fortune has so improved why can't you find a lady of your own standing? I am sure there would be plenty who would—"

He stopped her with a sardonic hiss.

"Such as the ones who looked down their noses at me in the past? You're better than any of them. In a year or two we can look down our noses at them. I'll be the envy of every titled land owner around here—if you marry me, that is. Will you marry me, Mary?"

Mary lowered her eyes, afraid Sir Roger could read the thoughts coursing through her mind. To be proposed to by a nobleman, even by one of dubious descent, was gratifying: but there were many considerations requiring reflection. First Sir Roger was a great deal older than she—twenty years at least. Then there were Mathias's warnings: they could be put down to plain jealousy, but it was best to be cautious. More important, how could she fulfil the role Sir Roger was so impetuously planning for her? For a moment she had a fleeting vision of herself purchasing new furniture for the castle and directing the renovation of its interior; but equally quickly she brushed it aside. The one vital ingredient was missing: love. At that moment she did not love Sir Roger, and so far he had not mentioned the subject. Gently she withdrew her hands.

"It is a great honour you bestow on me," she whispered. "No woman could have a greater compliment. But you must give me time to think. Your—your proposal is so unexpected—"

"Of course. Forgive me. I was so elated by my financial success that I rushed here without thinking. But please hear me out. Ever since I first saw you—even when you were wet and bedraggled with the rain—I have been thinking about you. You have rarely left my thoughts. I can think of no woman I would rather have by my side."

Suddenly he reached into his waistcoat pocket and produced a small chamois pouch. He opened it to reveal a fine gold ring.

"This will be yours if you consent to marry me. Will you try it on?"

Mary demurred but he took her hand again and placed the ring on her finger. It was too large and slipped down over the knuckle.

"I'll have it altered," he muttered. "Just a little off will do."

Mary studied the ring then, not to offend him, took it off slowly.

"It is beautiful. But please! I must have time—"

"Yes, yes—I understand, and in any case I must return to London almost immediately. I shall be away for a week—two at the most. But when I return will you give me your answer then?"

"Yes."

He seemed satisfied with that.

"Then I will pray that you will accept. If you consent do not fear the future with me, Mary. I will see that you have everything you desire, and after a time we will be accepted by the community. You will not be ostracised—I give you my word on that."

Mary glanced again at the ring then handed it back.

"I shall give your proposal every thought, Sir Roger, but I must be honest with you. It's better for you to know now for I do not want you to think me dishonourable in any way. I have been asked to go to a noson lawen with a friend."

Sir Roger's cleft chin jutted out suddenly.

"A noson lawen? Who with?"

"Daniel Mathias, the ostler."

"At Turberville's barn next month?"

"Yes."

"Is he—I mean, has he asked you to marry him?"

"Oh, dear me no! He's just a friend, but he's been very kind to me. I didn't like to refuse."

Suddenly his expression softened.

"Then you must go. When a person has been kind to you you must respond in like manner. Anyway, having a rival will put me on my mettle."

"He's hardly a rival."

Thoughtfully Sir Roger placed the ring in the pouch and the pouch in his pocket.

"Then I will be optimistic enough to have this altered. Please understand, Mary, that my feelings for you are genuine. I fell in love with you the first moment I saw you. We would be happy together, I am sure."

He was about to add something more but at that moment the door burst open to reveal a swaying Robert.

"Well, you two," he bawled. "Have you come to an arrangement yet? When's the nuptials?"

Sir Roger gave him a dark look then forced a smile.

"Hardly. We've not had time to discuss things fully yet."

The innkeeper put on a knowing, lascivious expression.

"Leave her to me; Mary obeys me in all things, don't you, m'dear? I'll get her to marry you if it's the last thing I do. It'd be nice to have a connection at Candleston. But come now. Your marriage may be important but there's a more pressing matter to attend to—one that won't wait."

He lurched back out through the doorway and waited expectantly. Sir Roger stood up, took Mary's hand and kissed it lightly. In a voice too low for Robert to hear he said:

"For the time being I am beholden to this man, but not for much longer. Now I must go. I will return with speed and await your answer. I pray God you will accept me."

He bowed and was gone, leaving Mary to contemplate the

112

fireplace and the all-important fact that Sir Roger had at last said that he loved her.

CHAPTER 16

MARY KEPT Sir Roger's proposal to herself and was saved from further embarrassment by the innkeeper going to Bridgend for a few days to visit his wife. But it remained constantly on her mind, especially as there was no one she could confide in or turn to for advice. Both Robert and Mathias, for reasons best known to themselves, were biased one way or the other, Gronow was unapproachable and Davies was worried about an outbreak of measles that had laid her son low. The final decision was therefore hers and hers alone, and she was tormented by doubts.

To clarify her mind she decided to go for a walk, for she had always believed that fresh air and physical movement were conducive to deep thought as well as good health. Also, just recently, she had heard a traveller extolling the virtues of Laleston, a pretty village about a mile distant; and so it was to see this place before the onset of winter and to attempt to reach a decision about the proposal that one evening she obtained leave of absence for an hour, little knowing that neither objective would be achieved and that fate was already conspiring to take her future out of her hands, whatever conclusion she came to.

It was the first week of September and as she set off across the forecourt the hem of her dress sent up a continuing flurry of russet-coloured leaves, an indication of the early approach of autumn and a long winter to come. She climbed the steep, tree-lined hill to Groes Gibbet, a place feared and avoided by the villagers because of its connotations with death, and as she walked past the ugly, menacing structure she said a silent prayer for all the poor mortals who had expired there, now buried namelessly beneath grass-covered mounds on the verges. Beyond the gibbet was the cross roads and there she paused, unsure which way to go. She found the sign-post eventually, half hidden in the branches of a tall elm, and was about to proceed in the right direction when she saw a group of men coming towards her. They were about a hundred yards distant, on the Laleston track, marching four abreast with slow, measured tread. Then she saw a coffin in their midst and, behind the coffin, a fine white horse ridden by a middle-aged man resplendent in army officer's uniform. Not wishing to obstruct a funeral procession in the narrow confines of the lane she looked around for a place of retreat and saw a small arbour near the elm. She ran to it, pressed herself against the hedge and waited for the cortège to pass.

After a few moments it struck her as strange that, although the men must now be very close, she could not hear a sound: there was no tramping of feet, no hymn singing, not even a cough or a clearing of a throat. Thinking that the procession had come to a halt, or turned off at the cross roads, she peeped through the foliage and was startled to see the front file of men almost on top of her, still marching steadily onwards. For all the noise they were making they might well have been walking in deep snow, and something about their demeanour struck her as strange. She shrank back again into the hedgerow.

Then the men were opposite the arbour, marching past with their slow, almost automatic gait, but still not making the slightest sound. She glanced at their feet to see if they were muffled in any way, but they were not. They merely glided past, their pallid faces gaunt and cadaverous, intent upon getting to their destination. No one looked at her, although now she was clearly visible to the nearest file; and for a moment she thought the figures appeared vague and indeterminate, as though she was having an hallucination. But the coffin was real enough, made of light oak, and there was no mistaking horse and rider. She could see the man's face clearly now, haughty and aristocratic, with white streaks in his hair, and she could even make out his epaulettes gleaming in the sun. Strangest of all was the fact that the horse, like the men, went past quite soundlessly, without even the creaking of a harness or the jingle of a bit. It was past Mary's comprehension and she began to wonder if her hearing had become defective. Wax in the ears, she knew, would cause that, but she could still hear the birds, particularly a vociferous

114

black bird in the hedge just behind her. Suddenly she felt chilled, as though the temperature of the air had dropped sharply.

She waited until the horse had passed, then stepped out into the roadway and stared after the strange procession. She could still see the swaying hind-quarters of the horse and also the coffin, bobbing up and down on the shoulders of the bearers. There was no doubt in her mind that what she had seen was a real funeral, but why it had been so eerie and silent was beyond her comprehension. Then another strange thought struck her. The cortège had come from Laleston, where she knew there was a cemetery, yet it was heading for Merthyr Mawr, which had its own burial ground; was it possible, she wondered, that one of the villagers had died without her knowing and that the coffin had been empty? It was better to forsake Laleston for a while and find out: and in any case she felt a strange and irresistible compulsion to follow the cortège. She gathered up her skirt and went after it, keeping a safe distance for the weirdness of the occasion still worried her.

Down the hill the funeral went, as soundlessly as before, and eventually arrived at the part of the road that curved past the New Inn. For a moment Mary lost sight of it so hurried to catch up, and then received her biggest surprise. Instead of going on over the bridge towards Merthyr Mawr as she expected, the funeral had come to a halt in the inn's forecourt, facing the front door. As she watched, the bearers placed the coffin on the ground and two men changed places; then they shouldered their burden again and the entire procession filed into the inn, leaving only horse and rider outside, with the animal pawing at the gravel. Greatly concerned now Mary ran to the back of the building and flung open the kitchen door. She expected to find the place in turmoil, with a flustered Davies busy over her pots preparing a funeral supper; but to her surprise both Davies and Gronow were sitting at the table, the accounts books open in front of them. They looked up, startled by her sudden appearance.

"The funeral!" cried Mary. "Who's died here?"

Gronow's eyes narrowed but Davies's face showed consternation.

"What funeral?" asked Gronow sharply. "What are you talking about, girl?"

"The funeral," repeated Mary. "It's here now. I saw the men coming in through the front door. With a coffin."

"There's no funeral here. We're not expecting any. Do you think I'd have allowed you to go off if we were expecting a funeral?"

"There'd be no funeral this time of evening," added Davies, her voice sepulchral. "No one buries after five o'clock. And no one's died here."

"Then what are they doing here?" gasped Mary. "I followed them all the way from the top of the hill. They stopped outside the front door and brought the coffin in. I saw them! They're in the hall now."

Without a word Gronow got up and went to the inner door. She opened it and listened.

"There's no one there. You must be mistaken."

"I'm not mistaken." Mary ran past her into the hall. It was completely empty. "They must be in one of the other rooms."

Followed by Gronow and Davies she went first to the packmen's room and then to the dining room. In each there was only a solitary man drinking ale. There was no sign of a funeral, or even a coffin.

"Only two people are staying here," said Gronow. "A pedlar and a farmer from Swansea. You saw them for yourself."

"But the horse is still outside," said Mary, almost beside herself with vexation. "Open the front door and ask the rider. He's an officer. He'll tell you I'm speaking the truth."

With an arch glance at the cook Gronow went into the passage and pulled back the heavy door. The forecourt was completely deserted. There was no sign of horse, rider, mourners or coffin.

"But they were there," cried Mary. "Don't look at me like that. They must have gone out again."

"Then where are they now?" Gronow's voice was harsh but there was a look of fear in her dark face.

"Come back to the kitchen, Mary." said Davies soothingly, "and tell us all about it there."

They trooped back to the kitchen and sat down at the table.

"Now, then," said the cook. "What exactly did you see.?"

Mary told them. She described how the funeral had passed her near the cross roads and how she had followed it back to the inn. She made a special point of remarking about its strange silence. When she had finished Gronow and Davies exchanged glances.

"Did you see the canwyll corff?" asked Davies.

"The canwyll corff? What's that?"

"A candle. Did you see a candle above the coffin or flying through the air?"

"Of course not. What would a candle be doing at a funeral?"

"That's a help, then," said Davies with something akin to relief. "When Uriah Gruffydd saw a candle his wife died within the week. It had a blue light. Are you sure you didn't see one?"

"Of course I'm sure."

"But you did see a funeral," probed Gronow. "You're sure of that?"

"Yes. As God is my witness."

The two older women began conferring.

"She's telling the truth," muttered Gronow.

"Yes—but without the candle. It's not so bad, then, perhaps."

"Don't be too sure. Eifion Jones didn't see a candle."

"I was told he did. When was it? Six years last Easter?"

"But she's sure about the horse. Eifion Jones saw a horse, too—a roan."

"It don't always happen. Eluned Hopkins saw a carriage before her baby died, not a horse."

"What I want to know is why she's started seeing things. Why her of all people?"

"Anybody can see them. Anybody chosen, that is."

"Please!" ejaculated Mary. "What are you talking about? Have I seen something dreadful—something I had no right to see?"

The other two looked uncomfortable. After a pause Davies said:

"It do look like it, Mary. What you saw were phantoms."

"Phantoms! D'you mean ghosts? But I'm not like that. I mean, I don't see ghosts. I never have. I'm not superstitious."

"Eluned Hopkins wasn't superstitious either, but she saw them."

"Then what does it mean? Am I going mad?"

"Oh, no!" Davies tried to sound reassuring. "You're not going mad, Mary. It don't mean that at all. But it do mean that you've seen into the future. What you saw was somebody's funeral—somebody who's not dead yet."

"And it had to come here," snapped Gronow. "Why did she have to see it?"

"I don't understand," said Mary. "Do you mean to tell me that because I've seen this—this thing somebody around here is going to die?"

"That's it," said Davies placidly, "otherwise you wouldn't have seen it. Some people do see a candle as well burning with different colours. Red for a man, blue for a woman and yellow for a child. But if you didn't there's no way of telling who it'll be. Did you know the man on the horse?"

"No. He was aged about forty, with greying hair. Dressed in an officer's uniform. How could I recognise him if he was a phantom—if what you say is true?"

"Give it a fortnight," said Gronow darkly. 'We'll know in a fortnight."

Suddenly Mary felt angry.

"It's all nonsense! Old wives' tales. I've never heard anything so ridiculous."

"It's not ridiculous," replied Davies with conviction. "You don't hear about many but when you do it's a sure sign. Mark my words! The real funeral will travel on exactly the same path as you trod today."

Suddenly Gronow jumped to her feet. Malevolently she stared down at Mary.

"And this girl had to see one—coming here. I knew there was something odd about her the first time I clapped eyes on her."

118

She gave Mary a final, glowering stare then stalked from the room.

"Oh, dear!" said Mary. "She does hate me. I've never been able to do anything right for her."

Davies patted her hand.

"Pay no attention. She's worried, see, because the funeral came here. That do mean somebody at the inn might die. She's afeared of death."

"So am I."

Davies gave her hand another pat.

"Of all people you do have the least to fear. Nothing ever happens to the one who saw it. Whoever it'll be it won't be you."

"But why did I see it? Gronow's right. Why did it have to be me? Because see it I did—there's no doubt of that."

"Because you were chosen, Mary, that's why. It don't happen to many. Many years ago our Saint David gave the power to some, so's they could warn that death was coming. Then people could atone for their sins. Mark my words! When news gets around of what you've seen there'll be much praying for forgiveness in the villages around here. But you're safe. No evil will come to you. You've been favoured."

Mary shook her head.

"Oh, dear! I liked it when I came here first but recently I've been having a terrible fear that something dreadful was going to happen. I've had it for weeks, ever since I saw a robin, and now this—"

Davies bustled over to the hearth. She took the big iron kettle off its hook and slammed it down on the fire.

"Tomorrow I'll get you some ivy to wear in your bodice. That'll keep you safe. In the meantime a cup of tea'll do us both good."

Mary watched the cook preparing the pot, then she said:

"Aren't you afraid? I mean, the funeral came here, and you work here."

Davies put the tea pot on the hearth to warm. When she straightened up she was smiling.

"Bless you, no child. I don't live here, see. Nothing will happen to me, but them—" she pointed upwards, "them up-stairs had better watch out. The devil don't always look after his own. We'll know in a fortnight."

CHAPTER 17

MARY WOKE BEFORE midnight to hear the trees rustling in the wind. She had heard the same sound before only now the rustling was more pronounced and the inn sign was creaking as well, a sure indication that stormy weather was approaching. But it was not merely the trees that had awakened her: it was the memory of what she had seen at Groes Gibbet. It had continually intruded upon her sleep, giving her barely ten minutes rest in the short time she had been in bed; and now that she was awake Davies's assertion that she had been favoured with supernatural powers was calculated to keep her mind active for a further few hours. Interwoven with these reflections were thoughts of a more physical connotation, such as Sir Roger's proposal of marriage and Mathias's assault on his character, all enough to tax the mind of a Solomon leave alone that of a simple country girl. Knowing that sleep was impossible she got up, went to the window and watched the violent swaying of the tree tops.

Then it occurred to her that she was thirsty. Having no appetite after her encounter with the funeral she had not eaten or drunk since Davies's cup of tea, and now her throat demanded the solace of water. She lit the candle and picked up the water jug. It was empty and so was her cup. Petulantly she flung herself back on the bed, annoyed at her forgetfulness and determined to will herself to sleep. But the thought of no water being available made her even more thirsty and soon she realised that she must have a drink or spend the night in torment. She flung off the bedclothes, put on her old shawl and, armed with the candle, made her way downstairs.

Except for the usual creaking and groaning of the woodwork

the inn was quiet, not even a snore emanating from the pack-men's room or from the better room where the Swansea farmer was sleeping; but to make sure she disturbed nobody Mary trod each stair carefully. A draught on the landing nearly blew out her candle causing her to stub a toe on the big, long chest that took up one wall, but eventually she reached the kitchen. She made straight for the pitcher and gratefully poured a cupful of cool well water down her throat. Feeling better she saw the embers of Davies's fire and, knowing that sleep was as far away as ever, she decided to sit by it for a while. She drew up a chair, placed her bare toes on the warm stones of the hearth and began another attempt to work out her problems.

She had been sitting there for only a few minutes when she heard a sound, as though of a door closing upstairs. She listened intently but again all was silence. Then, with a suddenness that stopped her heart in mid-beat, a scream rent the air, the same, piercing scream she had heard in the nightmare about McGregor. But this time it terminated abruptly as though the victim's mouth had been quickly gagged. Petrified, she remained in her chair, certain that Davies's prognostication had already come true. A few moments later she heard other sounds: a scraping that seemed to emanate from the landing, which was above the kitchen, and then the unmistakable creak of a stair. She folded her hands in her lap, composed her trembling limbs and stared at the fire, determined to pretend she had heard nothing if challenged. But mercifully the kitchen door remained closed: instead she heard the bolts of the front door being stealthily withdrawn and a faint draught brightened the fire. Except for the scream the sequence of sounds had been exactly the same as on the night McGregor had disappeared, and she had a premonition of what would happen next. Fearfully she stared at the window.

Outside the wind was gusting more strongly than ever. From her chair she could just see the tops of the bushes on the perimeter of the inn waving madly and making the whorls of glass shimmer as though alive. She waited another few minutes then, summoning her last reserves of courage, she went to the window and

121

peered out into the darkness. The clouds were racing past a large harvest moon, giving her only brief opportunities to see things clearly, and for a while nothing of importance occurred. Then, momentarily, one of the bushes parted, and she saw the figure of Mathias. He was staring at the upper windows of the inn and in his hand was a spade, an ordinary long-handled spade such as farm labourers used. A moment later he was gone, melting into the shadows like a wraith. Mary returned to the chair and sat down again.

Seeing the ostler had come as no surprise. She seemed to be living in a dream world in which events could be foretold; and the fact that Mathias had been carrying a spade merely confirmed the suspicions she had tried so hard in the past to discount. Now the proof was apparent: what explanation could there be for a man with a spade at the dead of night other than that he was the perpetrator of a crime, or at least an accomplice to it, possibly removing the evidence of a terrible deed? And that a terrible deed had been committed she had no doubt. No one screamed like that without a cause, even in a nightmare. She could hear its piercing cadences now, with that sudden, strangulated, cut-off ending.

For a moment sorrow mingled with her fear. Her fondness for Mathias had been gradually increasing of late: he had helped her when help was most needed and she owed him a debt of gratitude. Against her better judgment she had hoped that he was honest and above-board: but now she could see that his kindness had merely been a cloak to allay her suspicions. Now there was no one in the world she could turn to. Sir Roger had not returned, and even if he had, she could hardly rush to Candleston with an hysterical and unproved account of what she had heard and seen. Neither was there any hope from the innkeeper. Generous though he had been, bringing her a present all the way from France, she thought of him now as nothing more than a Cap Coch, the smuggler; a magnanimous one no doubt but a smuggler nevertheless, and it was unlikely that he was unaware of what was going on in his own establishment. And as for Mathias's suggestion that she should go and see Colonel Nicholl, that was

122

out of the question. Anything emanating from Mathias was suspect from now on. The more she thought the surer she became that there was only one defence against the evil surrounding her: prayer. With a fervency she had never before displayed she prayed for strength and guidance for herself and Davies, but when she had finished she remained sitting, resolved not to venture out of the kitchen until day break.

When at last the first faint rays illuminated the room she stood up and threw some logs on the fire. The wind had now risen to such a pitch that the bushes outside were dancing in a frenzy and she thought she could even feel the walls of the inn shudder. But she could see the furniture and pots and pans clearly, which was a comfort, so she went out into the hall and glanced at the main door, noticing that it was again properly barred and bolted. At that moment the grandfather clock struck six, her normal rising time for September. Pulling her shawl more tightly about her shoulders she ran upstairs, and on the landing ran straight into Gronow.

"What are you doing here?" Gronow's voice was hard and sibilant, her one good eye boring into Mary like a gimlet. "Why are you still in your night dress?"

"I—I went down for some water," stammered Mary. "I'd forgotten to fill my jug. I was thirsty." Then she noticed that Gronow was carrying the heavy mop used for waxing the floors.

Gronow saw the direction of Mary's gaze.

"I rose early," she said in a low voice. "I couldn't sleep because of the wind, so I thought I'd do a few jobs. You didn't do this floor properly yesterday. You're slipping, my girl."

Mary, who knew very well that she had polished the landing to perfection, stared at the floorboards.

"It's all right now," added Gronow hastily. "I've done it. You go and get dressed. Come down to the kitchen as soon as possible. I want this inn cleaned from top to bottom today."

"What about the beds? Shall I do those first?"

"You can do the pedlar's. I've already done the farmer's. He left an hour ago for Swansea. Come down as soon as you can."

Gronow pushed past her, still carrying the mop. Mary waited

until she was out of sight then darted into the room previously occupied by the farmer. As she expected the bed had been done and the floor swept. She went next to the pedlar's room. He was still asleep and snoring with a resonance that matched the storm. She closed the door quietly, went to her own room and sat down on the bed.

Another fact was now obvious: Gronow was an accomplice as well. The landing floor had been spotless, so the only explanation was that the woman had been obliterating some sort of evidence, probably scuff marks. Mary remembered the previous occasion when she had seen such marks, and Gronow's glib explanation for them. Saying that the farmer had left was also a lie. No one had come down the stairs at five o'clock, unless he had been carried, and vaguely Mary remembered the Swansea man: a short, red-faced individual, obviously affluent from his clothes. How long would it be, she wondered, before his body, too, was found on the beach?

Suddenly another problem loomed. In a short while she would meet Mathias. Having seen him in the bushes how could she act as though nothing had occurred? Going to the noson lawen with him was out of the question now. Feigning sickness was probably the best way out, but that was only a partial solution for she had to work with him every day and sooner or later he would guess she knew his secret. The outcome of that did not bear contemplation, for a man involved in murder would not hesitate to commit another to silence a possible informer. Numbly Mary completed her toilet and went downstairs, aware that her nerves were now so bad that she was incapable of coherent thought, a state made worse by finding Gronow in the hall, this time holding a heavy cane brush. She thrust it into Mary's hand.

"Start in the cellar and work your way up. Every room must be done. I shall see that you do it thoroughly this time."

Mary took the brush and went down into the cellar, wrinkling her nose at the pungent smell of ale and wine, always more pronounced in early morning. Without enthusiasm she brushed at the flags, gathering the dirt into a small, tidy pile. She was about to shovel the dirt into a bucket when the cellar door opened and Mathias clattered down the steps.

"Hullo, Mary," he called out cheerfully. "How are you this morning?"

"Not too bad, thank you."

"Looking forward to tomorrow? I hear they're having Noah Watkins the fiddler from Corntown to play, so it should be a good evening."

Mary pretended to dust the table and the heavy oak chair.

"Oh, good!"

"I've borrowed a horse to take us," Mathias went on. "A fine one—a chestnut—from a friend. All of seventeen hands and goes like the wind. You'll enjoy riding pillion on Twm."

"I'm sure I will."

"I tried to get the trap, but Robert is using it—or so he says. Anyway, Twm'll be better than walking. He's a beauty, believe me. You'll feel somebody arriving at the noson lawen on Twm."

He levered the keg from a pile of barrels and Mary watched the powerful sinews working on his forearms. There was enough strength in those limbs to snuff out a life in seconds. She picked up her bucket and made for the steps.

"I must go. Gronow wants me to clean all the rooms today."

Mathias looked up in surprise.

"Are you all right, Mary? You don't look too well this morning."

"I've got a cold, that's all. I hope it doesn't get worse."

She ran up the steps before Mathias could say anything more and closed the cellar door behind her. At least she had dropped the first hint that she could not go to the noson lawen. The next step was to say her cold was worse. She put the bucket down and prepared to start on the hall, first getting down on her knees to scrape away some candle grease.

Then, unexpectedly, like a bolt out of the sky, the solution to all her problems came to her. Of course there was someone she could turn to in her distress—someone who would not only be able to advise her about events at the inn but who would give her spiritual guidance as well, especially in the affair of the funeral.

125

He might even be able to help in the problem of her possible marriage to Sir Roger. She had been a fool not to have thought of him before.

She straightened up, the load already slipping from her shoulders. At the first opportunity she would go to Merthyr Mawr and pour out her troubles to Parson Newman.

CHAPTER 18

THE OPPORTUNITY ARRIVED in mid-afternoon when Gronow, driven by Mathias in the trap, went to Bridgend to order a fresh supply of victuals. Mary put away her cleaning implements, safe in the knowledge that however hard she laboured Gronow would find fault with her, ran into the kitchen to tell Davies she would be away a short while, and changed hurriedly into her best day-dress.

The walk to Merthyr Mawr was not as pleasant as on previous occasions. The wind, roaring in the tree tops, sent flurries of dust into her eyes, already tired after a sleepless night; but she struggled on, determined to accomplish her mission. With only a vague idea where the parson lived she intended asking a villager for directions, but was saved from that task by seeing Newman himself riding towards her on a small piebald mare. As soon as he saw her he reined in the horse and doffed his hat.

"Why, Mary Tudor! Of all people! I was just on my way to visit you."

"Were you, sir ? And I was coming to see you."

"Ah! Good! Then you have saved me a journey. There is a matter of some import I wish to talk to you about."

He dismounted clumsily, puffing with the exertion.

"Come to the vestry. We will have more privacy there. I cannot tell you how pleased I am to see you."

He led the horse, with Mary by his side, through the short village street. At the church he tethered the animal to the lych gate and opened it for her.

126

"Come. I've been hearing some interesting things about you and I wish to hear them first hand."

They walked up the path into the musty-smelling church. Newman opened a narrow door and ushered Mary into a small, sparsely-furnished room. He pointed to one of two rickety chairs standing by a table strewn with tattered tracts.

"Sit down, Mary. Now then, what's all this I've been hearing about you seeing phantom funerals?"

Taken aback by his brusque, direct manner, Mary groped for an answer.

"I—I don't know whether they were phantoms, father. I have been told so, but I'm not sure."

Newman lowered his ample frame into the other chair.

"The whole village is humming with gossip, but I try not to listen to rumour mongers. I would rather hear the story from your own lips. Kindly describe everything you saw in the fullest detail. Do not omit anything, however trivial it may seem to you."

Mary collected her thoughts then told her story as well as memory would allow her. Newman listened intently, never taking his bright blue eyes off her for a moment. When she had finished he began drumming his fingers on the table. He drummed for so long Mary began to think he had forgotten her existence. Suddenly he stopped and began plying her with questions.

"Did the men seem unreal to you? You know—ethereal, ghost-like?"

"Yes."

"But you saw the coffin plainly—and the horse and rider."

"Yes."

"You didn't recognise the officer, though?"

"No."

"And the procession stopped outside the inn. Did all the men go in?"

"Yes. All except the officer and the horse."

"But there was no one inside when you went in?"

"No."

"And you didn't see a candle?"

"No. Davies, our cook, asked me about that."

Newman restarted his drumming.

"Tell me, father," said Mary. "Is there any truth in it? I mean, is it possible to see phantoms? Can't there be some explanation—a trick of the light or something like that?"

"I don't know, Mary. All I can say is that we cannot discount such things. There have been too many authenticated and recorded instances around here to dismiss them lightly, otherwise I would say they were merely aberrations of country folks' minds. Had you not heard of them before coming here?"

"No."

"I don't suppose you would, living up in the hills where you did. So you see, I cannot put this—er—phenomenon down to mere superstition in your case. You are a sensible, level-headed girl, not an old crone half out of your mind. And you've no cause to lie, I'm sure."

"I'm not lying, father. I really did see a funeral."

"I believe you. The last instance of one around here was about six years ago."

"So Davies told me. It was followed by a death she said."

"Yes, it was. All these things are supposed to be followed by death in one form or another. I cannot explain it. I believe there are strange forces at work in the world about which we know nothing. The actual sightings may be figments of imagination but why they occur I cannot say. As a man of the cloth I should berate those who believe in them—but that probably means every member of my congregations. But do not let it distress you. I am told that no harm ever comes to the beholder."

"So I have heard, but I would like you to bless me, nevertheless."

"Of course, my child. We will go to the altar before you leave and I will pray for you. But now that I am in possession of the facts do not let us dwell too long on ghostly matters. There is something of a more immediate and pressing nature I would like to talk about. It has come to my ears that Sir Roger de Cantelupes has proposed marriage to you. Is that true?"

"Yes. It is true."

"You don't seem too happy about it. Is there anything worrying you?"

Mary lowered her eyes. The subject of Sir Roger had been one she wanted to discuss but she was not sure how to start.

"I am honoured by the proposal," she managed, "but there are matters beyond my understanding. I—I have heard things about which—"

Newman held up a peremptory hand.

"Don't tell me! Let me guess. Is it because you've heard that Sir Roger's no right to either land or title? To his name even?"

"Well, yes. Partly that, anyway."

"Well, Mary! I can vouchsafe that what you've heard is correct. If he is a Cantelupe it's along a very devious and indeterminate route, but do not hold that against him. He is a gentleman, is he not?"

"Yes. He is indeed a gentleman, and has been so to me."

"Well, then, what perturbs you? No one round here's going to dispute his right to the castle. If he had not come along—dubious though his lineage may be—the place would have fallen down years ago. Only the county families will disapprove, but that won't deter him. He's come into a little money, too, I believe, and I have a feeling he'll revitalise the estate, enormous task though that is. If he wishes to marry you, Mary, my advice is to accept him. He's a better prospect than marrying a farm labourer, don't you think?"

"That's what Mr. Robert says."

"And yet you still do not seem happy about it. Is anything else the matter? Have you sinned?"

Mary seized her opportunity with alacrity.

"No, father, I have not sinned, but there are other things that worry me greatly, although they have nothing to do with Sir Roger. It's what goes on at the inn that troubles me. That's mainly why I came to see you."

Newman sat back, folded his plump hands on his cassock and twirled one thumb around the other.

"And what is troubling you at the inn, pray?"

"Noises, father. Strange noises, especially at night."

Newman stared at her then, to her surprise, he began laughing. At first he laughed quietly then with mounting crescendo until his hands were bouncing up and down on his ample stomach. Eventually he stopped and wiped his eyes with a handkerchief.

"Oh, Mary, forgive me, but surely you've been there long enough to know what sort of place it is. Your master could never be the affluent person he is on the proceeds of the inn alone. His principal occupation is smuggling. Don't tell me that you, an intelligent person, have not realised that."

"I have realised it but—"

"Well, then, don't you see? If Robert is a smuggler—a very successful one too I'm told—then there's much going on there, especially at night, so no wonder you hear noises. Please don't think I condone it—I do not—but much smuggling goes on these days. You'd be surprised who's involved in it altogether. I could name one or two titled persons if I'd a mind to. But the point is this—you're bound to hear strange noises. You've come to no harm, though, have you?"

"No, but last night I heard a scream as though someone was being murdered."

"Murdered? Oh, come! I grant you Robert's not the most genteel of men and he has some very rough companions, but none of them would stoop to murder, I'm sure of that. You're mistaken, Mary."

"Then how do you account for Mr. McGregor? He was at the inn, too, and I was there when his body was found on the beach. He'd been hit on the head."

Newman's expression changed.

"McGregor? What's all this about McGregor?"

"I believe he was murdered, too. You see, he'd promised me a gift—a book mark—which I was to receive in the morning and—"

Again Newman held up a hand.

"Wait, Mary, wait! You are saying and implying things about which I know nothing and I can see you are agitated. Please compose yourself and tell me everything. As with the funeral, start at the beginning and leave out nothing. Then perhaps I will be in a position to dispel your fears. Now speak slowly and I promise you I will listen carefully."

Mary took a deep breath and began her account. She described the noises that had frightened her the night McGregor had disappeared, the finding of the book mark and her suspicions about the marks on the floor. She mentioned Sir Roger's theory about the wound in the packman's head and her disappointment that no enquiry had followed. Then she narrated her experiences of the previous night, but when she had finished she realised with surprise that she had made no mention of Mathias. It was as though her subconscious mind was trying to protect him; but it was an omission Newman was quick to seize upon.

"Noises and marks, Mary! Is that all you have as a basis for your fears? Did you not see anything more substantial—someone coming down the stairs immediately after you heard the cry, for example?"

"I was afraid to look."

"Then let us consider what you have said. Noises can be made by anything—particularly in a house at the dead of night. Even a scream can be the result of an accident—a finger caught in a door, a hand gashed by a broken bottle. And as for McGregor, was he not fond of his drink? He could have fallen into the river in spite of what you say. And scuff marks! The inn must be full of those. Until you can give me facts of a more material nature, Mary, I cannot reconcile your story with anything more unlawful than smuggling. Are you sure you didn't see anybody? What about those two—Ebenezer and Benjamin? Did you see them?"

"No. Oh, dear! I don't know what I saw. Probably shadows."

"Mary!" Newman's voice was stern. "I believe you are withholding something. If you are it is wrong of you. What's the point of telling me all this if you're not entirely truthful? Please remember—what you say has the secrecy of the confessional. I shall do nothing except what is in your own interest. Now, then! Is there anything further you wish to tell me?"

Mary remained silent, still puzzled by the inner prompting of her mind. Seeing her confusion Newman pressed further.

"I am good at divining people's thoughts, Mary. Are you shielding anybody? If so I must know, otherwise I cannot help you."

131

"I did see somebody, but he has been good to me. I cannot believe he is a criminal, or if he is he has been driven to it— made to do something against his nature. Oh, father, I am so afraid—"

"Who was that person? Was it Mathias?"

Mary stared at him with wide open eyes.

"How did you know?"

"It's my business to know what goes on in the parish. Let that be a sufficient reason for now. Tell me how Mathias comes into these—er—activities that have worried you."

Forced into it at last Mary described the two occasions she had seen Mathias, ending with the final episode when he had been carrying a spade. Newman nodded, sagely.

"You should have told me this before. It explains a lot. When last I spoke to the innkeeper he voiced some doubts about Mathias. Have you tackled him about it—Mathias, I mean?"

"No. That's why I've come to you."

"Very wise of you. Now, Mary, I'll tell you what you must do. Return to the inn and act as though nothing has happened. Say and do nothing that will arouse suspicion, especially to Mathias. In the meantime I will make enquiries—discreet, of course, not to harm you—and we will try to get to the bottom of this affair."

"But what about tomorrow? I'm supposed to go to the noson lawen with him."

"Then you must go. Not to do so will make him suspicious and I do not want that until I have looked into the matter. You must be courageous, Mary, but always remember that if anything transpires to threaten you you may come to me. I will be your refuge. You will always find me here or at the vicarage."

"Thank you, father."

"And now let us go and pray."

He led the way to the church. They knelt before the altar and Newman intoned in Latin and in English. He blessed her and after the final genuflexion he took her arm and accompanied her to the porch.

"Let us part on an optimistic note. I believe most of your fears

132

to be groundless, but neither will we tempt fate. Give no indication of what you know and try and appear happy at the noson lawen. In a day or two I will be in a position to put an end to this business, if business it is, and all will be well."

He patted her shoulder and Mary went to the gate feeling relieved that her burden was no longer hers alone and that she had received God's blessing. But as she walked along the lane doubts again began to assail her and when she reached the inn she could see in her mind's eye the white horse pawing at the ground, its rider staring intently at the door. It was as though the place radiated unseen, malignant waves, destroying her new-found sense of calm; and as she pushed open the kitchen door she felt that an evil greater than any yet experienced was lying in wait for her.

CHAPTER 19

MARY STOOD ON the mounting block waiting for Mathias to back the stallion towards her.

"Now!" he shouted.

Mary jumped, slewing sideways as she did so, to land squarely on the horse's rump. Quickly she shot one arm around Mathias's waist and with the other smoothed down the gown Sir Roger had given her. She felt to see if the extra ribbon around her bonnet was securely tied beneath her chin and wriggled into a more comfortable position. The ground seemed a long way away.

"Are you comfortable?" Mathias called.

"Yes, but don't go too quickly. I've never been on such a tall horse."

Mathias laughed and the horse bucked sideways, obviously objecting to the double burden.

"He'll get used to it in a minute. Hang on tight, though. He's raring to go."

They clattered over the bridge and headed for the Ewenny road; and there Mary was glad that her bonnet was double tied for the wind was gusting more strongly than ever. Fortunately they were sheltered from the worst of the blast by a long line of trees, which was just as well for the stallion was unpredictable, now trotting, now cantering and occasionally trying to break into a gallop. Mathias, however, was enjoying himself immensely.

"Isn't he a beauty? If I gave him his head we'd be in Cowbridge in ten minutes."

"It's all right for you," answered Mary. "You've got a saddle. I'm sliding off."

"Then grip tighter. I don't mind."

Mary strengthened her hold on Mathias's waist, feeling the strong muscles flexing under his jacket to the varying gaits of the horse, and marvelled that she felt so composed going to an evening's entertainment with a man she suspected of being a murderer. She could only put it down to the fact that they were attending a public function, with little chance of being alone, a feeling strengthened when they neared Ewenny bridge and met other couples riding tandem and several families travelling in carts. Mathias hailed a few of them and soon they were at the barn, a huge, rambling structure empty of its winter horde of hay and swept until the stone floor was shining. Mathias guided the horse through the crowds until they were near the big, half-open doors.

"You go in. I'll tether the horse."

He twisted in the saddle, placed an arm around Mary's waist, and with the strength with which she was now familiar hoisted her to the ground. Mary went into the barn, which was already crowded with farm workers and their wives, all dressed in their Sunday best, and untied her bonnet ribbon. The villagers had furnished the place with their kitchen tables and chairs, so there was plenty of seating, and along one wall was a long trestle and a battery of barrels. Mathias was soon back.

"Don't let's sit by the door—it'll be draughty. Over there!"

He led her to a table occupied by a jolly-faced farmer, his wife and two children and, after introducing themselves, they sat down.

"What'll you have to drink?" asked Mathias. "I'd better get it now before too many people arrive."

134

"I don't know."

"Try the cider. Ewenny apples. It's good."

"Very well."

Mathias pushed his way through several ranks of younger, sheepish-looking men all engaged in boosting their courage with ale and eyeing possible partners on the other side of the barn. In five minutes he was back with a glass of cider and a foaming tankard of cwrw da.

"Iechyd da, Mary."

"Iechyd da."

Soon the place was crowded and the impromptu singing started, mostly hymns in Welsh, which surprised Mary for her work at the inn had shown her how anglicised the Vale had become, and most of the customers spoke English. Afterwards a few of the men sang ballads with varying success, but the evening did not fully get under way until Noah Watkins, the fiddler appeared. He was greeted with a round of applause and, after a copious draught from a large earthenware pot, struck up a jig.

"Would you like to try it?" asked Mathias hesitantly.

"I'm not very good."

"Neither am I, but I'll do my best."

"Go on, merch fach," said the farmer grinning. "We'll keep your places."

Still Mary demurred but Mathias was already on his feet. They went to the floor and joined the throng, now so thick that there was little chance of finesse; but to Mary's surprise she began to enjoy herself. Mathias danced lightly, if erratically, and was so full of good humour that Mary forgot temporarily the true nature of her partner. The jig was followed by a reel and then a quadrille, at the end of which they were almost glad that Noah Watkins was in need of further alcoholic refortification. They collapsed back on their chairs to the applause of the farmer and his family.

"You do look a good couple," he beamed. "You do both dance well."

"Thank you," said Mary and was grateful for the cider, for the movement of the dancers in the draughty barn had raised the dust. Then, as she was raising the glass to her lips she saw Sir

135

Roger de Cantelupes standing by the door. He was dressed in a plum-coloured hunting jacket and white satin trousers and was with two companions equally well-dressed. His eyes were roving around the barn and when eventually they alighted on her they lit up. Mathias saw him at the same time but said nothing, although he glanced at Mary.

At that moment the director of ceremonies, whom Mary recognised as a smallholder from Southerndown, announced a new type of dance called the Corntown hop, which was greeted by a ripple of merriment and a general movement towards the dancing area. Mary saw Sir Roger detach himself from his companions and come towards her. She waited in trepidation, unsure whether or not she should dance with him if he asked. Mathias also waited, eyeing the approaching figure with dislike.

"Good evening, Mary." Sir Roger held out his hand and nodded perfunctorily to Mathias. "May I have the pleasure of this dance?"

Mary looked at Mathias who gave a surly nod. Sir Roger gently drew her away from the table and they took their place with the other couples.

"I must speak to you," he said, "but later, not in this din."

The Corntown dance was an energetic affair, consisting of many complicated hops and gyrations, so there was little chance of conversation. Sir Roger was slightly taller than Mathias and a more accomplished dancer. Mary did her best to follow him but they were frequently buffeted together, which seemed to please Sir Roger for he smiled and held her close. For a reason she was unsure of, Mary glanced several times in Mathias's direction, but he had disappeared from his chair and later she caught a glimpse of him renewing the contents of his tankard at a barrel.

Then, just as they had completed a half circle of the floor and were opposite the doors, the music faltered. Mary looked up to see Noah Watkins still fiddling but leaning sideways to listen to a man who was talking animatedly. His music became more ragged and disjointed, causing some of the dancers to slow down or give up altogether. One wag called out:

136

"What's the matter, Noah bach? Is the cwrw da too strong for you?"

In answer the fiddler stopped altogether, and now there were several men around him, all engaged in earnest conversation. Soon a hubbub of general talking developed, with the dancers waiting expectantly for Watkins to recommence. Sir Roger was staring over the heads of the crowd.

"Something's the matter. Come, let's go and see what it is."

He shepherded Mary through the waiting throng until they were near the dais on which the fiddler was standing. Sir Roger grasped a man by the elbow.

"What's happened? Why has the music stopped?"

"I don't rightly know," the man replied. "They're talking something about a wreck."

Impatiently Sir Roger pushed up to the dais itself.

"Watkins! Why have you stopped fiddling?"

Watkins grinned apologetically.

"Sorry, Sir Roger. I'll begin again in a minute. They say there's a big ship in distress off Sker. The men are debating whether to go or not. They won't, though. It's too far and the Newton and Kenfig people will be there by now. There won't be much pickings, anyway. It's a troopship."

"A troopship!" The words hit Mary like a bludgeon. "Did you say a troopship?"

"That's what I heard," replied Watkins, surprised at the vehemency of her question. "Dick, you said it was a troopship, didn't you?"

"That's right," said Dick. "Out from Bristol. Seven hundred soldiers aboard they say, making for Ireland. Gone ashore on the Scarweathers."

Suddenly the barn and the still-waiting people receded from Mary's view. She saw only her brother, smart in his infantry-man's uniform, and heard Sir Roger's voice.

"Hold her, I say. Help me hold her, somebody."

She was conscious of strong arms about her and the barn came slowly back into focus.

137

"What's the matter, Mary?" asked Sir Roger. "Are you unwell?"

"My brother! Jack! He's on the ship."

"Oh, God! Are you sure?"

"He was sailing from Bristol this week with his regiment, embarking for Ireland."

Sir Roger roughly levered a man out of a chair.

"Let her sit for a moment. Here, you, fetch some brandy. I'll pay you when you come back."

Mathias was standing over her now.

"I've just heard. Don't worry, Mary. They say the men are being brought ashore now. Jack'll be safe, never fear."

"I must go there," cried Mary. "However far it is I must go there."

"I'll take you," said Sir Roger. "My carriage is outside."

"What? With those nags?" Mathias's voice was harsh. "You won't get as far as Groes Gibbet before they'll drop on you. I'll take her." He seized Mary's wrist. "Come, Mary. Twm'll get us there in no time."

"You can't take her on a horse!" expostulated Sir Roger. "It's starting to rain."

"May be, but I'll get her there before you will."

Mary got unsteadily to her feet.

"I'll go with Daniel. I don't mind getting wet if it will be quicker. Please take me now."

"I'll get the horse."

Sir Roger consoled himself by supporting her.

"At least wait for the brandy. It will fortify you against the journey."

But Mary was already moving towards the door.

"I'll follow you," said Sir Roger. "I'll be there as soon as I can, I promise you."

Mathias was already outside mounted, the horse slewing around in circles.

"Give her a hand up," he called to a group of men. "Sit astride this time, Mary. It'll be quicker."

Willing hands lifted Mary on to the horse behind Mathias. She sat astride, as directed, with little thought for her gown or for her hair, now streaming in the wind. She encircled Mathias with both arms and immediately the horse surged away to the road, breaking into a gallop without hesitation. It was picking with rain and each drop felt like a pebble on Mary's face, so fast were they going and such was the power of the wind. She pressed her cheek into Mathias's broad back for protection.

Rapidly they traversed the same route back to the inn. Mary had a brief glimpse of its lights as they sped past and then they were galloping up the hill. There the stallion began to labour and Mathias reined him down to a walk.

"I've got to hold him back," he yelled over his shoulder, "otherwise he'd run his heart out. But don't worry. I'll get you there as soon as I can."

They proceeded at a walking pace for what seemed an interminable time to Mary, until she saw the lights of Laleston. Suddenly Mathias dug his heels into the horse's flanks and they tore down a hill at breakneck speed, at the bottom settling down to a loping canter which continued until they were half way up a long, gradual slope. Again Mathias checked the horse.

"This is Sturmi's Common. Once we're at the top we'll pick up speed again. Are you all right?"

"My fingers are numb, that's all."

Mathias vigorously rubbed her hands, clenched in the pit of his stomach.

"It won't be long now. Soon we'll be passing Pyle. We'll leave the main road there, so look out for branches. Hang on tight in case we stumble. There'll be no stopping until we get to Sker."

At the top of the common the wind was blowing with such force that even the indomitable Twm bowed his head and plodded forward like a farm hack; but as the ground levelled off and then began to slope downwards Mary felt the animal's muscles tense, and soon they were cantering again. They swung off through a village, twisting and turning along innumerable lanes, making her feel glad that she had chosen Mathias, for it was obvious that he knew every inch of the way, even in the dark. There was a final, sustained gallop and they came to a halt by an open gate. For the first time Mathias seemed unsure of himself.

"I think it's along here. I can hear the sea. Wait! Someone's coming."

Mary looked over Mathias's shoulder and saw an elderly man approaching, armed with a storm lantern.

"Which way to Sker?" shouted Mathias.

"Through that gate. Less than a mile."

Without hesitation Mathias spurred the stallion through the gateway to a rough track, but it was immediately apparent that they would have to be circumspect, for every few yards they came upon people, singly or in groups, hurrying in the direction of the deeply-roaring sea. A few were pushing hand carts, obviously intent upon getting their fair share of the flotsam they knew from experience would soon be theirs for the taking. From their snatches of conversation Mary and Mathias gathered that the local population had turned up in force, optimistic in spite of the fact that the prize was a troopship and not a merchantman.

Then, suddenly, Sker House loomed up in the darkness, a gaunt, eerie structure with many chimneys and gables, standing entirely on its own. Lights shone from every window and the entire area was alive with people, horses and carts. Mathias guided Twm to the front of the building and they saw that the main door was open. He slid off the saddle and held his arms up to Mary.

"Come. I know Black Evans. We'll get some information from him."

He tethered the horse to a cart with a broken wheel and they went up to the door. There several men were pressing around but Mathias forced his way through, with Mary in tow. Standing in the porch, silhouetted by the flickering light from within, was a heavily-built man with a black stubble of a beard.

"Mr. Evans," called out Mathias. "Can we come in, please? This lady had a brother aboard ship."

"Then God help her," said Evans. "There'll be few alive after this night, believe me." He stood aside to reveal the kitchen, filled to overflowing with red-coated corpses.

Mathias put his arm around Mary and they went into the kitchen.

140

CHAPTER 20

THE BODIES HAD been laid out in two neat rows, heads to the walls, feet a yard apart. All wore bright red tunics which, although stained with salt water, nevertheless still contrived to look smart. Every face was turned upwards towards the oak-beamed ceiling, some with their eyes still open. To Mathias, who held Mary tightly, it was the immovability of the figures that was unnerving, for they looked like toy soldiers lying in a gigantic box, waiting for some child to play with them.

A bleary eyed young officer with a large moustache hurried up to them.

"I'm sorry, you're not allowed in here unless you're connected with the house."

"This lady is a relative of one of the soldiers," explained Mathias. "Her brother was on the ship."

"Ah! That's different. What's his name, madam?"

"Jack Tudor," replied Mary.

"Jack Tudor! That's peculiar. I know of no Jack Tudor. What's his rank?"

"He's a private."

"Ah!" The moustache quivered. "Then you won't find him here. Only officers are being brought indoors. Other ranks you will find out in the yard at the front."

Mathias guided Mary back to the porch.

"Let me go and look first. It'll be better that way."

"No. I must come with you."

"He won't be there. I'm sure he's alive."

"I want to come all the same."

Outside a corporal was priming a lantern. Mathias explained again about Mary having a brother on the troopship.

"Come with me," said the Corporal. "I'll show you where they are."

He pushed open a wooden gate. In a small, walled enclosure

141

thirty or more bodies had been laid out with similar military precision. Most were wearing red tunics but some were attired in dark blue artillery uniforms. Even in the lee of the wall the wind kept whipping at the uniforms making it look as though the men were still alive.

"What arm, miss?" asked the corporal.

Mary stared blankly at him.

"Infantry," said Mathias quickly.

"Then follow me and see if he's here."

The corporal led the way along the row, dangling the lantern over the face of every red-uniformed soldier. When they came to the end of the line Mary shook her head.

"He's not there."

"They're being brought in every minute," said the corporal nonchalantly. "But it's best for you to wait until morning. You can see them proper then. Makes no odds, do it, I'm sorry to say. If he's alive, he's alive; if dead, dead."

At that moment a sergeant appeared.

"Go and get some sleep, Bickerstaff. I'll take over now. There'll be no more brought here tonight. They're coming ashore further up the coast—too far to bring here."

"How many survivors are there, sergeant?" asked Mathias.

"Survivors!" The sergeant laughed sardonically. "More than a dozen and we'll be lucky. The bloody ship should never have sailed. I said that at the time. It was blowing a gale when we set out from Bristol. Except for me, him, an officer and five gunners I've seen no one else alive. A whole bloody regiment and a troop of artillery thrown to the fishes!"

"But you said men were coming ashore further up the coast."

"Aye! That's right. Dead ones. What's it to you?"

For a third time Mathias explained about Mary. The sergeant looked at her with pity.

"I don't want to distress you, miss, but I don't hold out much hope. And don't try looking for him tonight. You can't do much in this dark and wind—and don't go down to the beach. It's dangerous. Go and rest and try again in the morning."

"We'd better do that," muttered Mathias.

Mary nodded numbly, and allowed herself to be led out of the enclosure.

"Come," said Mathias. "We'll seek shelter in the house."

But at the door an artilleryman barred their way.

"You can't come in here. Captain's orders."

"But I know Mr. Evans," remonstrated Mathias.

"Can't be helped. Captain's orders. The house has been requisitioned."

Desperately Mathias looked at Mary's sodden hair and dress.

"Lean up against the wall. At least the wind is less there."

Mary did as she was told and then began the longest six hours in her life. She was conscious of Mathias taking off his coat and slipping it over her shoulders and that he obtained a blanket from somewhere. They sat on the damp earth with their backs to the grey stonework of the house, listening to the shrieking of the wind as it tore over the roof; and always there was the deep booming and banging of the waves on the nearby beach. Men kept stumbling over them and Mathias, fearing the theft of the stallion, fetched him and haltered him to his leg with a rope. Neither of them slept and when eventually it was dawn they both had difficulty in stirring because of stiffness. Mathias was first on his feet.

"I'll just check with the sergeant."

He was soon back with the news that no other bodies had been brought to the enclosure. He insisted that Mary should sit in the saddle whilst he led the horse, explaining that a search would be easier that way. Mary complied with little hope and they set off for the beach. Mercifully the wind had abated a little and it had stopped raining. They reached the water's edge and stared at the broiling surf, their vision impeded by hurtling foam and spindrift. Then, as it grew lighter, they saw the ship, about a mile distant, keeling over at a terrifying angle. Even from that distance it was obvious that no living soul could be aboard. Without hesitation Mathias set off eastwards, keeping to a turf bank just above the sand. Soon they came to a jagged line of rocks and saw two red-coated bodies wedged in a gully.

"Hold the reins," he ordered and clambered over the rocks.

The faces of the two soldiers had been badly battered but, having met Jack during his brief sojourn at the inn, Mathias was able to breathe a sigh of relief. On his way back he shouted that all was well, mounted behind Mary and retrieved the reins.

"We'll go to the next beach."

Now they were able to move more easily for the wind, although still strong, was slanting diagonally behind them and soon they came to a small cove. There they found six more bodies, one still being trundled around by the hissing surf. Mathias steered the horse as near to the water as safety warranted and they stared down at each lifeless face in turn. None was Jack's. Without a word Mathias spurred Twm back to the grassy firmness of the bank and they traversed yet another ridge of rocks. There they met several people staring out to sea or searching in the ravines, and the reason for their interest soon became apparent when they found two further soldiers with their uniforms torn apart and their pocket flaps hanging out.

"Bloody ghouls," muttered Mathias and urged the stallion to the top of a small promontory at the base of the rocks. There the enormity of their task immediately became apparent to them for, from their slight vantage point, they could see inlet after inlet receding into the distance, each with its small quota of wreckage and corpses.

"I don't know what to do," said Mathias desperately. "We can't examine every one and I can't go over the rocks with the horse."

He strained his eyes through the swirling clouds of foam and could just make out a large beach beyond the inlets. On it figures were moving.

"We'll go over there. Perhaps we can find someone to ask."

Without waiting for an answer he kicked the horse into a gallop and they raced along the coastal track to the beach. There the scene was like a battlefield, with dozens of red and blue coated soldiers lying on the sand in grotesque positions as though they had been shot down by enemy bullets. A small group of men were sheltering behind a low ridge trying to light a fire. Mathias rode over to them and called out:

144

"Any of you men seen Jack Tudor?"

He was greeted with blank faces but one man, tunic-less, stepped forward.

"I know Jack Tudor."

"Where is he now?"

The soldier shrugged.

"The last I seen of him he was clinging to a spar. Perhaps he got ashore. I don't know."

A civilian who was fanning the flames of the fire looked up.

"If you're looking for someone, mister, it's best for you to ride on to Iron Gate Point. They're laying them out there and identifying them. Calling the roll, too, and there's a few men who're alive."

"Where's Iron Gate Point?"

"A mile further on. You can't miss it. There's no more soldiers beyond that, or if there are they'll be off Ogmore by tomorrow."

Mathias thanked him and they galloped off again. This time they crossed a small common, losing sight of the sea for a while, but when they returned to the shore-line they saw a sight that chilled even Mathias. On the green sward of a field, only yards away from a foam-bedecked line of rocks, stretching almost as far as the eye could see, about two hundred bodies had been laid out side by side, their legs pointing to the roaring waves that had killed them. Mathias reined in the horse and gaped. He felt Mary stiffen, then she began to cry.

"He's dead, Daniel, I know it. He's dead."

"Don't give up hope. You heard that man say there were a few alive. We'll find an officer."

They found an officer, a major, staring at the long line of corpses as though mesmerised.

"Major," shouted Mathias. "Can you help us, please?"

The major turned, revealing a cheek that had been gashed open from ear to chin. His eyes had the glazed, unseeing look of a man in shock. He cupped a hand around his uninjured ear.

"What did you say?"

"We're looking for a soldier named Jack Tudor, sir."

145

"Then look along the line. I don't know where he is. We haven't completed the roll call yet."

He turned away and directed two civilians to place yet another body in place. In desperation Mathias glanced about, hoping to find an ordinary soldier who was alive. Instead he saw Sir Roger's carriage approaching. It came up to them, stopped and Sir Roger got out. One look at Mary's face was enough to acquaint him with the position. He pointed at the carriage.

"Tell her to rest inside. I'll help you search."

Mathias handed Mary down. As though in a trance she allowed Sir Roger to place her in the carriage and shut the door behind her.

"She's done for," said Sir Roger. "At the end of her tether. Have you searched everywhere?"

"Not there." Mathias nodded grimly towards the line of corpses. "I'll do that now."

"What can I do?"

"Stay with her. You don't know Jack Tudor. I do. You'll do more good keeping her company. Turn the carriage so that she can't see anything."

Mathias rode over to the first body. Slowly he made his way along the line, bending low in the saddle so that he could study each man's face. Some had raw, gaping wounds that made recognition difficult or impossible, but he did not stop, intending to make a quick reconnaissance first. He passed small groups of civilians, the men sombre-faced, the women weeping, for the inhabitants of Newton-Nottage, although well used to wrecks, had never witnessed a calamity of such proportions before; and the sight of so many young men cut down in their prime was enough to incite pity in the most callous heart. He reached the end of the line feeling fairly confident that he had not seen Jack, but to make sure he rode back along the same path, dismounting now and again to make a more thorough examination. When he had finished he felt reasonably hopeful, and galloped over to the carriage. He knocked on the window and Sir Roger got out, carefully closing the door behind him.

"He's not there," said Mathias. "I'm fairly certain."

146

"Thank God for that. What will you do now?"

"I'll search among the inlets. You go across the common and shelter behind that rise, otherwise Jenkins up there won't be in a fit state to drive you back. How's Mary now?"

"Still the same. I'm trying to get her to take brandy, but she won't. She hasn't spoken a word—she's just staring into space."

"Then look after her. I'll return as soon as I get news."

Sir Roger climbed back into the carriage and held both Mary's hands in his. Wisely he said nothing. The carriage lurched across the common and stopped, much to Jenkins' relief, in the lee of a small hill. They remained there the best part of an hour, swaying occasionally when a gust caught them. At the end of that time Sir Roger could stand the waiting no longer.

"I won't be a moment, Mary. I just want to see if there's any sign of Mathias."

He clambered out and went to the top of the hill. The sudden force of the wind on the brow made his eyes water, but he stood there surveying the scene. The waves were still pounding the coastline, sending up huge sheets of spray and in the distance he could see the ship, now wallowing on her side like a giant whale. Few, he knew, could live in a cauldron like that. He turned and looked in the other direction and saw that a gang of civilians had already begun digging a long, shallow trench only a short distance from the soldiers' heads. How many relatives, he wondered, would know of the last resting place of their loved ones in such a grave on that bleak, wind-swept coast. Heavy of heart he returned to the carriage.

He sat for another hour, silently holding Mary's hands. Even in distress she looked beautiful and wryly he remembered his intentions of the night before. He had gone to the noson lawen to surprise her, to whisk her back to Candleston to ask for her answer. The ring with which he hoped to grace her finger was still in his pocket. Now events had made that impossible and unless her brother was found the opportunity would be a long time returning.

Then, interrupting his thoughts, he heard the sound of a galloping horse. Mary heard it, too, and for the first time looked up, hope in her eyes. Still afraid to say anything Sir Roger squeezed her hands more tightly. There was a sharp knocking at the window and through the salt-encrusted glass they saw the silhouette of a horse and rider. Sir Roger flung open the door and Mathias stooped and looked in at them.

"I've found him. Here he is."

He moved the horse forward and into Mary's view came Jack. He was sitting behind Mathias, hat-less and tunic-less and with his arm in a sling, but alive. Mary leaped from the carriage and Mathias helped her brother down.

"Don't hug him too hard. He's got a broken arm."

But brother and sister clung together, regardless of pain. Mathias turned to Sir Roger.

"I found him sheltering in a cave with two others."

Sir Roger nodded. Delighted though he was with Mary's happiness he felt a sudden sense of foreboding, compounded when Mary disengaged herself from Jack, threw her arms around Mathias and kissed him. He fingered the ring in his pocket and wished he could have done more.

CHAPTER 21

MARY RODE BACK to the inn with Mathias leaving Sir Roger to return alone in the carriage. She felt ungrateful about doing so, but Mathias had helped her so much it was unthinkable not to have gone with him, and she hoped Sir Roger would understand. As soon as she had the chance she would thank him properly for coming all the way to Sker to comfort her. In the meantime, as she sat behind Mathias in a more lady-like position, she felt deeply ashamed that she had been the instigator of an enquiry about him: no man who had acted so gallantly could possibly be a murderer or even be connected with one. She thought once of telling him what she had done and asking his forgiveness, but decided against it. That would look as though she had been prying into his affairs: it was far better to see Parson Newman as quickly as possible before irretrievable harm was done; and no

148

doubt the kindly cleric would be as pleased as she when he knew of the ostler's good deeds and realise the stupidity of her original suspicions. Perhaps tomorrow, when Gronow was taking her nap, she could slip down to Merthyr Mawr and put things to rights. And so when, by accident or design, Mathias's hand touched hers as they rode along she did not withdraw it, even when once he held it against his stomach for what seemed an unnecessary length of time.

Therefore although they were both heavy-eyed with fatigue and the tragedy of the wreck still lay heavy upon them, the journey back was pleasant compared with the outward trip. The rain had stopped, the wind was merely gusting and they felt uplifted by the knowledge that Jack was safe: moreover Mary had been told before leaving Iron Gate Point that, after attending a burial service for his comrades and a few days spent salvaging equipment from the beaches, he was to be posted to the midlands to help train recruits for his decimated regiment, a task that would keep him away from active service for at least a year. Accordingly, when she went to bed that night after completing her tasks and answering a multitude of questions about the wreck, she thanked God for her brother's safe deliverance and asked for a blessing on all the poor souls lost on that terrible night. Neither did she forget a request for comfort for the relatives who still had to hear the dreadful news and then, through sheer exhaustion, she fell asleep and remained so until morning.

But soon after getting up the inn began to re-exert its malign influence. The first indication that something was wrong came at about ten o'clock when, rushing through the hall to obtain ale for a group of travellers, Mary found two soldiers guarding the dining room door. At first she thought they had something to do with the wreck, then she noticed that they were troopers wearing cavalrymen's sabres. One of them stopped her and grinned.

"Hullo, my beautiful. Get us a noggin of porter, will you?"

"You can't drink here," hissed the other. "He'll have your guts for garters if you do."

"I'll stick it in the grandfather clock," replied the first. "Go on, my handsome. Get us one—just a small one will do."

"Who are you?" asked Mary. "What are you doing here?"

"Business," said the more responsible soldier. "Legitimate business on behalf of Colonel Nicholl."

Mary gave him an arch look and ran to the cellar. Mathias, she knew, was in the stable, so she poured the travellers' ale herself; but before she had filled the first jug she heard a voice coming through the serving hatch that stopped her in mid-action. It was the innkeeper's, angry and blustering.

"There's no need for you to bring half the army here, Colonel. You'll make it look as though I'm a villain."

"Well, ain't you?" The reply was dry, incisive and menacing. Mary poured the beer slowly, listening intently.

"Them's your words," said Robert, "not mine. Defamation of character, that's what it is."

"In that case you can take me to court."

"What! With you on the bench and all your friends magistrates. Fat chance I'd stand then. Ask the villagers if I'm a villain. They'll tell you."

"And I've no doubt about what they'd say. A good smuggler has to buy loyalty."

"Oh! So I'm a smuggler as well, am I? Then you prove it. Get the excise men to catch me then I'll admit it. Not before."

Nicholl let out a snort of exasperation.

"I'm not interested in your damned smuggling, at least not yet. You can go to France every day of the week as far as I'm concerned. You know why I'm here, Sioni Cap Coch."

Mary gasped. The malice in Nicholl's voice, especially the way he had mouthed Robert's nick-name, was chilling. She tiptoed to the hatch hoping to catch a glimpse of him but all she could see was his highly-polished riding boots. He was, she surmised, sitting on a chair by the fireplace, with the innkeeper opposite him.

Nicholl's voice reached her again.

"Now, then, let's get down to brass tacks. I hear you have a

150

carriage and pair that'd do credit to a nobleman in that house of yours in Bridgend. Do you dispute that?"

"Why shouldn't I? I've every right to them."

"A matter for debate. I also hear your house is full of plate and that your wife sports a great deal of jewellery. There are also rumours that you have money invested in France. Tell me, how does the income from a mediocre tavern such as this reach to such munificence?"

There was silence for a moment, then Robert laughed throatily.

"I see you've had your spies on me, Colonel. Well, I'll be honest. I do do a bit of smuggling on the side as you well know. It ain't no good my denying it. But don't hold that against me. I often meet one or two of your friends in my transactions and they wouldn't care to be named. I make a little extra that way—to put away for my old age."

"Not enough to pay for all you possess. You're lining your nest another way."

"You're going above my head now, Colonel."

"Am I? Then I'll make things plainer. Tell me. Do you do the murders yourself or do you get your minions to do them for you?"

Mary nearly dropped the jug. She was too late, after all, to stop the enquiry. Parson Newman had already spoken to Nicholl who, as chief magistrate, had acted quickly and come to investigate; although why Robert and the troopers had referred to him as Colonel she did not know. What unnerved her was the way he was setting about it, with all the delicacy of a cavalry charge. But she had no time for further thought for the cellar door opened and she heard Gronow's sharp voice.

"Mary! Where's that ale? The men are waiting."

Mary picked up the tray and hurried upstairs. She served the travellers as quickly as possible and was soon back. Robert was blustering again.

"You blacken my name, sir. You're using your position to malign me, knowing full well I can't defend myself. It's jealousy that's what it is—jealousy. Just because I've bettered myself and got myself looked up to round here you don't like it. I'm put in mind of that old saying: them as can, does; them as can't, cavil.

151

There's plenty ready to cavil about me round here and I can smell sour grapes a mile away."

There was a slight pause, then:

"I grant you you've bettered yourself, Sioni, but it's not sour grapes that've brought me here, I can assure you of that. I'd be obliged if you'd answer one or two questions—with a civil tongue in your head, if you please."

"What sort of questions?"

"First, what became of a man called McGregor?"

"Never heard of him."

"You ought to. He stayed here. We found him on the beach. My apothecary tells me his skull was half way through his brain."

"What of it? It's nothing to do with me."

"The last time he stayed here was the night before he was bludgeoned. Unfortunately for you his wife has made enquiries about him. She wrote a letter which came to me."

"My condolences to her. I know nothing about the man."

"Then perhaps you know something about a farmer from Swansea—named Eurig Jones. He stayed here, too—very recently."

"How d'you expect me to remember anybody called Jones? There are thousands of 'em in this part of the world—like Thomas and Davies."

"Only one Eurig Jones. Stop shilly-shallying, Robert. You know what I'm talking about. This time you've dunged up your own door step. Jones was the nephew of one of my bailiffs. His family still lives in Laleston."

"So what? It's nothing to do with me."

"Ain't it? When my bailiff tells me that his nephew is missing I look into matters, and I can tell you one thing: in the short time I've been here I've uncovered a few facts. A pattern is emerging, Sioni, a very interesting pattern indeed."

"What d'you mean, pattern?"

"Every time you go to France—or wherever it is you do go—it's peaceful around here. Very little happens, as you'd expect in a rural area. Yet the moment you get back people start disappearing—packmen usually or travellers with a bit of money or

152

valuable goods, and in every case they're strangers to the district. Now ain't that a pattern?"

"May be, but you're on the wrong track. Footpads is two a penny around Bridgend. Seek them out and you'll find the guilty party."

"No footpad has been as busy as that. Over the last eight years an average of one person a month has disappeared—that's about a hundred altogether, I'm informed. I blame myself for not having tumbled to you before, but I'm beginning to get the hang of things now. I'm not having people as far away as London saying my area is the most lawless in the country."

"Then why don't you start on them outlaws down at Ogmore castle? If there's any missing persons you'll find them there. Now if our positions were reversed—"

"There's no danger of that. I'm told my predecessor here was suspicious of you a few years ago when bodies were being found in the river, then it stopped. Now it's started again with McGregor. What happened in between? Where've you been putting the bodies?"

"Bodies! There ain't been no bodies as far as I'm aware."

"And what's happened to Eurig Jones? Mark this, Robert, if he's found in the river—or anywhere else for that matter—I'll come after you like the Llangeinor hunt. I'll make sure you swing on Stalling Down, damme if I don't."

"Now hold on, Colonel. I'm not saying I'm the best of men but I ain't as bad as you make out. Now if you was to be nicer to me I could help you. An innkeeper gets to know things, especially when he's a mind to. Instead of accusing me why don't you let me get some evidence for you. That'd satisfy you, wouldn't it?"

"Coming from you, no. I wouldn't trust you further than I could throw my stallion."

"But if I was to lay evidence before you—evidence that made no doubt about who the guilty party was—you'd have to act, wouldn't you?"

"What sort of evidence?"

"Well, Colonel, you've mentioned people disappearing. There's somebody around here I've had my eye on for some time—

somebody I never trusted from the beginning. If there's dirty work going on he's at the bottom of it, believe me."

"What are you getting at?"

"Now if I should tell you his name he'd get wind of it, and you wouldn't see him again. Give me a couple of days, Colonel, and I'll have him up before you. That'd clear my name, wouldn't it?"

Nicholl's chair scraped on the floor.

"'Pon my soul, Robert, you're a plausible rogue. You'd cut your best friend's throat to escape the gallows, and that's what I believe you're trying to do. Bring forward what evidence you may but I tell you this: if Eurig Jones is not found soon then may God have mercy on you, for I shan't. I'll have you up on the Downs before you can say Mari Lwyd."

Robert started to reply but footsteps on the floor signified an abrupt end to the conversation. Mary heard the dining room door open then close; and she stood for a moment, frightened and worried. As far as she was aware not once in the conversation had she heard Mathias's name mentioned, but there was no doubt who Robert was alluding to, or what he was getting at. If she did not act soon the ostler would be in trouble. It was too late now to explain her mistake to Parson Newman, but if she could see Colonel Nicholl for only a few moments she might be able to help. After that she would find Mathias, have it out with him once and for all about his nocturnal wanderings, and warn him of what was afoot. With this plan in mind she ran up the steps and reached the hall in time to see the front door closing. At that moment Robert brushed past her, his face black with anger. Normally he would have said something, or made some ribald remark, but he made straight for the stairs and went to his room.

Furtively Mary pushed open the heavy front door, afraid that someone would see her talking to Nicholl. It was her intention to run as far as the bridge and stop him behind a hedge, but she was impeded by one of the troopers' horses that circled around contrarily as he tried to mount. She dodged the horse and made for the bridge and at last reached the shelter of a hawthorn bush. With beating heart she waited.

Then, suddenly, she recoiled in shock. For the rider coming towards her on a magnificent white steed, resplendent in uniform, medallions and epaulettes, who could be none other than Colonel Nicholl, was the same man she had seen riding in the funeral.

CHAPTER 22

BEFORE MARY COULD recover, Nicholl and the troopers were away over the bridge and trotting up the hill; but although badly shaken she remembered the second part of her plan: to warn Mathias. She returned to the inn intending to look for him first in the cellar and then in the stables, but in the hall Gronow was waiting for her, looking like a dark wraith.

"Where have you been?"

"Out, Mistress Gronow. Just getting some fresh air."

"I'll give you fresh air. I've been searching for you. I want you to go to Bridgend."

"Now? But I have a few jobs to do first."

Gronow's bony hand poked her back out to the forecourt.

"They can wait. There are some knitting needles I want urgently. Here's the address and the size of the needles. Make sure you get the right ones." She thrust a piece of vellum into her hand.

"Very well. I'll just get my cloak—"

The thin arm came across like a toll-gate.

"You don't need your cloak. It's not going to rain."

Certain now that she was being got out of the way, Mary tried another ploy.

"Can't Mathias take me in the trap? I'll be over an hour otherwise."

"No. He's engaged on a task for Mr. Robert."

With Gronow standing on the step watching her Mary had no alternative but to set off down the path. Once around the side of the building she made a dart for the stables, but Gronow had anticipated that. She was standing in the yard, arms akimbo,

155

black eyes glowering. Quickly Mary retreated to the path, convinced without doubt now that she was being sent on a fool's errand. A pedlar called frequently at the inn with needles of all kinds and Gronow was no great shakes at knitting as far as she knew. She fought back a feeling of panic that welled up inside her and half ran, half walked in the direction of Bridgend. All this was her own doing. If she had not gone rushing to Parson Newman with her unfounded fears Colonel Nicholl would not have visited the inn and Robert would not have had the chance to twist things against an innocent man—a man who had done nothing but help her. Desperately she tried to think out ways in which she could retrieve matters but could come up with only her original solution: to warn Mathias. But now she would have to be subtle: she could not afford another mistake. First she must allay suspicion by returning the needles to Gronow whilst pretending that she had no inkling of what was afoot; then she must find Mathias and alert him to the danger, that is if it was not already too late. The thought added to her anguish but speeded her steps and in a very short time she reached the town's packhorse bridge.

She found the shop without difficulty, obtained the needles and hurried back. She went straight to the stables, opened the door and called out, but there was no reply. Next she went to the kitchen door and with a shock found it bolted. She looked through the window and tapped on it several times, but no Davies appeared. With a heart pounding from exertion and fear she went round to the front door and found that secured also. She was about to knock when she heard the bolts being withdrawn and a moment later the heavy structure swung back to reveal Gronow.

"So you're back already."

"Yes, Mistress Gronow. Here are the needles. Why is the door locked?"

"We are closed for the day."

"I couldn't get into the kitchen. Where's Davies?"

"She's been sent home."

"Why have we closed?"

Gronow swung the bolts to with a thud.

"Stop asking questions. Come with me. Mr. Robert wants to see you."

Mary's heart sank as she followed Gronow through the dining room to the parlour. Without customers the inn was strangely quiet, almost as though it was brooding, again giving her the sensation that something dreadful was afoot and that she was already too late. Gronow opened the door for her, thrust her inside and followed her in. Seated at the small Jacobean table, looking incongruous around such a delicate work of art, were Robert, Benjamin and Ebenezer.

"Ah, Mary!" said Robert, smiling, his humour evidently restored. "I'm glad to see you, m'dear. Sit down. There's a little matter to be dealt with."

Mary sat in a chair opposite the trio.

"You know our visitor, of course," said Robert. "He tells me he's had a few interesting chats with you."

Mary swung round to see Parson Newman standing by the door beside Gronow. She gasped in surprise.

"Why, father! What are you doing here?"

Newman avoided her gaze. His normally jovial face was pallid. He seemed shifty and ill at ease and when he spoke his voice was low and faltering.

"Good evening, Mary. I'm afraid my presence here is not of my choosing. I assure you I would not be here if it were not for—"

"But you are," interrupted Robert harshly. "And right glad I am because of it. Mary, I'm going to ask you a direct question in front of the parson here and I want a direct reply, if you please. Have you ever been to the big house to see Nicholl?"

"No. Of course not."

"Not at any time? Or spoken to him anywhere?"

"No." She glanced sideways at Newman as she spoke and Robert noticed the movement.

"Come over here, Newman, for God's sake, or you'll have Mary's head twisting round like a top. Sit there by Ebenezer so that I can keep an eye on you. Now I'll ask you the same question in front of Mary here. Have you spoken to Nicholl at any time?"

157

"No. How many times do I have to tell you? I've already sworn on my cloth."

"That ain't much, coming from you. Well, one of you's lying. Mary, why did you go to parson here with information about a certain person in my employ? It's no good you denying it. He's told me all about your visit."

Mary stared aghast at Newman who kept his eyes averted.

"I—I don't know," she stammered. "Certain things worried me, I suppose."

"Such as Daniel Mathias being seen with a spade at two o'clock in the morning. Why didn't you come and tell me that?"

"I don't know. I thought Parson Newman was the best person to see."

"You're right in a way. Parson here is a good friend of mine and so he came to me. But I'm hurt, Mary, that you didn't speak to me in the first place. I've been good to you, ain't I? I've let you live here after the death of your family. I've been like a father to you, yet in a matter that affects me considerable you ignore me."

"Leave her alone," said Newman, looking up suddenly. "I've done what you wanted. What more do you want?"

"Plenty. I'm not having a stuck-up aristocrat like Nicholl, who thinks he owns every stone around here and who ain't been here two minutes, coming here and accusing me of murder."

"Well, I didn't inform on you and I'm sure Mary didn't."

"No, perhaps not. You're too fond of your liquor to get rid of the one who supplies you. But Nicholl's not going to blame me when the guilty party is sheltering under my roof. Now, Mary, are you ready to testify that you saw Mathias with a spade the night a man called Eurig Jones disappeared?"

Already feeling faint Mary tried to gather up her courage.

"Daniel hasn't done anything."

"Ah. It's good of you to protect him. I respect you for that. He's helped you a lot, ain't he? Going to Sker with you and finding your brother, then there was that trip to your home. I can understand your feelings, m'dear, but you can't explain away a spade now, can you? Answer me that."

158

Mary tried to think of an answer, but failed.

"There you are!" cried Robert triumphantly. "And to think I've been good to Mathias as well. I took him on when nobody else would give him a job and look how he's repaid me. The master being blamed for the sins of his servant! I ain't standing for that."

"Where's Daniel now?" asked Mary.

"Where? I'm not telling you that, m'dear, for I see you're still not convinced about his guilt. I'll tell you this, though. We'll soon get the truth out of him. He ain't taking me for a scapegoat."

"He's done you no harm."

"Done me no harm you say! Only tried to put my neck in a noose. That's harm enough."

"Don't trust her!" blurted Ebenezer, speaking for the first time. "She knows too much. If she sneaked off to see Newman it's on the cards she's been to Nicholl as well."

"Quiet, Ebenezer. I'll do the talking."

"I agree with Ebenezer," said Gronow from her position by the door. "That girl's been nothing but trouble since the day she arrived. Why all that walking about she's been doing? If you ask me she's been nosing into things."

Robert raised his fist, intending to thump the table, but before he could do so there was a loud knocking on the front door.

"See who it is, Gronow. You know who to let in and who not."

Gronow left the room and for a few moments no one spoke. Then the door burst open and Sir Roger strode in. For the second time Mary stared in disbelief.

"What the hell's going on, Robert?" said Sir Roger angrily, then he caught sight of Mary. "What on earth are you doing here?"

"She's helping me," said Robert quickly. "I've been falsely accused and Mary's got evidence that'll put me in the clear."

Mary looked helplessly at Sir Roger who went up to the table and glared down at the four men seated around it.

"You look like a confounded court to me. Are you persecuting her in any way?"

159

"No, no," said Robert, shaking his head. "She's just helping, that's all. Like the fair-minded Methody she is, she wants to see justice done."

"And what's Newman doing here?"

"He's helping, too."

"By the heavens, Robert, if I thought you were harrassing her in any way I'd put a ball in you! What's this evidence you're talking about?"

"Mary here saw Mathias with a spade the night a farmer named Eurig Jones disappeared. Nicholl thinks I had something to do with it, but I ask you, what explanation can there be other than Mathias being the guilty party and disposing of the body? Caught red-handed by Mary herself."

Sir Roger swung round.

"Is that true, Mary?"

Mary shook her head.

"I did see Daniel with a spade but—"

"There you are," shouted Robert with glee. "So I'm not likely to harm her, am I? With a witness like that Nicholl can't lay a finger on me, so menacing talk ain't called for, Roger."

Sir Roger stared thoughtfully at Mary.

"So Mathias is the culprit, is he? By hell, Robert, you take some beating. Now that Nicholl's caught up with you at last you're getting out of it by putting the blame on a poor bloody ostler—and using Mary to do it. I've got a damned good mind to stop you."

Robert chuckled.

"You try that and I'll see that Nicholl knows we've been using your place to hide the contraband. There's enough still there to get you hooked. You're in this up to your neck so I wouldn't try any monkey tricks if I was you."

Sir Roger's face darkened and for a moment he seemed to be having trouble with his words.

"To hell with you, Robert. Smuggling's one thing but murder's another. I'd get away with a pardon but you'd damn well swing. I rue the day I had anything to do with you."

"Ah, but you have! Out of greed like the others. You didn't

turn your nose up at the money so it ain't no good complaining now we've struck a bad patch."

"Take care, Sir Roger," quavered Newman, swaying about on his chair as though in anguish. "Don't act too hastily. We're all in his clutches through avarice, miserable sinners that we are."

Sir Roger placed a hand on Mary's shoulder.

"He's not having Mary in his clutches. Mary, you've heard enough to think ill of me. My only excuse is that I wanted to better my lot so that I could save Candleston. I've had sleepless nights thinking about you in this den of thieves, but the time has come to put an end to it. However low your opinion of me you must come away now. Whether or not you marry me is for you to decide later, but leave you must. Come now. Knowing what I do of these men it's not safe for you to remain here."

"Well spoken," said Robert, clapping his hands. "A very pretty speech indeed. But I wouldn't try and take her if I was you."

"And as for you, Robert, I've had enough. I've gone along with the smuggling and blinded myself to the other things, God forgive me! But when you propose sending an innocent man to the gallows for what you've done I draw the line. I've no love for Mathias but I've learned to respect him. Leave him alone, d'you hear? Come, Mary. I'll take you now."

"Hang on!" said Robert quickly. "Now let's talk things over. If I allow you to take her will you promise to keep your mouth shut and produce her when I want her?"

"I promise nothing. You've had your reign, Robert, now it's at an end. If Nicholl is after you no amount of wriggling will get you out of it. You'll do no good keeping Mary here against her will."

"I can't come with you, Sir Roger," whispered Mary. "I can't leave without Daniel. They're holding him somewhere."

"There!" said Robert. "She won't come with you. Did you hear that?"

The pressure of Sir Roger's hand on Mary's shoulder intensified.

"Where's Mathias now?"

"She don't know," interjected Robert. "And I tell you this: in spite of your hard words Mathias is the guilty party. I'll get a confession out of him and march him in front of Nicholl. Now, Roger, I ask you again for a promise before you leave. Swear before God you'll keep your trap shut and keep Mary safe till required."

Sir Roger seemed to explode.

"By hell, are you deaf? I've told you once. I swear to nothing. Come, Mary."

But Mary was staring at Ebenezer who had produced a pistol. Mesmerised she watched the ugly barrel swaying slightly and saw its reflection in the table top, with Ebenezer's dirty finger around the trigger. Sir Roger spotted it at the same time. His lips curled in a sneer.

"Try that on, Robert, and you'll swing for it. You're not dealing with one of your unknown packmen now. It'd be the end for you and you know it."

"Maybe," said Robert, "but I'll take the chance. Now ain't you even going to promise not to bring men here to get Mary?"

"No—go to hell!"

"But you ain't in a position to argue, are you? Not with Ebenezer in the nasty mood he's in."

Mary saw Sir Roger lick his lips. His dark eyes had become even darker. For a full half minute there was complete silence, so complete that Mary could hear the distant ticking of the grand-father clock in the hall. Suddenly he pressed her shoulder reassuringly then took his hand away.

"Have no fear, Mary. As you can see this rogue has the upper hand of me for the moment. But I shall return and fetch you. You will come to no harm. I know too much about them for that to happen. Have courage and all will be well."

He turned and made for the door; but as his hand touched the latch Robert called out in a low, grating voice.

"Roger, my hearty, here's your last chance. We've been friends for a long time but I ain't letting you go without a promise."

Sir Roger kept his hand on the latch and his back to the room. His voice was steady when he replied.

162

"For the last time, Robert, understand this. I've finished with you. If you harm as much as a hair on Mary's head I'll deal with you myself.

He lifted the latch and swung back the door, but barely had it opened an inch when there was an explosion like a thunder-clap. A small, black hole suddenly appeared in the back of his jacket and he was flung violently forward, slamming the door to with a crash. He leaned against it for a moment, his fingers scrabbling at the woodwork, then he levered himself around, still on his feet. With an expression of surprise he stared first at Ebenezer and then at Robert.

"By hell, Robert, you've done for yourself now. You'll swing for this."

Slowly he slid down the door, leaving a dark stain on the already dark wood, until at last he was sitting knees-up on the floorboards. A trickle of blood oozed from his lips and gradually his eyes lost their lustre. Mary leaped to go to him but was roughly forced back in the chair by Gronow, who had come up behind her. For a while the only sounds were Mary moaning and Newman blubbering out some kind of incantation. Gronow was the first to break the silence.

"You shouldn't have done that. Now Nicholl will be down on us."

"It's done," replied Robert. "There was no alternative. He'd have bleated and brought men here to get Mary."

"What shall I do with him?" asked Ebenezer, blowing at the still-smoking barrel. "Put him in the chest like the others?"

"Aye. Bury him when it's dark."

"I'll have nothing to do with this," cried Newman, jumping to his feet and wringing his hands. "Nothing, d'you hear? I wasn't party to it. I—"

"Shut up," snarled Robert, "or you'll be the next."

"What about this one?" said Gronow, nodding down at Mary. "You'll have to deal with her now. She'll not keep her mouth shut."

Robert's brow puckered.

"Aye. Mary's going to be a problem. Lock her in her room

163

until I can have a word with her. Now, Mary, if you as much as shout to anybody through the window, so much the worse for you. I like you, m'dear, and I'm sorry about what's happened, but I ain't letting you spoil things now. You've seen how I deal with them that cross me."

Ebenezer and Benjamin picked up Sir Roger's inert body and carried it through the door. After them went Gronow, holding Mary's wrist in a vice-like grip. They went up the stairs and on the landing Mary watched horrified as the two men lifted Sir Roger into the long chest and closed the lid.

"He ain't the first," grinned Ebenezer brushing his hands together, "but I've a feeling he'll be the last for a bit."

Gronow forced Mary into the narrow well of the attic staircase, prodding her upwards until they reached her room. Without a word she bundled her inside and locked the door. Mary heard the key rattling as it was withdrawn from the lock, then she flung herself on the bed and wept for the man who had proposed to her.

CHAPTER 23

FOR AN HOUR Mary lay there, immersed in grief and horror, but also thinking continually about Mathias. Robert's threat of getting a confession out of him could mean only one thing: torture; and so gradually she pulled herself together and considered ways of escaping so that she could summon help. It was too far to the ground to make a rope of bedclothes and in any case she might be seen; then she thought of Gronow's knitting needles and remembered she had needles of her own in the wardrobe drawer. She searched among the clothes and, finding one, used the drawer as a vice to bend the sharp end. She probed in the lock and discovered that the bent part was too long, so she tried again with another needle. This time the bolt slid a little and, by adjusting the angle of the bend and using her full strength she eventually succeeded in withdrawing it completely.

Holding her breath she made her way down the stairwell. At

the bottom she could hear voices in Robert's room, so she tip-toed across the landing, stifling her revulsion as she passed the chest and slowly descended the main staircase, trying each board carefully before putting her full weight on it. Reaching the hall she found the cellar door locked and wondered for a moment whether she should go to the stables, but instead went into the dining room and knelt down by the serving hatch.

"Daniel," she whispered. "Are you there?"

A faint sound like a groan reached her ears, then she heard Mathias's voice.

"Yes, I'm here. Is that you Mary?"

"Yes. They've locked the door but there's a spare key in the kitchen. I'll get it."

She ran to the kitchen, retrieved the key from its hook under the mantel-piece and returned to the cellar door. The key was stiff but turned slowly and she entered the cellar which was lit by a single candle burning on the table. Mathias was sitting in the oak chair, his hands resting on its stout arms. Mary was relieved to see that he was not injured or tied up in any way.

He grinned at her.

"Hullo, Mary. It's good to see you."

"Come, Daniel, we must escape. They've already murdered Sir Roger. They'll be down any moment."

"Easier said than done, I'm afraid. You'll have to help me."

Mary stared at him, wondering why he did not get to his feet and rush with her out of the cellar: then something about his immobility struck her as strange, so she moved nearer to have a closer look. Suddenly, with a shock of horror, she saw that his hands had been nailed to the arms of the chair. In the flickering light of the candle she could just make out the rusty tops protruding above the skin. Her stomach turned to jelly.

"Oh, my God! What have they done to you?"

She knelt in front of him, petrified at the sight of the congealed blood on his hands and the wood of the chair.

"Don't be alarmed," said Mathias cheerfully. "I've lost all sense of pain. I can't move, that's all."

"What can I do?"

165

"There's a pincers in the table drawer that I use to draw bungs. Do you think you could use it ?"

"But I'll hurt you."

"Not if you use a bung as a base to lever. Then I won't feel a thing. If you can get one nail out I'll manage the other."

Feeling ill about what she had to do Mary found the pincers and a spare bung about an inch in diameter.

"That'll do," said Mathias coolly. "Put the bung on the wood near my hand and have a go at it."

Mary did as she was told but found that her fingers were trembling. The pincers nearly fell to the floor.

"Keep calm, Mary," said Mathias. "Remember, my hands are numb, so I can't feel anything."

Mary placed the jaws of the pincers around the nail-head and, holding the bung as instructed, tried to wrench it upwards. The nail refused to budge.

"You'll have to use more strength," encouraged Mathias. "Pull sideways. My hand will go with you. Don't worry."

Mary tried again, shutting her eyes as she pulled. The nail bent and appeared to loosen.

"One more go," said Mathias nonchalantly, "and you'll do it."

Almost weeping with anguish Mary pulled again. The nail came away with a rush. She stared petrified at the small jagged black hole in the back of Mathias's hand.

"Oh, Daniel, are you all right ?"

"I'm fine. Give me the pincers and hold the bung for me."

Using his free hand Mathias made quick work of the other nail. He flung the pincers to the floor.

"Now let's see if I can walk. Ebenezer tried the same thing with my feet before the fool realised it was a stone floor. He didn't leave the nail in, fortunately. Ebenezer doesn't like to waste things."

He stood and took a pace forward but stumbled. Mary threw her arms around him and looked down at his boots. The eyelets of one were steadily oozing blood. She struggled to keep calm.

"Take your boot off and let me bandage you. I'll do your hands, too."

166

"No, there's no time. Come, we must hurry."

Supported by Mary he limped up the uneven steps.

"Where shall we go?" asked Mary, breathless with the exertion.

"To Nicholl's place. I'll have to lean on you for a while."

Slowly they made their way across the hall and reached the kitchen. As quietly as possible Mary opened the outer door and they walked out into the cool September evening. It was nearly dark but a new moon cast a pallid light on the bushes.

"Keep to the shadows," said Mathias, "or they'll see us."

They skirted the perimeter but just as they reached the road they heard the inn door burst open and Robert's voice bawling out.

"They're out here somewhere. Get the bastards or you'll answer to me for it."

There was a flash of lanterns and Mathias pulled Mary into the hedge.

"Through here. Quickly."

They stumbled through a gap and went crashing through a plantation of buckthorn. The needle-sharp thorns tore at Mary's flesh but she hardly felt them. Panting, they found a path and went along it, with Mathias hobbling as fast as he could. Suddenly he slowed down.

"Not so fast. If we make too much noise they'll find us. Walk quietly and they won't know where to look."

Holding on to each other, with Mary's arm tight around Mathias's waist, they picked their way around the obstacles of tree or bush, and eventually came to a fork in the path.

"Which way?" whispered Mary.

"I'm not sure. Let's try the left one."

The route they chose was a narrow one with many twists and bends. After a while they stopped and listened. They could still hear shouting but now it was further away.

"We're losing them," said Mathias cheerfully.

They went on for several minutes until Mary noticed that the vegetation was getting sparser and that they were walking on sandy soil.

"We've missed the house. We must be near the dunes."

"Then we'd better rest—till daylight. It's no good blundering around here in the dark. There are too many nasty places to fall into. We'll just go a little further."

Suddenly the lane ended in a clearing surrounded by gorse, brambles and elderberry trees. They listened once more but now the only sound was the murmuring of the sea.

"I think we've shaken them off," said Mathias.

"Then I'll bind your hands."

"There's no need. They've stopped bleeding."

"You mustn't get dirt on them. It won't take a moment."

She reached down, pulled up her dress and tore a long strip off her petticoat. As gently as she could, still feeling weak at the sight of the wounds, she bound first one hand and then the other.

"You won't have a petticoat left," said Mathias, grinning.

"It doesn't matter. What shall I do about your foot?"

"Leave it. It's best to leave the boot on."

"Then let's find a place to hide."

They pushed their way through the nearest line of bushes and found themselves in the middle of a small rabbit warren. Without a word Mary knelt and began scooping away the sand between the holes. In a short while she had made a shallow trench.

"What's that for?" asked Mathias.

"For you to lie in. I shall cover you with branches."

"What about you?"

"I shall lie beside you."

Obediently Mathias levered himself into the trench, groaning as he stretched out one leg. Mary broke off several branches from the nearest elderberry tree and placed them beside the trench. She climbed in beside him and drew the branches over the lower part of their bodies.

"There! They won't find us now. We'll rest until you get your strength back." She slid one arm under his head to protect it from the sand and Mathias gave a contented sigh.

"Thank you. You're a marvellous girl."

"Nonsense! Now you must sleep. You've lost a lot of blood."

"I don't feel like sleep. I'd rather talk to you. There are many things I want to know."

"No. Later. They might hear us."

"There's no one near. And don't worry about me. I feel fine. Tell me, Mary, how did they kill Sir Roger?"

"They shot him. Ebenezer fired the pistol but Cap Coch gave the order."

"I'm sorry. Were you there when it happened?"

"Yes."

"Did you love him?"

"No. I didn't love him."

"But he wanted to marry you."

"Yes."

Mathias settled his head more comfortably in the crook of Mary's arm.

"Did they ill treat you in any way?"

"No. They locked me in my room. Robert wanted me to give evidence against you—because I saw you with a spade."

She felt his eyes boring into her in the darkness.

"When did you see me with a spade?"

"I was in the kitchen getting some water. I saw you in the bushes and like a fool I told Parson Newman. Forgive me, Daniel, I didn't know he was in league with them. They were going to prove that you were a murderer."

"You weren't to know about Newman. Few people did. You must have thought I was in with them as well."

"I didn't know what to think. What were you doing with a spade, Daniel?"

"Trying to find out where they'd buried Eurig Jones and the others. Nicholl asked me to do it."

Mary suppressed a sigh of relief. The long, lingering doubt was at last at an end, only to be replaced by curiosity.

"Why? Are you a servant of his?"

"No—not really. I'd promised to help him get rid of Cap Coch. That's why they were torturing me—to find out how much I knew, not to admit to murder. That would have come later."

"And thanks to me you were nearly killed."

"But thanks to you I'm here now, so don't reproach yourself."

Mary tried to digest the new information.

169

"This John Nicholl. Cap Coch kept referring to him as a colonel. Is he a colonel?"

"An honorary one. He uses the rank for recruiting and to do official business—such as when he came to the inn. He's a lawyer, really, a King's Counsel."

"But what he asked you to do was dangerous. Why did you agree to do it?"

"Somebody had to. Cap Coch's got away with things for too long. Why are you so interested in Nicholl?"

Mary took a deep breath.

"Because he's the same man I saw riding on a white horse in the funeral."

A long silence indicated Mathias's incredulity.

"You must be mistaken, Mary. You probably saw him before that—in civilian clothes quite likely, and got confused."

"No Daniel, I'm not confused. It was the same man. There's no doubt about it. I didn't know until I saw him at the inn, then I was sure."

Mathias's head settled back again.

"Well, I can't say I'm surprised, really, the more I think about it. That inn has a peculiar effect on people. The sooner it's closed down the better."

"Then go to sleep now and in the morning we'll go to Colonel Nicholl and tell him everything that's happened."

"It's no use, Mary. I can't sleep. I've told you, I'd rather talk to you. Anyway, it's not often I get the chance to lie down beside you. I'm enjoying myself."

"Hush."

"I won't hush. Tell me, Mary, when you say your prayers do you ever thank God for your beauty?"

She stared at him, afraid that his suffering had made his mind wander.

"No, I've never done that. I've never considered myself beautiful enough."

"Well you ought to. All beautiful people ought to thank God for their gift, just as other people with gifts should, too. You know—intelligence, wisdom, skills—"

"Daniel, please! You must rest."

He ignored the entreaty with a wave of a bandaged hand.

"Of course, beauty on its own isn't enough. There must be other things as well to make a person truly beautiful, such as kindness, gentleness, compassion, courage—especially courage. You've got courage in abundance, Mary."

"Pooh! That's the last thing I have. If only you knew how frightened I've been in that place."

"I know. I've been watching you. You've endured things that would have crushed a normal woman—the death of your family, the wreck at Sker, finding McGregor's body, and now the murder of Sir Roger. The wonder is you've not run away. You've come through it all. That takes courage, Mary, more than most people have."

"Well, if I ever had any it's all gone now. I couldn't stand it any more."

"I don't wonder. Mary, there are some things I can't tell you yet—later, but not now. But I can tell you this: ever since you came to the inn I've tried to look after you. You didn't know that, did you, but I have. Not perfectly, but I tried. I wanted no harm to befall you."

"Thank you, Daniel. That was kind of you."

"You didn't like me at first, did you? Do you remember the day we met? You fell backwards in the tumbril."

"Yes, and you laughed at me. I hated you then."

"But you don't hate me now, do you? I've made up for it, haven't I?"

"Yes, you have. Of course I don't hate you."

He reached up and stroked her hair, ruffling it slightly because of the bandage.

"It's difficult to say certain things, especially when you're talking to a person who has all the attributes I mentioned. It gives one a sense of inferiority. You see, when a woman is beautiful and brave, kind and thoughtful, intelligent and modest, a man must choose his words carefully, otherwise he may sound foolish and insincere. But when that woman has saved his life,

171

rightly or wrongly he is privileged, and I shall take advantage of that privilege. Turn your head a little so that I can see you better."

Mary turned her head, certain now that Mathias was delirious.

"I can't see the colour of your eyes," he went on, "but I can see the outline of your face. And I can't feel your hair because of this damned bandage—I'm sorry, I mean petticoat—but I can feel your body close to mine. And that's what I'd like more than anything in life, Mary—always to feel your body close to mine."

Mary held her breath.

"Please, Daniel. You'll be better in the morning and—"

"I'm better now. I love you, Mary. You have that effect on all men, and many must have told you that, but no one's watched over you as I have and come to admire you so much. I'll love you for the rest of my life. Will you marry me?"

Mary lowered her head on his shoulder, suddenly afraid. She remembered Sir Roger's proposal and his fate at the hands of the men at the inn.

"You must rest. We'll talk about it tomorrow."

"No. I want to know now." He went on stroking her hair. "Please, Mary, will you?"

Suddenly, startlingly, a curlew called, its plaintive cry in sharp contrast with the deeper note of the sea, yet blending with it. In spite of all that had happened a feeling of serenity stole over Mary. Out there in the open she felt safe with Mathias, injured though he was, and already the inn seemed to belong to another world. Slowly the serenity was replaced by a feeling of excitement, for deep in her heart she knew what her answer must be, and had known for a long time. Gently she arrested Mathias's hand and held it to her cheek.

"Then I will, for I've come to love you too."

He sighed, closed his eyes and settled into a more comfortable position. He muttered something that sounded vaguely like 'thank you' and within seconds appeared to be asleep. Without moving her arm Mary turned her head so that she could see the stars. Gradually and inexorably her arm became numb, but she kept it around his head until the first light of dawn showed above the trees.

CHAPTER 24

MARY WOKE WITH a start, certain that she had heard voices. It was light and she could see Daniel's face plainly. He had been asleep most of the time although occasionally he had groaned as the pain of his wounds pierced his sub-consciousness; but now his sleep was deep, the breathing regular and even. Making sure she did not disturb him she withdrew her arm from under his head, wincing with pain as the blood re-commenced flowing in the numb limb. Silently she climbed out of the trench and went to the edge of the thicket.

Again she heard voices, coming from somewhere on the other side of the clearing. Using the bushes as cover she walked towards the sounds, but as the trees thinned she froze into immobility. Fifty paces away, coming towards her, was Ebenezer, stabbing into the bushes with a long, pointed stick. To his left was another man and on a nearby hillock yet another. Cap Coch had sent out a search party.

Without hesitation Mary moved quickly and silently to the next grove, then walked towards the men, giving them little chance of seeing where she had come from until the last moment, for her only thought was to prevent them discovering Daniel's hiding place. She was almost upon Ebenezer before he realised she was there. He stared at her with blood-shot eyes.

"So it's you. Where did you spring from?"

Mary ignored him so he blocked her progress with the stick.

"Where's Mathias?"

"Out of your reach. He's gone to Colonel Nicholl."

"You're lying. He's out here somewhere with you."

"Then search. You won't find him."

Ebenezer studied her, doubt all over his ugly face. Suddenly he called out.

"Over here, Jake, and bring the others with you. I've found the girl."

The man called Jake came up to them and quickly four or five others gathered around, one of them Benjamin, wearing an old sack over his shoulders.

"She says Mathias has gone to Nicholl," said Ebenezer. "I think she's lying."

"Why?" asked Jake. "We ain't found him, have we? If he's gone to Nicholl I'm off. I ain't staying here with things getting as hot as they are."

"Me neither," said another. "I got a family in Bettws, anyway."

"Stay," shouted Ebenezer in a voice loud enough to make Mary afraid Daniel would hear. "You go now and that'll be the end of you around these parts. Cap Coch'll see to that."

"Go to hell," said Jake and trudged off through the trees, quickly followed by the other dissenter. Ebenezer looked dubiously at Mary.

"If she's telling the truth it don't look good. Anyway, we can't search this bloody warren any more. We'll take her to the inn. Walk in front of us, girl, and no nonsense or you'll be for it."

He pushed Mary up the path and he and the others fell into step behind her. Her fear of what lay ahead was overcome by elation at leading them away from the hiding place, but as they came within sight of the inn dread again seized her. Her only hope was that Daniel would wake, realise what had happened and summon help, and she prayed that it would be soon. As they reached the road Ebenezer took the precaution of grasping her arm and pulling her roughly round the side of the inn and in through the kitchen door. The fire, which Mary had never before seen out, was extinguished. They went through the hall to the dining room where they found Robert, sitting in front of an equally cheerless hearth. He looked up as they entered, a lack-lustre expression on his face.

"We've got the girl," announced Ebenezer, "but we can't find Mathias."

"A pity," said Robert, "but Mary's a help. Where's Mathias, Mary?"

"She says he's gone to Nicholl," said Ebenezer. "If he has we'd best look out."

174

"Mary," said Robert, "it's a pity you've been a thorn in my side, for I wish you no harm, but you've been shielding a murderer."

"Daniel's no murderer," cried Mary. "You are. You and your gang."

"Come, come, now, no temper."

"And you tortured him. I won't forgive you for that. I pray you'll get what you deserve."

"Ebenezer," said Robert reproachfully, "have you been too hard on Mathias?"

"He wouldn't talk. I couldn't get anything out of him."

"Then it's his fault, ain't it?"

"What are we going to do with her?" asked Ebenezer. "She won't testify, I'm sure of that."

"We'll see."

"But what if Nicholl comes here?"

"What if he does? There's no evidence that I know of, is there? And if he brings Mathias Mary'll see her way to telling the truth. If not she ain't a proper Methody."

"I don't like it," said Ebenezer. "Two of the men've gone already, and this one's thinking about it. It's best we clear out for a bit."

"What, and make it look as though we're the guilty party! Not on your life, Ebenezer. I take it you and Benjamin ain't thinking of leaving yet awhile."

"We've not let you down so far, have we?"

"No, you're good lads. Stick by me as you did before Nicholl came here and we'll soon be out of the wood. Now, then, I've got a spot of checking to do before he gets here. Don't let Mary get away like last time. Stay with her in this room and don't let her out of your sight, even if she wants to go to the privy."

He rose and went out of the room, taking the third man with him. Ebenezer immediately sat down on a chair by the door and Benjamin did likewise by the window. Mary glared disdainfully at the both of them then perched herself on the edge of the settle. No one spoke and the only noise was Benjamin taking out a pistol and blowing down the barrel, a task that occupied him for

175

about ten minutes, after which he got bored and replaced the pistol. Mary remained on the settle, ignoring them.

Robert was away for an hour, and when he returned he seemed cheerful.

"All's well, lads. Nothing to worry about. Nicholl can come any time he likes now and bring that bastard Mathias with him. We'll have it out on the spot with Mary here and there'll be an end to it. Benjamin, go and get me some brandy."

Benjamin obediently got to his feet, but as he reached the door they heard the sound of horses clattering over the bridge.

"Leave it," ordered Robert. "They're here. Keep your mouths shut and leave the talking to me. That goes for you, too, Mary."

Mary looked out through the window. From her position on the settle she could see about twenty cavalrymen dismounting on the forecourt and she thought she caught a glimpse of Colonel Nicholl's white horse. A moment later there was a loud banging on the front door and a frightened-looking Gronow came into the room.

"What shall I do? Shall I let them in?"

"Of course, woman," snapped Robert. "And for God's sake look more cheerful. You've got a face as long as a bloody fiddle."

Mary heard the bolts of the front door being pulled and a sound as though of sabres being drawn, followed by a sharp, barked order. Into the dining room strode Colonel Nicholl, followed by a sergeant and a dozen troopers. Without hesitation the soldiers made for Robert and his henchmen. There was a brief struggle and then Mary saw that all three had been manacled. Bellowing loudly Robert tried to wrench his off, but two burly cavalrymen held him fast. The onslaught and the apprehension had taken barely five seconds.

"What's the meaning of this?" Robert yelled. "You ain't got any power of arrest that I know of."

Nicholl ignored him. His piercing eyes swept round the room taking in Mary and everything else. A soldier brought in a struggling Gronow.

"I caught her getting out of the back, sir. What shall I do with her?"

176

"Hold her! Sergeant, see to it that all entrances are guarded, then bring in Bevan."

"I demand my rights," ranted Robert. "The right under law of every King's subject to know cause of arrest. I ain't committed murder and you know it."

Nicholl turned his back on him and went up to Mary. He smiled down at her, his stern, forbidding expression temporarily softened.

"I take it you are Mary, the young lady who saw me at a funeral?"

"Yes, sir," said Mary, rising.

"Very interesting. We must speak about that later. In the meantime I have a message for you. Daniel is well. He will be here presently."

Mary sank back again on the settle, weak with relief.

"And as for you, Robert," said Nicholl swinging around, "I am aware of your rights. The charge against you is not murder. It is theft."

Suddenly there was a commotion outside and with astonishment Mary heard the bleating of a sheep. Into the room came a bow-legged, be-smocked man carrying a crook, followed immediately by two soldiers dragging a fully grown sheep. Robert stared open-mouthed at the animal.

"Watcyn Bevan," said Nicholl in his cold, dry voice. "Repeat the information you have already laid before me as magistrate."

Nervously Bevan cleared his throat. He glanced at Nicholl but avoided the gaze of Robert then began speaking in a low voice. To Mary he seemed to be reciting a well-rehearsed speech.

"Yesterday, your honour, I missed one of my sheep. I searched for it everywhere but could not find it. Then, acting on information received I came to this place and found it here, tethered at the back of this inn. I examined the sheep and found it to be mine—my master's that is."

"There's no doubt the sheep is your master's, Bevan? You examined it carefully?"

"I did, your honour. No doubt at all. It's got my master's markings on it and anyway I recognise it."

177

"And was it tethered outside this inn?"

"Yes, sir."

"But the rope around its neck is not yours?"

"No, sir. Never seen the rope before."

"Now wait a minute," shouted Robert. "Watcyn Bevan here is Lord Carne's man, and he's got it in for me. I've stolen no sheep and you know it. How much've they paid you to lay this charge, Watcyn?"

Bevan stared uneasily down at the floor.

"Watcyn!" Robert went on. "Ain't I been kind to you in the past? Didn't I help you get a strip of land a year or two ago? Is this how you repay me now—with false evidence? And you, Mary—you remember how I saved you from Carne. Ain't you got a word for me?"

"Enough!" roared Nicholl. "Now then, Bevan, who gave you information that the sheep had been brought here?"

"My wife, sir. She saw him take it." He pointed at the inn-keeper.

"And are you prepared to testify that it is so in court?"

"We are, sir."

Robert, his face livid, struggled to get at Bevan and it took two more troopers to restrain him.

"I'll get you for this, Bevan," he shouted, "and you, too, Nicholl. You ain't trumping me with a charge like this. I'll—"

Nicholl's cold voice cut him short.

"The charge is one of theft, the stealing of a sheep, the penalty for which is hanging by the neck until you are dead. You will be incarcerated in the House of Correction at Cowbridge pending trial. Take him away."

For a moment Mary was afraid Robert would break his manacles, and it took the full strength of the four soldiers to drag him from the room. Ebenezer and Benjamin, after grimacing at each other, went quietly, followed by a weeping Gronow. Through the window Mary saw a dozen soldiers mounting and then heard the rumble of a cart. She had a brief glimpse of the inn's tumbril with the four conspirators in it before Nicholl

178

blocked her view. He bent forward and stared out at the forecourt, turning only when the noise of cart and horses had died away.

"There goes a villain, young lady. If stealing a sheep is the only way we'll get him, so be it."

Mary tried to smile. It needed little intelligence to guess that the charge had been fabricated and the memory of the incident with the pig flooded back to her; but now it was out of her hands, a matter for the law. Of more immediate concern was the whereabouts of Daniel. Nicholl seemed to sense her thoughts.

"Well, Mary, by my reckoning Daniel will be here within the hour. I insisted he had proper treatment for his wounds, so be patient a little while longer. He is as anxious to see you as you are to see him. He has told me a great deal about you. If only half of what I hear is true I ought to enlist you in the militia. You'd make a good soldier."

He laughed and was about to say something more when they heard the sound of a horse.

"'Pon my soul," said Nicholl, "I believe it's he now. He's even more anxious than I thought."

Mary ran to the window but saw only a rider-less, untethered horse which a soldier was trying to catch. Then the door opened and in came Daniel, swathed in clean bandages and wearing a felt slipper on his injured foot. In two paces he was across the room and had Mary in his arms. Nicholl turned again to the window and contemplated the view.

"How are you, Mary?" asked Mathias when he had got his breath back.

"I'm well. How are you?"

"Fine. Never felt better. You won't go back on your word, will you?"

"What word?"

"That you'll marry me."

"I never go back on my word."

He picked her up and swung her round several times.

"Put me down," cried Mary. "You'll hurt yourself. Your hands—"

179

"To hell with my hands. Who cares about hands? I'll make you the best husband in the world, see if I don't."

There was a discreet cough behind them.

"I don't want to intrude," said Nicholl, "but if marriage is in the air, as I believe it is, then I must warn you that it has legal as well as romantic implications. My congratulations, of course, but I believe it my duty to introduce you properly. Mary, allow me to introduce your future husband—Lieutenant Mathews of His Majesty's Customs and Excise."

Mary stared at him.

"Lieutenant Mathews?"

"I'm sorry," said Daniel from behind her. "I couldn't tell you before—I had orders to tell no one."

"Quite right," said Nicholl. "He's been here for two years keeping an eye on those rogues. A very dangerous assignment. But thanks to him we've the names of every smuggler between Newton and Nash. So you must forgive the subterfuge, Mary."

"It's still Daniel, though," said Daniel hopefully. "That hasn't changed."

"Dammit, woman," said Nicholl, his eyes twinkling. "What difference does it make. He's the same man underneath, ain't he? Tell him you'll marry him and have done with it."

Mary did not know whether to laugh or cry. Her attempt at controlling her emotions merely resulted in her eyes moistening, which set Nicholl off again.

"'Pon my soul. You don't know where you are with women. They cry when they're happy and laugh when they're sad. Never know when to make up their minds. Not good soldier material after all. Kiss her Mathews and make it up for her."

Shyly Daniel stepped forward and kissed her on the lips. Mary hesitated for a moment then placed her arms around his neck, and the kiss became a very long-drawn-out affair, terminated only when a cough from Nicholl indicated that his patience had finally come to an end.

CHAPTER 25

AFTER NICHOLL HAD departed for Cowbridge to supervise the incarceration of Cap Coch and his gang, Mary and Daniel breakfasted together in the small dining room. Not having eaten for so long they were ravenous and did full justice to a meal of bread, cheese and honey, washed down, at Daniel's suggestion, with a bottle of Robert's best claret. Although happy they spoke little for events and the impact of love had made them thoughtful; moreover Daniel knew that the inn had not yet revealed its final secret so, as soon as they had finished eating, whilst contriving to sound light-hearted and casual, he said:

"You mustn't stay here now, Mary. I've engaged a room for you at the Wyndham Arms. I'll get a soldier to take you in the trap."

"What will you do?"

"I must stay on here for a few days. There are several things to attend to. The place must be closed down pending the result of the trial."

"Then I shall stay with you. Those bandages will need changing before long."

"I shall be all right. I'll come and visit you every evening."

"No, Daniel. I'm not leaving you, if it's only to see that you eat properly. You're still weak after what's happened and tonight I shall cook a decent supper for you. Davies isn't here but I know where everything is in the kitchen."

"But this place isn't good for you. The sooner you're out of it the better."

"It's not so frightening now that Cap Coch and the others have gone. Thank you for engaging a room for me but I shan't leave until you do."

Daniel smiled, secretly pleased at her determination to look after him.

"Very well. I see I can't convince you. Anyway, it will be

181

perfectly safe here now. There'll be about a dozen troopers bivouacing in the orchard."

"Then we are indeed protected. Where will you sleep, Daniel ?"

"In the stable. I've got quite attached to the place."

"But you'll leave as soon as you can, won't you ?"

"Of course, and take you with me." He reached out and held her hand. "But if I allow you to stay you must do one thing. I want you to go to your room and remain there until I call you. Will you promise me that ?"

"Yes, if you wish. But why ?"

"There may be things I don't want you to see."

"What sort of things ?"

"I don't know yet."

"Is there any danger ? For you, I mean."

"Of course not, otherwise I'd pack you off now."

She studied him, tempted to press him further, but thought the better of it.

"Very well. If I didn't think you were serious I'd come to the conclusion that you were trying to get rid of me. Anyway, I don't really mind. I have several things to see to myself."

Still holding hands they went into the hall. There the sergeant was waiting. He saluted.

"The men are ready, sir."

"Thank you, sergeant," said Daniel. "Now, young lady, to your room and don't stir until I come and fetch you."

Obediently Mary ran upstairs, secretly pleased to have some time to herself. Discovering that Daniel was an officer and not an ostler had been a shock and presented certain problems. One day, she knew, she would meet his parents and must be dressed appropriately. From then on she would have to lead the life of a lady in a higher position than she had expected and be prepared to entertain other officers and their wives. There could even be balls and banquets, taxing her knowledge of etiquette. It was a great and sudden change from being a serving maid and she had no doubt that some who knew her background would disapprove of her. But she would meet that when it came and she knew that, whatever the future held in store, her main task in life from then on was to make Daniel happy and, God willing, to bear his children. The thought of God suddenly made her remember Daniel's words about her beauty and so she knelt by her bed and said a prayer of thanks for the good fortune that had befallen her.

Her prayer over, she examined the contents of her wardrobe. Except for the dress Sir Roger had given her and the best home-spun cotton frock, which she knew made her look attractive, she was badly off for clothes. Her serving dresses could now be discarded, along with a collection of aprons and most of her shoes which had seen better days. The sooner she got down to making new clothes of materials she had fancied in Bridgend the better, and a new bonnet would not come amiss either. The only item she had doubt about was the shawl Robert had given her, and she decided to ask Daniel's advice about whether to keep it or not.

She had got as far as examining her underwear when suddenly she became aware of voices in the forecourt. She looked through the window and saw that a small group of people, some of whom she knew, had gathered near the roadway. They were being kept back by two soldiers and all were staring at the inn and talking animatedly. As she watched some women joined the throng and they, too, stared at the inn, or at something at the side of it, with expressions of intense interest. Mary shrugged, remembering Daniel's request that she should stay in her room and, whatever was causing the crowd to collect, she intended carrying out his wishes. Marriage vows embraced obedience as well as love and she intended to start as she meant to go on, so she returned to her underwear and began sorting out the acceptable from the unacceptable.

But after half an hour's work the noise outside had gradually increased in volume until now it was a constant, buzzing hubbub. She looked out again to see that many more people had con-gregated, including several horsemen and a stage coach full of gawking passengers. As before everyone, not least the two soldiers, had their eyes riveted upon the inn. Torn by curiosity Mary's resolve wilted. Surely she thought, if people were watch-ing something of such absorbing interest Daniel would not mind if she had a peep, too. In any case, whatever was intriguing the crowd was now public knowledge and she saw no reason why she should be excluded. She placed the underwear on the bed and went downstairs.

In the hall she noticed that the front door was still bolted so she made for the kitchen, intending to go through it to the yard. She pushed open the door but found that it moved only a few inches, so she pushed harder and was suddenly confronted by a red-faced, tunic-less soldier. He stared at her in surprise.

"What d'you want, miss ?"

But Mary was looking beyond him, at a sight she was never to forget. The kitchen, which she knew so well, was unrecognisable. Every flagstone had been pulled up and lay stacked in a neat row against the opposite wall. Five or six shirt-sleeved soldiers were toiling with spades, digging out the earth and throwing it on a central pile. In one place they had excavated a trench the entire length of the kitchen and in it, still encrusted with lime, were two skeletons. On a mound of earth, looking like a recumbent scarecrow, was the remains of a body, the flesh of its face and hands half rotted away. To complete the macabre picture a skull lay on the hob where the kettle usually rested and, even as Mary watched, two soldiers hoisted pieces of a decomposed carcase out of a hole. She stepped back, aghast.

"You can't come in here, miss," said the trooper superfluously. "Lieutenant Mathews's orders."

Frantically Mary searched for her handkerchief and held it to her nose, for the stench was unbearable. With mounting horror she remembered the many hours she had spent with Davies in the kitchen, gossiping and surrounded by the pleasant odours of cooking and all that time what she had just seen must have lain beneath their feet. She ran to the front door, tore back the bolts and stood outside, gulping in the fresh, life-giving air.

But barely had she recovered when a sudden movement in the crowd made her look up. Some of the spectators were pressing forward, making it difficult for the soldiers to restrain them, but all eyes were still riveted on something at the side of the building. Still feeling faint Mary walked to the corner of the inn and peered

184

around it. The sight that met her eyes was as frightening as that in the kitchen.

In the enclosure between the bushes and the inn, and in the orchard beyond, soldiers and civilians were digging furiously. Some of the piles of earth they had excavated were small, as though they had started a hole and then given up, but other mounds were large and near many was either a skeleton or a tattered, grotesque, figure, ominously still. It looked for all the world like a vast graveyard where the grave-diggers had gone berserk. On a cart near the bushes was a pile of thin pauper coffins and canvas sheets such as those used to bury drowned sailors.

Then Daniel saw her. He hurried up to her, a look of concern on his face.

"Mary! I told you to stay in your room. Why didn't you?"

"I saw the people watching. I didn't know what was going on, so I came to look."

He put his arm around her.

"I should have insisted upon you going to Bridgend, then you wouldn't have seen this."

"What's happening, Daniel? Have all those—those people been found here?"

"I'm afraid so. We've dug up about thirty so far, including six in the kitchen. All Cap Coch's victims."

"What will happen to them?"

"They'll be re-buried I suppose. I don't know where. Paupers' graves mainly, I expect. Most of them are unrecognisable, so there can't be any identification. Some of them must have been there for years I'd say. We've found Eurig Jones, though. sent word to Colonel Nicholl."

As he spoke a commotion in the crowd made them look up. The ranks of people parted to make way for a group of soberly-dressed men carrying a coffin made of light oak. With grim faces they passed within a yard of them and made for a mound at the far end of the orchard. They placed the coffin near the newly-turned earth and one of their number removed the lid and took out a shroud. They knelt near the stout, recumbent figure of a partially-clothed man and, after a few minutes, placed the body in the coffin. Watched by the other diggers, who had stopped work as a mark of respect, the lid was screwed down. Amid a murmuring of 'amens' the men re-shouldered their burden and retraced their route to the front of the inn.

"Eurig Jones," breathed Daniel as the group passed.

Suddenly, splitting the silence that had descended on the whole area, there was a clattering of hooves and Colonel Nicholl came riding across the forecourt on his white horse. He stopped by the door of the inn and waited for the men to come up to him, the horse pawing impatiently at the gravel. When they reached him they placed the coffin on the ground and re-arranged themselves according to height for the march that lay ahead. Other men detached themselves from the crowd and joined them, forming a procession four abreast. When everything seemed ready Nicholl gave a signal and the men shouldered the coffin; a further signal and the leading file moved off. Slowly the line made its way to the road, Nicholl taking up a position at the rear. Daniel's grip on Mary's shoulder tightened.

"You've seen that before, haven't you?"

"Yes."

"And it's taking the same route you described, isn't it?"

"Yes."

Fascinated Mary watched the retreating procession. She could see the coffin bobbing on the shoulders of the bearers, hidden occasionally from view by the tall, upright figure of Colonel Nicholl and the swaying hind-quarters of his horse. Every detail was as it had been in the other, previous funeral. Suddenly she leaned heavily against Daniel.

"I'm sorry, Daniel. I can't stay here any longer. Will you take me to Bridgend, please?"

"Yes, of course. I understand."

He beckoned a soldier and ordered him to get the trap. When it arrived he helped her into the seat.

"Go now. Don't delay. The trooper will see you safely to the hotel. I'll pack your things and bring them to you tonight."

Mary nodded and the trap lurched away, swirling the leaves

on the forecourt. The crowd parted for it, staring curiously at its occupants, then they were bumping over the bridge. Before rounding the corner that led up the hill Mary glanced back and saw that men were digging even as far as the river bank. Suddenly she thought of Sir Roger and of her brief encounters with him, and a vision of his eager face when he had proposed came to her, superseded almost immediately by his sad expression when she had declined to ride back from Sker with him the day after the wreck. Then she remembered their walk on Ogmore beach and the shy way he had held her arm, and how he had slid down the door after he had been shot, staining it with his blood. She had wept enough in that place but she could not prevent the tears coming again.

CHAPTER 26

DANIEL ESTABLISHED Mary in the Wyndham Arms and gave her money to buy dresses, insisting that she made no more of her own until they were married. She found it strange staying at the hostelry, waited upon hand and foot, her slightest whim granted at the touch of a bell pull, in great contrast with her previous mode of life. She bought a book entitled 'The Art of Genteel Living' and studied it avidly; and carefully observed the mannerisms of the well-to-do ladies who frequented the establishment.

Daniel visited her every evening, bringing news from Merthyr Mawr and Cowbridge. Parson Newman, he informed her, had disappeared, no doubt afraid that his complicity in smuggling would be discovered, as had a few local men known to be members of Cap Coch's gang. The bodies unearthed at the inn were being buried, as found, in paupers' graves, the yard and the orchard having yielded about sixty so far. Of Sir Roger there was still no sign, and Daniel voiced his opinion that he would never be found. Orders had also been received that the inn was to be pulled down when the last body had been recovered, thus ensuring that all trace of its notoriety would be obliterated.

The trial of Cap Coch was arranged with great speed, its date coinciding with the announcement that John Nicholl had received a knighthood, granted for loyal service to the legal profession. Sir John, as he quickly became known, was therefore anxious to return as quickly as possible to London to undertake his duties as Member of Parliament and to receive the further honour of being appointed Privy Councillor, but was loath to do so until the innkeeper had been well and truly put below ground and the Merthyr Mawr area made safe. It was no secret that he was bringing heavy pressure on the magistrates to complete the trial as quickly as possible, and to that end the original charge of sheep-stealing was retained rather than one of murder, which would entail lengthy litigation and irrefutable proof. Watcyn Bevan was duly produced in court, his statement made under oath, and judgment passed. Robert was sentenced to hanging without even mention of a corpse. Benjamin and Ebenezer were given transportation for life on a charge of complicity and Gronow, after the prosecutor had demanded death by boiling, received five years imprisonment with an annual appearance in the stocks. From start to finish the arraignment had taken no more than a quarter of an hour.

Knowing that Robert was still popular with many local people because of his acts of generosity, a rumour was then deliberately started by the clerk of the court that the hanging would take place at Groes Gibbet, whereas in fact arrangements were made to complete the course of justice at Stalling Down, a hill-top near Cowbridge. Few people were privy to this at the start but Daniel, conscious of his previous deception, told Mary, who was grateful for the trust shown in her.

On the day of the hanging Daniel appeared early at the Wyndham Arms dressed in the full uniform of an excise officer. It was the first time Mary had seen him so attired and her first reaction was to wish that her father was alive to witness her pride and joy in being loved by such a man; and her second was to fall even more deeply in love and hope that the day of marriage was not too distant so that she could prove with body and soul the depth of her love. But before that happy occasion could arise there were other, more pressing, matters to attend to, principally Daniel's unpleasant task of attending Robert's execution and afterwards meeting his wife at the New Inn, from which she had obtained permission to remove her husband's personal effects. An inventory then had to be made of the inn's furniture and fitments, which had to be sold to defray the cost of the trial. It was this latter imposition that depressed Daniel most of all, for he had no wish to meet a hanged man's wife, especially Cap Coch's, so Mary hit upon the idea of travelling with him to Merthyr Mawr, ostensibly to see Davies, the cook, who was now without work, but actually to keep him company on such a harrowing assignment. Daniel seized upon the suggestion eagerly, with the proviso that on no account should Mary enter the inn, and departed for Cowbridge in a happier frame of mind.

He was back by mid afternoon, grim-faced and serious, with no appetite for a meal. Mary's now sharply-developed intuition told her that it could have been no easy matter to witness the judicial killing of a man they had both worked for, so she said little; but after they had been for a leisurely walk along the river bank and returned for tea she adjudged it time to elicit a few details.

"Was it carried out properly, Daniel?"

"Yes. There was no trouble."

"Were there many people there?"

"More than I thought there'd be. Word got round."

"So it's all over."

"All over. He's properly dead. I saw him swing. They'll bury him in lime."

"It must have been horrible, in spite of what he'd done."

"It's strange. Knowing what he was I wanted him hanged but at the last minute I couldn't look. It's a funny thing, death. You forget a man's villainy and remember his good points. When he thought I was just an ostler with no work he gave me a job. I can't forget that."

Mary took Daniel's hand.

"Don't reproach yourself. He was good to me, too, but he was evil. Remember what the soldiers found."

He squeezed her hand.

"You're marvellous. A few words and you make me feel better. I don't know what I'd do without you. I'll see his wife tonight and then there'll be an end to it. We'll never see the New Inn again. We must leave soon."

He fetched Poppy and the trap, which he was allowed to use pending the sale of the inn's chattels, and they set off for Merthyr Mawr. It was a fine, late autumnal afternoon, with just a hint of cold, and they made good time until they reached the cross roads. There Daniel jumped out and handed Mary the reins.

"You go on to the village and I'll walk to the inn. Give me an hour—no longer or it'll be getting dark. Here, give this to Davies with our best wishes."

He reached into his breast pocket and took out a sovereign. Mary leaned over and kissed him.

"You're a thoughtful, generous man. I love you."

Daniel smiled, the first time that day, and started off down the little leaf-strewn hill.

"Don't forget," he shouted over his shoulder. "Don't come into the inn. Wait for me by the bridge."

Mary jerked the reins and within five minutes was outside Davies's cottage. The cook heard the wheels and ran to meet her, then insisted upon giving her mint tea and Welsh cakes. Davies was full of news of recent events, some of it factual, some gossip. She told Mary that many villagers had gone to Groes Gibbet that morning hoping to see the hanging, and some were furious at being cheated of the final spectacle. After expressing horror that she and Mary had spent so much time in the inn's kitchen without knowing what lay beneath their feet, she re-iterated Daniel's view that the body of Sir Roger would never be found. The rumour was, she said, that Cap Coch, out of spleen or fear, or because it was the only murder actually wit-nessed, had buried him somewhere on the dunes, probably near Candleston Castle itself. Jenkins, Sir Roger's servant, was still in the building for he had nowhere to go else, but the death of his master had affected him so greatly that it was feared he had not long to live. Within a few years, Davies averred, the place would be little more than an unrestorable ruin. From that she turned to the subject of Mary's forthcoming marriage, which was now common knowledge, stating that she had known all along that Daniel was something more than an ostler.

"I was sure about it," she cried. "You could see he was a gentleman. Oh, my dear! I'm so glad you accepted him before you knew he was an officer. That showed you loved him for what he was, don't it? I'm so glad for your sake."

Blushing, Mary concurred, and Davies waxed indignant about the torture inflicted upon Daniel.

"Can you think of anything more cruel than driving nails through a man's hands? If I had my way the whole lot would swing. Are his wounds healing?"

"Yes, thank you. The physician bled him a little to get rid of the infection and is applying wych hazel poultices. He is responding well."

"I'm so glad. Will you have more tea?"

Mary refused and took the opportunity to bring the conversation round to Davies's financial position. She was relieved to hear that the imbecile son had been given a job on the Nicholl estate as a tree feller, work for which he had shown aptitude, and so with his small income and a fair-sized garden mother and son would be able to live in tolerable comfort. Nevertheless, after a token show of resistance, Davies accepted the sovereign and made Mary promise to bring Daniel to see her as soon as he was free from his duties. Then, knowing that her hour was nearly up, Mary begged leave to go.

Davies accompanied her to the trap, pressing a small parcel of Welsh cakes into her hand, and after a farewell that was both happy and tearful Mary sent Poppy clip-clopping back up the lane, and was soon descending the hill leading to the inn. Obeying instructions she pulled in on a grass verge just short of the bridge and settled down to await the arrival of Daniel. It was then that she noticed that it was starting to rain. Praying that it would not continue she pulled her cloak hood over her head.

At that moment she saw that a horse and small cart were waiting outside the door of the inn, and a few minutes later a tall, strongly-built woman appeared, carrying a sack. She placed the sack in the cart and was then joined by two fair-haired stalwart youths, struggling with a chest. Mary recognised it immediately as the one in which Cap Coch had kept his armoury, and so she surmised that the dark woman was the innkeeper's wife, but whether the youths were his sons she did not know. With a start she realised that she knew little about her previous master. He had kept family life completely separate from his inn-keeping duties and so she did not know whether he had been happily married or what was the size of his family. She was only conscious of being sorry for the woman and for the boys, if they were his sons, for they now had to pay in public acrimony for the sins that had been committed.

After tying the chest securely to the low-sided cart all three went back indoors and when they reappeared a soldier was helping the boys carry the large chest that had always been on the landing, the one in which the body of Sir Roger had been placed. Mary averted her eyes, her memory flooding back of the other man who had loved her, and for a moment she wished she had not come. But voices made her look up again and she saw that the woman had mounted the cart and that one of the youths was delightedly twirling a brace of pistols. There was a sharp command from the woman and the pistols were handed to her. Then the boys climbed in and the cart moved off. Soon, thought Mary, Daniel would come, and she would never see the hated place again. To add to her depression the rain came down in a steady drizzle.

She waited in the trap for a further half hour, gradually getting wetter. It was also starting to get dark, and when a small pool of water had gathered in the seat beside her she made up her mind. As much as she hated the inn she would have to go inside for shelter. Daniel had either forgotten the time or was unaware that it was raining, and in any case he would not like it if her new dress was ruined. She flicked the reins and guided Poppy to the spot on the forecourt where the cart had been. Dismounting she ran to the inn and stood just inside the main door, grateful for the comparative warmth and comfort.

"Daniel," she called, but there was no answer. The only noise was the ticking of the grandfather clock in the hall. The door of the large dining room was open and she peeped in. It smelt musty and damp without a fire but there was a chair just inside so she sat on it, safe in the knowledge that three paces would get her outside again if fear overcame her.

The inn remained silent except for the regular tick-tock of the clock, which seemed to coincide with the beating of her heart, making her feel nervous and apprehensive. Surely, she argued with herself, nothing dreadful could happen now. Cap Coch was dead and his confederates under lock and key, so no further harm could befall her. But whilst she was reassuring herself she had a sudden premonition that she was not alone. Someone, she felt sure, was in the small dining room beyond. Holding her breath she listened intently. Not a sound came to her ears but the uneasy feeling that someone was there remained, almost as though she could sense a presence.

"Daniel," she called again, adding, "is there anyone there?"

Her voice sounded sepulchral in the emptiness of the room, but there was no reply. She stood up, went to the front door and looked out. The rain was now slanting down with intensity and it was nearly dark. She had the choice of either returning to the trap and getting soaked or waiting in the hall constantly afraid that someone would come up behind her. Suddenly she made up her mind. She crossed the dining room, boldly pushed open the parlour door and again called out, but without response.

At first she could see little for the room was in almost total darkness, then she saw the bulky figure of a man hunched up on the window seat. Her premonition had been correct all along.

"Who are you?" she demanded angrily.

The figure turned and then, as her eyes finally mastered the gloom, she saw who it was. It was Cap Coch, still wearing the same suit as on the day of his arrest. She opened her mouth to scream but failed, and clutched at the lintel to support a body that had suddenly become icy cold.

"Hullo, m'dear," said Cap Coch cheerfully. "Sorry to startle you. Don't shout. I ain't going to harm you."

Mary struggled to find her voice which, when it came, was high pitched and hysterical.

"What are you doing here? You're dead. You've been hanged. Everybody knows that."

"You're mixing me up," said Cap Coch. "My name's Twch."

Mary shook her head, afraid that her reason was leaving her.

"You're not Twch. You're Cap Coch—Mr. Robert who owned this inn. I'll tell Daniel."

"Wait!" Robert's voice was both peremptory and coaxing. "Don't tell Daniel, leastways not yet. He'll only think you've been seeing things, like that funeral you saw. I tell you again, Mary, I'll not harm you. I ain't never touched a woman."

"But you are Cap Coch. I know it. Oh, God, am I going mad?"

"No, Mary, you ain't mad, but I see it's no good trying to fool you. Everybody thinks I'm dead but I ain't. It's no good you telling anybody that, though. They won't believe you."

"But—"

"I know what you're going to ask. How come I'm alive? Well, Mary, seeing as how I like you and I ain't going to be around for some time I'll tell you. Remember Martin Llewelyn? You met him early on here. He was dispossessed if you remember. I couldn't get his land back so I did the next best thing. I got him a job as assistant hangman at Cowbridge. And bless me, who do you think one of the hangmen turned out to be? Why, none other than Martin Llewelyn, and you know the old saying, Mary: one good turn deserves another. What did that there Martin do but go and put a proper knot in the rope. Not a slip-knot, mind you, but one that wouldn't shift, so although I dangled I wasn't hanged, if you know what I mean. Look, here's the proof."

He stood up and held his neck at an angle. Mary could see an ugly, red weal around his throat.

"There!" said Robert triumphantly. "See what comes of good deeds, Mary? Martin cut me down when the magistrates thought I was a goner. Mind you, I was nearly done for. Two minutes holding the breath ain't conducive to good health, but what's a little hurt compared with a real stringing?"

194

To her amazement Mary found herself becoming angry.

"Good deeds! Who are you to talk of good deeds? What about all those people they found in the yard and the kitchen? You murdered them."

Robert put on a contrite expression.

"Well, now, murder's a comparative word, Mary. Put it down to the times we live in. One day there'll be no poverty, then there'll be no need for the likes of me. But remember this: I did a lot of good. Many's the people I helped—many's grateful to me beside Martin. I ain't a villain entirely so don't judge me too harshly."

"But you killed innocent people. Not once but scores of times."

"I'm sorry about that but these is violent days and violence begets violence—and remember, some of them merchants were misers. I did more good with their money than they did—ask some of the poor and needy around here. Now say no more, and I'll go in peace. If you ever meet me again, m'dear, remember my name's Twch, not Robert, and it ain't no good you saying otherwise or they will think you mad."

He made to push past her but at that moment Mary heard Daniel's voice in the hall. She turned and ran towards it, flinging herself into his arms when she saw him.

"I'm sorry, Mary," Daniel began, "but I was in the stables. I didn't even know it was raining." Then he caught sight of her face. "What's the matter? You look as tho' you've seen a ghost."

Mary fought to get her words out.

"It's Cap Coch! He's still alive. He's in the parlour—he's there now."

Daniel stared at her.

"Keep calm, Mary. That's impossible. I saw him dead myself."

"He's there, Daniel. I tell you I saw him. Come and see for yourself."

She dragged him along, giving him barely time to draw his cutlass. At the door of the parlour she stood back for him to enter, sword at the ready. Still weak with shock she waited, expecting to hear voices or the sound of a struggle; instead there was a short pause and then she heard Daniel's voice.

195

"There's no one here. Come and see for yourself."

She went into the room. Except for Daniel it was empty. There was no sign of Cap Coch. The only sound was the clacking of the casement window as it swung to and fro and the steady hiss of the rain on the forecourt.

CHAPTER 27

MARY AND DANIEL were married at Merthyr Mawr church. It was not Mary's intention to do so but Sir John Nicholl insisted upon giving them a wedding breakfast in his big new house overlooking the river; and on the day of the ceremony she was glad that she had agreed, for the church was a perfect setting for a wedding in spite of the fact that the New Inn was but a mile or two distant, and during the service she thought occasionally of Parson Newman. Afterwards Sir John introduced her to many of the gentry who attended, treating her as though she had come from a county family herself, for which she was grateful; and then capped a happy day by saying that he would personally see to it that Daniel gained promotion as a just reward for his two years of danger at the inn.

After a short honeymoon on the Gower Peninsula Daniel was back at his task of chasing smugglers, so they bought a house in Wick, which was convenient for his jurisdiction over the coast from Ogmore to Barry. His promotion duly arrived and they were able to employ a female servant and purchase a phaeton and a matched pair of sorrel horses, which Mary quickly learned to handle. They remained at Wick for eleven years and in that time produced three children, a boy and two girls, and were completely happy except when the subject of Cap Coch's last appearance cropped up, as it frequently did when they were entertaining Daniel's fellow officers. Incredulous at the time Daniel had closely questioned Martin Llewelyn, who denied any attempt at dereliction of duty, and was adamant that he had placed the body in the authorised lime pit, an assertion difficult

196

to prove. Daniel, Mary knew, had come to the conclusion that what she had seen was a figment of her imagination, the product of an over-wrought mind. He never said so openly but he implied it, a view strengthened as the years went by without further sighting of Cap Coch, either by the authorities or anybody else, and the failure to discover the whereabouts of a man called Twch. Mary knew otherwise but, because she desired harmony in her home, she ceased to labour the point, and in any case wanted to forget everything connected with the New Inn.

Then, in their eleventh year at Wick, Daniel received news that he was to be posted to Bristol and the multitudinous tasks of removing house began. When arrangements were nearly complete Mary realised with a stab of guilt that she had never returned to the scene of the wreck of the troop-ship to lay as much as a flower on the mass grave. The reason she had not done so was that the only direct route to Iron Gate Point passed the New Inn, and she had resolutely refused to go anywhere near there. But now, eleven years later, her fears having receded, she knew she could not leave the region without placing a wreath on that hallowed spot and saying a prayer of thanks for the deliverance of her brother, who was still safe and well. Daniel acceded to her wish and so, although pressure of work prevented him from going, on a fine day in June she made a wreath of roses and carnations picked in the garden and, accompanied by her eldest daughter, ten-year-old Samantha, set off on the journey.

The run as far as Ewenny was pleasant, but as she turned the horses on to Merthyr Mawr road her pulse quickened. Instinctively she urged the pair into a fast trot, keeping them at it even as they descended the hill to the little bridge. There the narrowness of the structure forced her to slow down. Samantha leaned out, crying with delight at the sight of the river, but Mary was determined to go as fast as possible. Then, as she surmounted the hump of the bridge, she saw with a shock that there was no sign of the inn. She had heard that it had been dismantled and expected to see merely a ruin, but now there was nothing except an expanse of blackberry bushes covered with bindweed. Not even the forecourt was visible, and it was as though the building

197

had never been. She slowed the horses to a walking pace and stared open-mouthed.

"Can we stop here, Mama?" shouted Samantha. "It's such a lovely place."

Mary hardly heard her. She was still stunned by the total disappearance of a place that had left such a mark on her, but subconsciously she kept the horses going. At last she replied.

"No, not here. We haven't much time."

Then they were round the bend and going up the tree-lined hill where she had seen the funeral. The trees seemed taller, their topmost branches touching, blotting out the sun's rays entirely. Beautiful place or not Mary was glad when they reached the top and were once more in clear daylight. They sped past the gibbet to the open road, following the route Daniel had taken on the night of the storm, but turned off at a toll road marked 'Newton', which was the easier route for a carriage, the one which Sir Roger had taken. When they came in sight of the sea Samantha demanded to hear again the story of the wreck and of how her papa had found Uncle Jack in the cove. Mary had told the story a hundred times to her children, who never tired of it, especially the part where Mary admitted that it was on that dreadful night that she knew for sure she loved their father. Samantha listened again and caressed the small posy she had made ready to lay on the grave.

A further sign-post indicated the village of Nottage and then they were bumping along an uneven track to the edge of the sea itself. Samantha, who had been promised a picnic, clapped her hands and the day was so fine that Mary herself felt in good spirits, although their task was sad. They skirted a rocky bay and came to a small common, where Mary slowed the horses to a walk for she knew they were near their destination. She recognised the landmarks she had noticed on that dreadful night: the track leading to a bigger common, the promontory of cliffs beyond and the long field where the soldiers had been buried. But there was no sign of a grave now. Where the bodies had been there was nothing but grass as far as the eye could see. Puzzled, she stopped the carriage.

"Where is it, Mama?" asked Samantha. "Where are the soldiers buried?"

"I don't know. I thought it was here."

Mary's eyes swept along the coastline. She had made no mistake. There were the inlets where the bodies had been washed ashore: there was the path along which Daniel had ridden to search along the line of red-coated figures: that was the field where they had been buried. There was no doubt about it, but there was not even a mound to mark their last resting place.

Then she caught sight of an old crone coming from the rocks carrying a sack of seaweed. She waited until the woman came level with them then called out.

"Excuse me. Can you tell me where the soldiers from the troop-ship are buried?"

The woman shielded her eyes from the sun with a bony hand.

"You mean the one that happened eleven years ago. Why there, of course." She pointed at the field.

"But there's nothing there. Only grass."

"Why, yes, they let the grass grow over it."

"Isn't there even a tomb stone?"

"No tomb stone's ever been laid. No one comes to look at the place, leastways not now. There used to be a few who put down flowers but no longer. You're the first I've seen in years."

Mary stared at the flat, green sward.

"But over two hundred soldiers lie buried there."

"That I know. I remember the night. Terrible it was, the worst storm we've ever had. There was talk of making a proper grave but the authorities wouldn't pay, so nothing came of it. They're all forgotten now."

She humped her sack over the other shoulder and made to move off, then changed her mind.

"Anyway, there's talk of building a dock here and some say there'll be a town as well to be called Port Call, so they'll want this land for building on, I dare say. Then it'll be convenient to forget who's buried here. Don't say much for humanity, do it?"

With that final, piercing remark she shuffled away.

"What will we do, Mama?" asked Samantha who had been listening.

Mary dismounted and helped her daughter down.

"We'll place the flowers over there."

They walked along the track, the sun hot on their backs, until Mary adjudged that they were half way along where the trench had been. There she knelt and placed the wreath on the grass, and Samantha did likewise with her posy. Silently Mary prayed and heard Samantha intoning the Lord's Prayer, ending with "God bless Papa and Uncle Jack". Then they returned to the phaeton.

Samantha, with the exuberance of childhood, soon forgot about the grave and did full justice to the hamper of food they had brought with them. Afterwards she played happily on the grass but Mary kept looking at the field. Only someone who had been there at the time and seen all those young men lying lifeless could understand the full implication of the tragedy, but it had been cruel not to have marked the spot, if only with an obelisk. She thought, too, of poor Sir Roger coming all the way from Ewenny with his decrepit horses and carriage and then foully murdered, and of the thousands of men killed in the interminable war that was still dragging on. It seemed that since going to the New Inn the whole world had been full of violence and destruction, and that the two hundred sleeping near her were only a tiny fraction of all those killed. Suddenly a mood of despondency seized her which she knew would not lift until she returned home and saw Daniel again. She allowed Samantha a few more minutes then called out that they were returning.

Knowing that they were stable-bound the horses made good time on the return journey and they were passing Laleston almost before they realised it. Descending the hill, Mary again made up her mind that she would not stop: a final, passing glance at the place where it had been, perhaps, but nothing more; and after an hour's trotting she would be out of the region for ever, with all links with a dreadful period of her life finally broken.

But as she rounded the bend at the bottom she saw that the

bridge was crammed with sheep, with dogs running up and down the parapets. The air was filled with the sound of a hundred bleatings and the sharp cries of shepherds. Samantha, who had never seen sheep being dipped before, cried out in ecstasy.

"Oh, Mama! Look at the poor animals falling into the river. Why are they making them do that?"

"To clean the wool before shearing."

"Isn't it cruel? Won't they be drowned?"

"I don't think so. They'll swim to the bank, and any that can't will be saved by a shepherd."

"Can we stay and watch?"

Mary glanced at the bridge, packed tight with woolly backs.

"We may as well. We can't go on for a moment, anyway."

Samantha jumped out of the carriage and ran towards some sheep, which scattered. A gruff rebuke from a shepherd made her stand contritely still. Mary joined her and put an arm around her shoulders.

"Don't go further than here. The shepherds won't like it if you do."

She watched the familiar spectacle for a few minutes then, keeping an eye on her daughter, she walked a few paces to where the forecourt of the inn had been. It was even more overgrown than she had first thought, with no trace of the gravelled surface. She fancied that in a briar bush she could see the remains of the mounting block which she had used to climb on Daniel's horse, but where the building had been was now nothing but a twisted mass of thorn, blackberry and convolvulus, with here and there a sapling. The perimeter bushes had become lank and over-grown, their bases smothered in weeds, and the apple trees in the orchard were covered with mould and fungus. A dank smell of decay seemed to pervade everything.

So intrigued was she with the spectacle that for a moment she forgot about Samantha. She was brought to her senses by the sound of many sheep scampering up the hill, and when she turned she saw that the dipping was over and that the flock was being driven away. She ran to the bridge, reproaching herself for having let Samantha out of her sight even for a moment in that place. To her relief she saw her daughter come skipping over the bridge towards her.

"Mama, Mama! Come quickly. There's a gentleman here who knows you."

Sudden, unaccountable fear seized Mary. She grasped Samantha's hand.

"What gentleman? Where?"

"On the other side of the bridge. He said he knew who I was for I look exactly like you."

Still skipping, Samantha dragged Mary reluctantly across the bridge. Sitting on a stile near the end of the parapet was a man wearing a tricorn.

"Here she is," shouted Samantha. "Here's my Mama."

Mary pulled Samantha to a stop.

"Wait. Don't go further."

Surprised by the tone of her mother's voice and hurt because of the rough way she had been halted, Samantha looked petulantly at her.

"But, Mama—"

Mary drew the child to her and held her fast. She had not been sure at first but she was now. The man was Cap Coch.

"What are you doing here?" she cried. "How dare you molest my daughter."

Cap Coch shook his head.

"Go away," Mary shouted. "Why do you torment us?"

Again Cap Coch shook his head.

"Samantha," said Mary. "Go back to the carriage. Wait for me there. I'll come to you in a moment."

Samantha hesitated, so Mary pushed her to the apex of the bridge.

"Go this instant."

She watched to see that Samantha had safely boarded the phaeton then turned, intending to berate the innkeeper for his insolence in talking to her daughter and to threaten him with arrest by Daniel. But Cap Coch had gone. She went to the end of the bridge where he had been but there was no sign of him. He had disappeared so quickly it was as though he had melted into

202

thin air. Suddenly a sensation of intense cold enveloped her and the smell of decay she had noticed before assailed her nostrils. She could hear the distant bleating of the sheep from far up the road but in the immediate vicinity of the bridge there was a strange silence. With heart thumping she gathered up her dress and ran back to the carriage.

"Why didn't he speak to you?" asked Samantha reprovingly. "He spoke to me. He seemed such a nice man."

Mary ignored her. She lashed at the horses with the whip, galvanising the startled animals into instant action. They sped over the bridge to the road beyond and as they passed the place where Cap Coch had been the horses shied, although there was no sign of him. Mary lashed out again and they raced up the hill, reverting to a stumbling trot only when exhaustion set in.

Then, when they were out of the hollow and on the road to Ewenny, a strange thought struck her. Except for an uncharacteristic sadness in his expression Cap Coch had appeared exactly the same as when she had seen him last. Eleven years had lapsed but he had not seemed a day older; moreover he had been wearing his familiar day-to-day clothes: a dark-blue, high-collared coat with long tails, cut away in front to show the yellow, embroidered waistcoat and buckskin trousers, and on his head had been the battered tricorn of which he was so fond. Mary shivered, remembering the intense cold she had felt when near him, and the strange way he had remained silent, merely shaking his head in answer to her questions; and for a moment she wondered if her imagination had played another trick on her. But Samantha had seen him, too, and actually spoken to him; and suddenly Mary remembered another aspect of Cap Coch's appearance—one that had eluded her in the sudden excitement of meeting him: there had been weals on his throat similar to those he had displayed on that last frightening night at the inn. They should have disappeared by now but they were still there, as red and as raw as though the rope had just been removed from his neck.

She struck out again at the flagging horses, certain now only of one thing. She must get out of the region as quickly as possible and never return, for if she did she would see Cap Coch again.

Always he would be there, sitting by the bridge or wandering about where the inn had been, chained there by the ghosts of a hundred men. Beautiful though the place was it would never be free of him, even to the end of time.

EXPLANATION OF WELSH WORDS AND LEGENDS

p. 44:   *Spirit hounds:* harbingers of death and always found in remote places, they hunted singly or in packs and were greatly feared in country districts. Their favourite haunting places were cross roads where a hanging had been carried out or a murder committed.

Mallt y nos: a beautiful but wicked lady who loved riding to hounds and was, according to local legend, brought over from Normandy by Robert Fitzhamon, the Norman conqueror of Glamorgan. "If I cannot hunt in heaven," she once remarked, "I would rather not go there"; thus after her death she was directed to the spirit hounds to hunt with them for eternity. Though she repented of her evil, it was of no avail and, with her braying hounds, she was greatly feared by the villagers of the Ogmore area.

p. 58   *Cawl*—broth: the traditional farmers' winter diet.

p. 66   *'Machgen 'i:* my boy.

p. 70   *Merch fach:* little girl.

p. 75   *Uffern:* hell!

p. 79   *Da iawn, merch fach:* very good, little girl.
Cwrw da: good beer.
Diawch: Devil!
Iesu Grist: Jesus Christ.
Diolch yn fawr: thank you very much.
Weddol: fair.

p. 84   *Brawd:* brother.

p. 104   *Nosen lawen:* traditional evening of Welsh dancing and singing, etc. (*literally* 'cheerful evening').

p. 113   *Groes Gibbet:* Gibbet Cross.

p. 154   *Mari Lwyd:* possibly *literally* 'the grey mare'. Old Christmas-tide custom involving a party of young people, one inside a white sheet with a bleached horse's skull bedecked with ribbons and streamers, who would tour the streets of a village and attempt to gain entry to individual houses by engaging in witty verbal exchanges with the occupants.